GINNY SWART

HEART OF AFRICA

Complete and Unabridged

LINFORD
Leicester

First published in Great Britain in 2006

First Linford Edition
published 2007

Copyright © 2006 by Ginny Swart

British Library CIP Data

Swart, Ginny
    Heart of Africa.—Large print ed.—
Linford romance library
    1. South Africa—Fiction
    2. Love stories
    3. Large type books
    I. Title
823.9′2 [F]

    ISBN 978–1–84617–759–0

Published by
F. A. Thorpe (Publishing)
Anstey, Leicestershire

Set by Words & Graphics Ltd.
Anstey, Leicestershire
Printed and bound in Great Britain by
T. J. International Ltd., Padstow, Cornwall

This book is printed on acid-free paper

1

All Aboard!

Helen McLeod leaned back against the seat of the rackety old bus and, for the first time since arriving in South Africa two days before, tried to relax.

Her travelling companions made that somewhat difficult, especially the toddler on the seat behind her. With enormous brown eyes in a chocolate brown face, he stood on his mother's lap and gently stroked Helen's fine blonde hair with a chubby hand. When she turned round, his mother gave her a wide smile.

'He like your pretty hair,' she explained, and carried on chatting loudly to her friend across the aisle.

The next thing Helen knew, he was clambering over the back of the seat on to her lap, grinning angelically and

1

patting her face.

'He like you very much!' His mother laughed, making no attempt to pull him back. Helen felt ridiculously pleased to have the approval of this friendly little fellow.

'What's his name?' she asked.

'Bongani.'

'Well, Bongani, I hope you're comfortable.'

He proved that he was by snuggling up and falling asleep almost immediately, his thumb in his mouth. As Helen felt his little body relax warmly against hers she gave up all thoughts of a nap and concentrated on the scenery shimmering in the heat.

The travel agent had assured her that an air-conditioned coach would take her the five hundred kilometres to the farm, but when she'd arrived at the bus station in Cape Town there had been a mix-up with the bookings.

'I'm sorry, miss, you'll have to wait until tomorrow for the next coach. Of course, there is the Mawasa bus, but I don't think you'd like that.'

'Why not?' Helen had queried. She'd checked out of her hotel and was already wishing her backpack wasn't quite so heavy.

'That's it over there,' he'd said simply.

The name *Mawasa Cross-Country Super Luxury Bus* was emblazoned in silver across the side of a vehicle decorated with vivid pictures of animals and people. The luggage was being stowed on top of the roof, tied on with fluorescent orange rope. Bulging suitcases, cages of live chickens and crates of vegetables were jumbled together with bags of sugar and cornmeal.

Passengers were milling around, shouting instructions to the men tying on the luggage above, buying cool drinks and packets of food for the journey.

It was all a far cry from the sleek coach she'd been expecting, but then, this was Africa! And Helen had promised her grandfather that she'd make herself try everything new that came her way.

'I want you to enjoy it as much as I did,' Albert McLeod had said. 'Don't try to find things that remind you of home — learning about people and places that are completely different, that's what travel is all about.'

And this would certainly count as something completely different! Any doubts she had were overcome by the pair of cow's horns fastened to the front of the bus.

Helen handed her backpack up to be tied on and, following the example of the other passengers, bought a can of lemonade from the street vendor and something wrapped in waxed paper which looked like a long piece of fried dough but which smelled deliciously of curry. Then she boarded the bus and found an empty seat next to an elderly man who smiled at her.

'You go to Johannesburg?' he asked.

'No, I'm getting off long before that, at a place called Hartley's Drift,' she said. 'It's a little town close to the farm I'm visiting. It's called Kasteelpoort and it's near a place called the Three Castles.'

'Ah yes, the three big mountains. I know them.'

'Oh, good, then maybe you can tell me when we're getting near?'

When Helen had told the Bissington travel agent where she was going, he'd been unable to find it on his map. She was relieved to find someone who'd heard of the place.

People waved and shouted cheerful comments as the bus made its way through the crowded streets and on to the freeway out of Cape Town.

Colourful

She could feel the excitement as they left the city behind and headed over the mountains. Behind her, someone started singing, a woman's clear strong voice.

5

She was joined by others all lifting their voices in harmony, the men adding deep bass rumbles to the melody. She couldn't understand the words, but Helen shivered from the sheer beauty of it.

Great blue-grey rocky sentinels reared up on either side of the bus as it struggled noisily up the pass. A colourful patchwork of vineyards and orchards threaded with silvery rivers spread out in the lush valleys below.

Farmhouses and clusters of small cottages surrounded by oak trees dotted the lands as far as her eye could see. Helen couldn't help smiling as she thought back to another, more familiar bus trip taking her home from Bissington Infants' School for the last time as it chugged around the narrow lanes between the English hedgerows.

★   ★   ★

She'd spent that journey staring out of the window, blinking away the tears

6

she'd held in check all morning. Saying goodbye to her class of five-year-olds had been difficult and she'd struggled not to cry as they heaped her desk with little gifts and lovingly drawn farewell cards.

Her two years at the school had been her first job after college, and Helen had enjoyed every minute. But when her boyfriend, Mark Milne, announced that he was being transferred to Leighton, she'd felt she had to resign. He hadn't actually asked her to, because he knew how much she loved the children and her work.

She hadn't relished the thought of moving away, but had been confident of finding another post once they'd married and settled in Leighton.

A pain had started behind her eyes and she'd wondered briefly if she was coming down with flu, but decided it was the emotions of the morning getting the better of her.

No doubt a cup of tea would banish the headache and she'd feel fine by the evening, when she and Mark were due at Angela's twentieth birthday party. Not that she expected to enjoy the disco that her younger sister had planned, but they had to put in an appearance.

She'd even hoped they'd be able to leave early . . . Angela's friends were great fun but awfully rowdy! Helen had been surprised that her quiet, rather shy boyfriend had even agreed to go. He'd been so distracted over the past few weeks. But he'd had a lot on his mind with his recent promotion and the forthcoming move to Leighton.

She knew Mark so well. From the moment they started going out together after their first meeting at the tennis club five years before, she'd known this was the man she'd marry one day.

Not too flashy, quiet and thoughtful in his ways, Mark was everything she'd ever wanted in a man. He was ambitious and took his job at the computer company seriously, spending most weeknights doing courses related to his work. He didn't go out drinking with his mates and disliked noisy clubs and discos as much as Helen did.

'Mark and I are really well-matched,' Helen had said contentedly to her mother. 'We enjoy doing exactly the same things, going to concerts, playing tennis, going for walks. And he's so nice, isn't he, Mum? Everyone likes Mark.'

'Well, Mark's a lovely lad, but don't be too quick to settle for anyone yet, love,' Gwen had cautioned. 'You're young and you haven't met many boys. Maybe you should take a job a bit further away from home, see a bit of life outside Bissington before you decide? Marriage is a big step.'

'Mum, I *have* decided. I would never marry anyone except Mark!'

'Has he asked you?'

'Not yet. But we both know.'

'Tell me, darling,' Gwen had said seriously. 'Does your heart give a little leap every time you see Mark?'

Was it supposed to?

'Why? Was it like that for you and Dad?'

'Yes.' Her mother smiled. 'Seeing your dad come through the front door of an evening made everything feel better. There was always that little spark.'

'You miss him, don't you, Mum? I do, too.'

'Well, I've twenty happy years to look back on,' her mother said briskly, clearing her throat. 'And I'm just worried that there's no spark between you and Mark. No magic.'

'Oh, Mum, you're a hopeless old romantic!' Helen had laughed. 'You sound just like Angela. Mark and I are a perfect couple. We're very comfortable together. We don't need magic . . .'

'I'm So Sorry . . .'

But when Mark had called for Helen on the evening of Angela's birthday bash, he'd kissed her briefly, and there had

10

been a strange expression on his usually cheerful face.

Something's wrong, Helen had instantly realised, with a little flutter of alarm. His job? Maybe his mother was unwell again?

'Helen, let's sit down. I've something I need to tell you.'

It must be his work, she'd thought, her mind racing. Maybe something had gone wrong with his promotion . . .

Mark had looked wretched and white-faced. He'd gently taken her hand, then turned her safe and predictable little world upside down.

'I don't know how to say this, Helen, so I'll just tell you. I'm in love with Angela and she loves me. I've asked her to marry me and she's said yes.'

Angela? Her *sister*?

The silence seemed to stretch between them for ever. Helen had felt cold all over and words refused to come.

'I'm desperately sorry,' he'd added miserably. 'I know we'd . . . that you'd thought . . . '

'I thought we both thought,' she'd retorted.

Helen had pulled her hand away from his, realising starkly for the first time that there never had been a ring on her finger, never an official declaration of love.

Mark and Angela? How could she have missed this?

'I didn't know you even saw much of Angela,' she'd said evenly. 'When did this happen?'

'I was in charge of installing a whole bank of computers at her college some months ago. We had lunch together in the canteen there a couple of times . . . then she asked me to help her with some computer programmes so I went round to her flat to upload them and show her how they worked. And we were drawn for mixed doubles at the club when you hurt your ankle, remember?'

He'd run his hand through his hair.

'It was then I started seeing Angela as a person on her own, not just as your younger sister. There was this sudden, I don't know, electricity between us.'

Her younger sister, whom she'd always loved. How could she do this to her?

'And I could tell she was . . . I don't know, she felt the same. Then we finally admitted our feelings for each other. I'm sure it sounds clichéd, but we couldn't help it. Angela's been so anxious and guilty about the whole thing and wanted to tell you, but I thought I owed it to you to be the one to speak to you, to explain . . . '

Owed her? Yes, five years of her life!

Opposites Attract . . .

Angela had been fifteen when Helen and Mark had met. In Helen's mind, Angela had always been the pesky little sister who made Mark listen to her playing the guitar and asked for his help with maths homework. Mark had been endlessly patient and Angela had adored him, treating him like an older brother.

Helen had taken it for granted that Angela would be her bridesmaid one day, and they'd even discussed the colour of the dress she'd wear. Peach satin.

'But how could you let me resign from my job when you knew I . . . that you . . . ' Helen had said raggedly.

'Helen, my dear, I only really knew for sure two days ago! Up till then I just let everything between you and me jog along as usual. I suppose I assumed we'd get married in the end and move together to Leighton. I realise now I shouldn't have been so indecisive. I feel awful.'

'Good. So do I. And don't call me your dear!' she'd snapped. 'Well, off you go to Angela's party.'

'I hardly feel like it, to be honest. Shall I make us a cup of tea first?'

'JUST GO!' she'd shouted.

When Mark looked shocked, Helen had almost smiled. She'd never raised her voice to him before. It felt quite liberating.

'I'll be fine,' she'd added quietly. 'Please . . . just leave.'

As he shut the door behind him, Helen realised her headache had vanished. She was thinking quite clearly.

They said opposites attract, and she'd always known that Angela was everything she wasn't — full of crazy ideas and mad enthusiasms which changed from one week to the next. Angela was able to charm the birds from the trees, as her mother often said.

Whereas Helen, with her quiet commonsense and dependability, had often felt overshadowed by her younger sister, wishing she could be more like her. Angela had plenty of boyfriends, but none for longer than a few months. Would she drop Mark in the same way?

Suddenly Helen had felt like a cup of tea after all.

Waiting for the kettle to boil, she'd wondered why she didn't want to cry,

15

and tried, in her usual orderly way, to analyse her feelings. *If I were Angela,* she'd thought ruefully, *I'd be devastated, throwing things and bursting into tears.*

Was she devastated? Not really, but her very foundations had been severely shaken. For as long as she could remember, she'd pictured a future with Mark, buying a house and starting a family. Now Helen couldn't imagine anything else, and she was frightened of the big black hole where her cosy, uncomplicated future used to be . . .

Was she sad? Strangely, only a little. It was as though she'd said goodbye to an old friend whom she knew she'd see again somewhere. As of course she would. Mark would be part of her family, her brother-in-law.

It struck her then that most of all she was dreading telling their friends and family. Everyone she knew had always assumed she and Mark would get married, just as she had. Now the man who'd been her boyfriend for five years was going to marry her little sister, who loved dancing and clubbing and all the things Mark had said he disliked!

She went to bed and lay staring into the dark. People will pity me, she thought in horror. I won't be able to bear their sympathetic looks and the whispering behind my back at the tennis club. I'll have to leave Bissington.

Helen had allowed the hot tears to come at last, sobbing silently into her pillow. Then she'd fallen into a deep, dreamless sleep.

'You Must Hate Me'

The following morning there had been a tentative knock on her door. Through the glass, she'd recognised Angela, and paused before she opened the door, feeling hollow.

Helen had wondered what she'd say to her sister, how she'd cope, whether she'd be able to look her in the face and speak normally.

She needn't have worried. Angela burst into tears and flung her arms around Helen, hugging her so tightly she could hardly breathe.

'Helen, I'm so sorry,' she'd sobbed. 'I never, ever thought I'd fall for Mark. Until now, I've never even fancied him! But suddenly we just fell in love. Really in love. I'm sorry. Please forgive me.'

Helen found herself patting Angela comfortingly.

'Don't cry. It's all right,' she'd soothed, slipping into her usual role of older sister, the one who bandaged Angela's knee when she fell, who listened to her side of impassioned arguments with her friends at school.

'No, it's not! I know you've always loved him. I did, too, but not this way.'

Angela had sniffed and wiped her eyes with her sleeve.

'It's like, suddenly, you know, there's this thing between us. I can't explain it, I've never felt this way about anyone before.'

The spark, Helen had thought sadly.

Mum had never thought Mark was right for me. And she'd been right.

'Here's a tissue. Come into the kitchen and I'll make us some coffee.'

Angela blew her nose.

'Any toast? I'm starving.'

'Have you told Mum yet?' Helen had asked carefully.

'No, Mark and I are going round this afternoon. I guess she'll be shocked, although I know she's always liked him.'

'Perhaps she won't be all that surprised. Mum doesn't miss much,' Helen had said as she'd spooned coffee into two mugs.

'She never felt I should marry Mark. She was always telling me to go out and meet other people before I made up my mind.'

'Really?' Angela had given her a watery smile. 'Well, I've met loads of guys so she can't object on that score.'

'I expect she'll be very pleased, once she's got used to the idea,' Helen said wryly.

'Yes, but *you're* not — you can't be. You must hate me and I don't blame you.'

'No, I don't hate you, Angela. If I'm honest with myself, there was never that 'thing' you're talking about between Mark and me. We'd just got into a very comfortable groove. Now I feel as though I've been standing on a rug that someone's pulled out and shaken. And I'm up in the air not knowing where I'm going to land.'

Gwen's Advice

As soon as Angela had left, Helen had tidied her flat and walked round to her mother's house. She'd found Gwen McLeod doing the ironing in the kitchen.

'Mark and Angela are getting married,' she'd said flatly. 'He told me last night.'

Her mother had put her arms around Helen and hugged her.

'Darling, I'm so sorry.'

'You don't sound very surprised,' Helen had remarked. 'Did you know about them?'

'Not officially. But I could sense something between them at the tennis club last month — a sort of connection that wasn't there before.'

'I missed it completely.' Helen had sighed. 'Oh, Mum, I feel like such an idiot. Here I've been thinking that Mark and I were going to jog along, as he put it, for ever. But all the time he wanted that romantic magic you've always said was missing, and now he's found it with Angela, of all people!'

'It must be very hard for you, darling. I just wish you hadn't been hurt by all this. How do you feel about her? Have the two of you spoken?'

'Yes, and we're fine. Really. I didn't think we would be, but we are. We had a long talk this morning. I just hope this doesn't turn out to be another of Angela's many mad passions. Mark would be so hurt if it didn't last.'

'No,' her mother had said slowly. 'I

think it will last. Mark's just right for Angela when you think about it. He's solid. And she's a bit . . . well, you know what Angela's like, she needs someone like Mark to steady her. She knows him very well after all this time. I think they're very well suited.'

'Not like we were, you mean,' Helen had rounded bitterly. 'Both of us solid and steady. And boring.'

'Darling, I didn't mean that at all. But I've always thought you needed to spread your wings a bit, and meet different people. You've never even been out with anyone except Mark since you left school.'

'I think I'll leave Bissington anyway. I can't believe he didn't say something to me before I resigned.'

'Mark's always been slow to decide things. But Helen, dear, don't run away. I know things will be difficult for a week or two, with people talking, but that'll blow over. You need to face them and show you're not too upset about Angela and Mark.'

'I suppose you're right,' Helen had conceded. She'd started to put away the dishes on the draining board. 'I'll look around for another teaching post somewhere near, although I'll probably not find one for next term. It's a bit late.'

'You could always give me a hand at the herb centre for a while, until you find something.'

Perhaps that's what I need, Helen had thought, quiet time among Mum's pots of marjoram and basil.

In The Middle Of Nowhere . . .

'All out!' Helen's thoughts were jolted back to the present by the raucous shout of the bus driver who had skidded to a halt.

'Flat tyre! All out!'

On her lap, Bongani stirred, and she handed him back to his mother as she stood up and followed everyone out on to the side of the road. They had left the mountains far behind, and without her noticing it, the countryside had completely changed.

'Eh, eh, this is bad luck,' the old man said. 'Maybe he has no spare. We sit here a long time.'

'No spare tyre? Surely he has one?'

'Maybe yes. Maybe no.'

Helen watched anxiously as the driver, helped by several young men, crawled under the bus and reappeared laughing triumphantly. They were dragging a well-worn tyre behind them. The passengers gave a collective sigh of relief and settled on the grass, opening packets of food and passing them around.

'You like some chicken?'

Bongani's mother shyly offered Helen a plastic container of fried chicken wings. She was about to refuse automatically, but they smelled delicious and she didn't want to offend her, so she took a small piece. It didn't taste like any chicken she'd ever eaten. It was crisp and fiery, and she nearly choked.

'Thank you,' she spluttered, and reached hastily for her canned drink.

'Very hot,' the woman said complacently. 'Sharp-sharp!'

'Yes, indeed.' Helen laughed and saw with amazement that little Bongani was wolfing down the spicy chicken with evident enjoyment.

The bus had stopped in the middle of nowhere. Towards either horizon, the tarred road stretched ahead and behind them, and on either side lay flat land covered in low, greyish-brown scrub.

The Three Castles

In the distance a tall windmill clanked around, and she could hear the distant bleating of sheep although she couldn't see them. There was no farmhouse anywhere and no sign of life, not even a passing car.

'This the Karoo,' the old man explained, indicating the endless space around them. 'Very big farms. Plenty sheep. No water here.'

'How do they live?' she wondered.

'Water under the ground. Windmill pump it out.'

'Oh. How far is it now to Hartley's Drift?'

'About one hour. But the Three Castles mountains, they come before Hartley's Drift. You get off there.'

'No, the people I'm staying with are going to fetch me. I have to phone them from a call-box in Hartley's Drift.'

The old man smiled.

'You will see. The bus stop for you where you want to get off. It is our way.'

She noticed that he spoke to the bus driver before they climbed on board again.

'All fixed!' He smiled when he sat down beside her. 'He drop you off. No worry.'

Sure enough, they'd been on the road again for about half an hour when the bus slowed down and stopped.

'Three Castles!' the driver shouted. 'Miss, you get off here.'

Two of the young men climbed the metal ladder on to the roof of the bus and started untying her backpack.

'But I don't even know where this farm is!' Helen protested.

'Is right here, miss.' The old man pointed to a pair of gateposts with a white-painted sign that read *Kasteel-poort. G. Smit and family*.

'Is your farm.'

A dirt road led off into the distance.

'Go well, miss.' The old man stood up and gave a half-bow.

'Thank you.' She smiled. 'Goodbye, and goodbye to you, Bongani.'

To her surprise there were murmurs and smiles of farewell from the rest of the passengers, and as she stood on the side of the road, they waved until the bus was out of sight.

Helen struggled into her backpack, which somehow seemed heavier than before, and started up the farm road, her thoughts crowding in.

G. Smit. That would be Amelia's son, Gerard, who'd died two years ago, she thought. Married to Cora. And her children are Adam, Flippie and Anna-Marie. Amelia's grandchildren. I wonder if she has changed a lot since Grandad knew her?

Well, she was about eighty so she must have.

At the thought of finally meeting the Smit family, butterflies started.

What must they think, she wondered, with Grandad asking their grandmother if she could come and stay with them? They didn't know him, and their grandmother could hardly remember Grandad after fifty years, Christmas cards or not!

The sun beat down directly overhead and she had to screw up her eyes against the glare. The grey-brown land on either side shimmered in waves from the heat and she wished she'd brought sunglasses and a hat. Worse, after a few minutes, she was desperately thirsty.

The Three Castles loomed ahead in the far distance. The farmhouse can't be too far now, she thought, plodding on and licking her dry lips. I wonder if it was as hot as this when Grandad stayed here, she thought, as memories of home flooded back.

A Strain

Mark and Angela had announced their engagement, then their marriage, just weeks apart. Well, it made sense. Mark was due to move to Leighton and they wanted to go as a married couple.

Helen had gradually become used to the fact that she and Mark were no longer together, but knew she was going to find the ceremony difficult. When Angela asked her hesitantly if she would be her bridesmaid, she'd refused.

'It just wouldn't work, Angie,' she'd said. 'Even if I wanted to, which I don't, people would spend half the wedding muttering about how it used to be Mark and me and now it's Mark and you. I truly, truly have got over that, but I just think it wouldn't be right. Besides, I can't stand myself in peach satin!'

'Mark said I shouldn't ask you,' Angela had said sadly. 'But if I can't have you, I don't want anyone.'

'Don't be daft, Angie, ask Cathy. You can't have a wedding without a bridesmaid!'

'Well, all right. But I'd much rather it was you. You could wear any colour you like!'

But Helen had stuck to her guns.

At first, she had found it a strain talking to Mark when they met again. It was as though she were making polite conversation to a stranger, and it was obvious he felt awkward, too. It was Angela who'd broken the ice, her bubbly personality making it easy for them all to be friends again.

But Helen realised sadly that the old familiar closeness with Mark would never return.

Gwen McLeod had happily thrown herself into the wedding arrangements, making ever-increasing lists. Helen had found herself unwillingly drawn into the excitement and preparation of it all and the wedding day arrived almost before she knew it.

Standing next to her mother in the church, she'd felt quite calm, and forced herself to smile at old Mrs Webster, who'd patted her arm consolingly as she passed.

'Never mind dear, you'll get your turn one day!' the old lady had whispered.

Watching her radiant sister walking towards Mark on the arm of her grandfather, and his look of adoration as she came towards him, Helen had known they were meant for each other. Mark had never looked at her with such obvious devotion in his eyes.

In the end, it had been her grandad who had helped Helen through the weeks after the wedding.

'I'll let you into a secret,' he'd told her. 'I haven't mentioned this to your mother or anyone else, but I've decided to put together a sort of biography. The story of my life.'

'Really, Grandad? That'll be interesting.'

Helen knew her grandfather had enjoyed a full life. During the war, he'd been awarded a medal for bravery, and had come home to start the first newspaper in Bissington, which was later bought out by a bigger newspaper group. Afterwards, he'd been active on the local council and later, a Justice of the Peace.

He'd twice been to London, heading up protest groups — once against the planned widening of the road, and once against an airport which would have destroyed a wetland where wading birds nested. Both times he'd been successful, and although he was now past eighty, he was still known in the town as someone who'd fight for a cause he believed in.

'An Old Girlfriend?'

Lately, Albert had taken up organic gardening and was now so enthusiastic about it he ran a weekly newsletter aimed at spreading the word against chemicals and insecticides.

'I want to write something to leave behind when I go,' he said. 'So my grandchildren and great-grandchildren can continue the fight!'

'You old stirrer,' Helen had said affectionately. 'So why are you telling me this?'

'I need someone to get my paperwork in order, and you, my dear, are just the right person! You could come and stay with me for a month or two until you find another post as a teacher.'

It was just what she'd needed. Helen had found her grandfather's papers were indeed in a mess. In his attic he had boxes and boxes of photographs from the war, pamphlets about protest marches, newspaper clippings and old letters, all jumbled together.

She'd brought them downstairs and looked at them silently.

'You see what I mean,' Albert had said. 'Try sorting them out into letters, newspaper articles and so on. Once you've done that, we can go over them together and see which are important.'

Helen had started on the bundle which looked the oldest, and was soon fascinated by his wartime correspondence. There were many flimsy letters from his mother, addressed in a careful, sloping hand to *Engineer A. McLeod, HMS Howe*, telling him that all was well at home despite the bombing.

They were praying for his safe return and hoping he was sleeping well in those nasty hammocks.

She'd mentioned the family's delight at receiving some dried fruit he'd sent from Cape Town and hoped he'd be able to post more.

I made us a wonderful boiled fruit cake, used the whole month's sugar ration but Dad agreed it was well worth it, she'd written.

Helen had opened the next bundle, all postmarked *South Africa, 1943*, and found letters written in a big round hand by someone called Amelia, who sounded young and full of fun.

Her letters were illustrated with little

cartoons in the margins and she said she missed Albert and his funny jokes, and hoped he'd come back to the farm one day.

'Grandad, who was Amelia?' Helen had quizzed mischievously at lunch. 'An old girlfriend?'

'Amelia? My goodness . . . Amelia. Haven't thought of her in a while. Well, Amelia and I are distantly related, but yes, we were very fond of each other during the war.'

'In South Africa? I didn't know we had cousins out there.'

'Well, pretty distant by now. Amelia's father was my dad's step-brother and he went off prospecting for gold there when he was just a lad. My dad always kept in touch at Christmas.'

Character

'So Amelia lived on a gold mine?'

'Goodness, no. Her father became a farmer, miles from anywhere in the middle of a desert. But wealthy, mind. They had an enormous farm, thousands of acres.'

'How did you meet them?'

'That was just luck. I was an engineer on *HMS Howe* and round about 1943 we put in to Durban for a major refit. It was going to take about five months and the top brass didn't know what to do with the crew so they decided to offer our services to local farmers!'

He'd laughed at the memory.

'Some of the lads were a bit cross, but I was delighted. I didn't fancy sitting around on a beach with the water full of sharks. I managed to wangle permission to work on my cousin's sheep farm, although it was a long way from Durban. So that's how I met Amelia.' He paused. 'I had a very happy time on that farm. Learned to love the country.'

'Amelia sounds awfully nice in her letters. Very jolly.'

'She was a real character, full of pranks. She had bright red hair and freckles and she loved music and dancing. And painting. She always dreamed of being an artist, going off to Cape Town and studying art.'

'And did she?'

'No. She was an only child and her parents wanted her to marry a lad who could take over their big farm. In those days, lasses obeyed their parents! A couple of years after the war she wrote and told me she'd wed a man called Pieter Smit. She sounded happy enough.'

'And you never went back to visit?'

'Never had the opportunity. But in her Christmas card every year, she always invites me to come and stay.'

Helen had raised her eyebrows.

'Your gran and I sent her a Christmas card every year and kept up to date with her,' he'd explained. 'We told her our family news over the years, so she knows all about our David marrying your mum, and you and Angela being our grandchildren.

'Amelia had just one child, a son called Gerard who inherited the farm when her husband died. But several years ago he was killed in a fall from his horse. That was the same year your gran passed away. So his wife Cora runs the farm now and she's got three grown-up children. I expect they help her. They're still on the same farm.'

Helen had been dumfounded.

'Grandad! That's fifty years you've been sending Christmas cards to Amelia and you've never mentioned her!'

'Well, it was long ago. Here, I'll show you something.' Albert had led the way to his bedroom. 'See this picture? Amelia painted it for me when I went back to my ship. It's their farm, Kasteelpoort. It means 'Castle Gate'. Those three mountains behind are called the Three Castles.'

'They look like giant's castles, with great rocky crowns.'

'Climbed to the top of all three while I was there,' Albert had added proudly. 'Amelia made me. Said it was tradition. I found out later she was fooling me

She was a great one for jokes, was Amelia.'

'A Warm Welcome'

'Grandad, why don't you go out for a holiday?' Helen had asked. 'Wouldn't you love to see her again?'

'No, I'm much too busy here. Too much to do.' He'd looked at her, bright-eyed. '*You'd* enjoy a trip out there, though. South Africa's a wonderful country. You could stay on the farm for a while and then tour around, see a game park or two.'

'Don't be daft, Grandad, I couldn't just arrive on their doorstep!' Helen had protested. 'Besides, I don't want to travel anywhere. I've applied for a post at Great Hamwood Infants.'

'Nonsense. Amelia would be delighted to see my granddaughter! I've told her all about you. South Africans have a reputation for being hospitable, especially the farmers. They're so remote they welcome anyone with open arms. And a bit of travel would do you the world of good.'

Helen had stopped arguing, sure her grandfather would forget all about it. But a fortnight later she'd received an airmail letter from South Africa, stamped *Hartley's Drift* and written in a vigorous, upright hand.

Dear Helen,

Your grandfather, Albert, and I have been friends for many, many years and I have very happy memories of the time he spent on our farm during the war. I would like to extend an invitation to you to visit our farm and stay with my family for a while. Your grandfather tells me you are at a crossroads in your life. Why not take the road less travelled, to Kasteelpoort?

You are assured of a warm welcome by everyone here and especially . . .

Your friend and cousin,
Amelia Smit.

And although at first Helen had argued and protested, she'd been persuaded to reply, arrangements were made and six weeks later she'd found herself on a plane to Cape Town . . .

★ ★ ★

Helen had lost track of time and was plodding mechanically along the road when a big pick-up stopped next to her. The blood was pounding in her ears with the effort of walking and she hadn't heard it approaching.

'Taking some exercise for your health, are you?' A ruddy, smiling face looked down at her. 'You don't want to be out in the sun at this time of day. Visiting the Smits?'

'Yes,' she croaked. 'They're my cousins.'

'Hop in. I'm on my way to deliver something there, anyway.'

'Thank you.'

Helen climbed gratefully into the passenger seat while he took her backpack and tossed it in the back on a pile of fence posts and cans of sheep dip and old rope.

'From England, are you?'

'How can you tell?' Helen smiled.

'You don't speak like anyone round here. And you've caught the sun quite badly, young lady.'

Helen could already feel her shoulders starting to burn.

'Jacob de Wild.'

He thrust out a huge paw.

'Helen McLeod.'

'I farm next door on Blouberg. The name means Blue Mountains. See those three over there?'

'The Three Castles, you mean?'

He looked at her in surprise.

'Ah, you've heard of them. Well, on winter evenings those mountains turn a shade of blue that you only see in the Karoo. Very beautiful. My grandpa named the farm after them.'

'And the Smits named their farm after the mountains, too.'

Jacob de Wild frowned.

'The Smits. Yes. Your cousins are nice people but I'm afraid their place . . . well, it will take a lot to make a success of that farm. Young Adam does his best but you can't farm a mountain. Nothing but stones.'

'I thought their farm was big?'

She remembered her grandfather saying it was enormous.

'Used to be, but not any more. Old Gerard Smit was a hopeless farmer. He lost most of it to the bank.' He smiled briefly. 'Mind you, one of these days, when Adam and my Marita get married, he'll have the run of both farms. He's got a good head on his shoulders and he'll have me to guide him.'

Helen was silent, thinking that the man shouldn't be so free with his criticism to a total stranger.

The truck bumped along and finally, near the foot of the three mountains, Helen saw the first signs of life.

In a paddock, several horses cropped the brownish grass, and further away, there was a big barn and some outhouses. Behind it, tall trees formed a pool of shade over a low, rambling farmhouse surrounded by a wide verandah, and in the distance, there was a scattering of round thatched huts.

Jacob skidded to a halt next to the barn.

'Tell you what, why don't you give this to your aunt? Cora, I mean.' He handed her an envelope. 'She's expecting this. I haven't time to stay and chat, much as I'd like to. Give her my regards and tell her I'd like her reply by tomorrow.'

Mystified, Helen thanked him for the lift and shouldered her backpack for the last fifty yards to the house as Jacob reversed and drove away noisily in a cloud of white dust.

The Girl From England

'Who on earth is that girl Jacob has just dropped off?'

Cora Smit put down her coffee cup and walked to the edge of the verandah.

'And that heavy backpack she's carrying!'

She turned to her younger son.

'Flippie, go and give her a hand. She looks so hot.'

The young man bounded down the steps and jogged easily along the rutted track to the girl, who stopped and wiped her flushed face when she saw him approach.

'Hi, there,' he said. 'Are you lost? Let me take that.'

The girl shrugged the pack off her back and smiled at him thankfully.

She's so small, Cora thought, watching, like a delicate bit of china. That rucksack's almost as big as she is.

'I'm Flippie Smit.' He grinned at Helen. 'Come up to the house. You look as though you could use a cool drink.'

'Thanks. But I'm not lost at all. This is Kasteelpoort, isn't it? I'm Helen McLeod. You must be one of Cora's sons? Your grandmother invited me to stay here for a couple of weeks . . . '

He looked at her in some dismay.

'But my mother thought you were arriving next week!'

'No, sorry, it was this week. The twelfth.'

'But Ma's got the nineteenth marked on the calendar! And she's been talking about getting ready for you for ages. Oh, boy, she's going to be so upset. She really wanted to do everything nicely for you. The first visitor we've ever had from overseas.

'Ma!' he called. 'Guess what — this is the girl from England!'

★   ★   ★

Helen gulped down the glass of iced water Cora had offered and accepted a refill gratefully as the Smit family watched in silence. She felt a hot, sticky mess and wondered what they must think of her.

This girl looks badly sunburned.

46

Cora thought anxiously. She's such a fragile little thing. I wonder how she's going to enjoy our rough and ready ways for two whole weeks?

Flippie looked at her in undisguised admiration. She's the most beautiful girl I've ever seen, he thought. She beats Marita de Wild and all the girls of Hartley's Drift by a long way. She looks friendly, but she'll probably think I'm an oaf.

Anna-Marie studied their visitor and noted her hairstyle and the cut of her skirt. She's a natural blonde, I can tell, she thought. I wonder if she'd let me make a pattern from that skirt of hers?

Only Adam spoke.

'A hat would have been a good idea, Miss McLeod,' he said with a slight smile. 'Now I know why they say 'mad dogs and Englishmen'.'

'Adam! Don't call our visitor mad!' Cora exclaimed.

''Go out in the midday sun',' Helen finished weakly. 'He's right. If it hadn't been for Jacob de Wild giving me a lift halfway along I'd still be walking!'

Adam's lips tightened.

'That man's not exactly welcome on this farm.'

'Oh . . . well, he seemed nice to me, and I was very pleased to see his pick-up,' Helen answered, puzzled. 'He seemed to like you, though.'

Adam snorted.

'I can't imagine what he — '

His mother interrupted him.

'Oh, dear, we were supposed to pick you up from the village! I don't know what you must think of us, getting everything so wrong.'

'I meant to phone you, but the bus just stopped next to the signpost for Kasteelpoort and the driver told me to get off there. He seemed to think the farm was just over the hill.'

'Bus? Didn't you come by coach? The coach always stops at the service station at Hartley's Drift and you could have waited for us in the tea-room there.'

'I caught the Mawasa bus.'

Bad Timing . . .

Cora almost choked. The Mawasa bus! Full of workers returning upcountry, overloaded and overcrowded, with no air-conditioning. Probably the brakes weren't all that good, either.

'You're lucky to have got as far as you did, my girl,' she said grimly. 'Those old buses break down all the time and their drivers take terrible chances with passing on the wrong side of the road. Some of them don't even have proper licences.'

'Actually, I really enjoyed the trip!' Helen laughed. 'Everyone was so friendly. And I loved the horns.'

Cora exchanged looks with her elder son. Perhaps their visitor had a touch of sunstroke . . .

'Well, Helen, I'm just glad you managed to get here at all, after that long walk. Let me introduce everyone. This rude fellow is my eldest son, Adam. You've met my little boy, Flippie, and this is my baby, Anna-Marie.'

The reference to 'little' was obviously a family joke, as Flippie stood a good few inches taller than his older brother, although Adam, five years older, was well over six feet tall, dark eyed and serious.

'Ma!' Anna-Marie said in exasperation. 'I'm eighteen. Stop calling me your baby!' She turned to Helen. 'I'm glad to meet you. It'll be nice to have another girl around for a while.'

'Give you a hard time, do we, *baby*?' Flippie mocked, dodging his sister's energetic swing.

'Flippie! Anna-Marie! You two, really!' Cora smiled apologetically.

Helen had liked Cora at once, with her plump, motherly figure and open, rather weatherbeaten face.

'It's very kind of you to have me to stay when you don't even know me, Mrs Smit,' she said a little shyly.

'Call me Cora. Of course we're pleased to have you. Your grandpa was a friend of Ouma Amelia's from long ago. It's a nice change to have a visitor, especially from so far away.'

'By the way, what did Jacob want, coming up our road?' Adam asked in a neutral voice.

'Oh! I'm sorry, I almost forgot. He asked me to give you this.' Helen handed the envelope to Cora, who glanced uneasily at Adam and passed it over.

He ripped it open and read quickly, his face darkening.

'Just what we thought, Ma,' he said harshly. 'He wants the bottom fields. Well, Jacob de Wild can go to hell! I'd rather give them away than sell to him.'

Cora stood up and gripped the railing, her knuckles whitening. She gazed out at the farm in the shimmering heat.

'We won't sell them to anyone,' she said shakily. 'We have to keep those fields. Without that land, this farm will be finished.'

Helen felt acutely embarrassed and totally out of place. It was all so different from what she'd expected. Talk about bad timing! It looked like coming to Africa might not have been such a wise decision after all . . .

2

An Argument Flares . . .

Helen, Flippie and Anna-Marie sat silently watching Cora and Adam. 'We'll never give up this place, Ma,' Adam said softly, hugging his mother. 'This is our home. I'll think of some way to keep the bank happy and that won't include selling any part of Kasteelpoort.'

Cora nodded and gave him a watery smile, then wiped her eyes and turned to Helen.

'I don't know what you must think of me,' she said apologetically. 'Let me take you to your room. I'm sure you're dying to unpack and have a shower. You've had a long day.'

The message seemed clear — Jacob de Wild and any trouble on the farm was none of her concern. But it was something that affected them all deeply . . .

By evening, Helen felt much better. After an invigorating shower, she lay on her bed intending to have only a short rest, but fell deeply asleep. She awoke completely refreshed, but for a moment she was unsure of where she was. Then she remembered. Kasteelpoort farm. South Africa.

She looked around her room. Cool and spacious, it had wide sash windows opening on to the verandah. The walls were covered with faded wallpaper and the flowered curtains were drab from years of washing. The old-fashioned furniture was dark and heavily carved, but there was a pleasant smell of beeswax polish and the wood gleamed with care.

While she slept, someone, she suspected Anna-Marie, had placed an arrangement of daisies on the three-mirrored dressing-table, making a cheerful splash of colour. Helen got up and combed her hair, hearing voices raised in argument on the verandah.

It was Cora's sons, Adam and Flippie. They appeared to be discussing sheep and Adam's deep rumble seemed to be getting the better of Flippie.

'OK, have it your own way — as usual,' the younger brother snapped. Helen heard angry footsteps and the sound of a door slamming somewhere in the house.

Anna-Marie's Ambition

Helen wondered what to do ... she didn't want to walk out and have to speak to Adam if he was in a bad mood. His whole demeanour towards her seemed distant and rather cold, although he'd been the first one to comfort his mother.

But his younger brother was fun and she was sure she and Flippie would be friends. And she liked Anna-Marie, who had looked very different from her brothers who were dressed for work in T-shirts and khaki shorts. Anna-Marie was smartly dressed, her auburn hair gelled saucily into the latest style and her nails painted bright red. Clearly, fashion meant a lot to her.

There was a gentle knock and Helen opened the door.

'Won't you join us for drinks on the *stoep*?' Cora invited. 'We always have a glass of wine about this time.'

She had changed from an old housedress into a darker frock and applied a touch of lipstick.

'That would be lovely, thanks.'

Helen followed Cora outside to the verandah where Anna-Marie was already settled with a magazine open on her lap. The girl had also changed clothes and was wearing a beautiful hand-printed kaftan. Helen guessed this was another of her own creations.

Adam was pouring wine from a frosted bottle and gave her a brief smile as he handed her a tall glass.

'Thank you.' She hesitated. 'Cora, I'm looking forward to meeting your mother-in-law. The older Mrs Smit?'

Helen felt awkward referring to someone of her grandfather's generation as Amelia, but she'd been wondering why the woman who'd invited her was nowhere to be seen.

'Is she an invalid?'

Cora gave a snort of laughter.

'Not at all! You'll meet her any minute. I phoned to tell her you'd arrived and she's coming straight over.'

'She doesn't live on the farm, then?'

'No, last year she moved to a little flat in Hartley's Drift. She was born on this farm, you know, and one day she announced that nearly eighty years in one place was quite enough! Most women her age would stay put, but not Ouma Amelia.'

Cora smiled affectionately.

'She comes out most weekends and still keeps her room here. And she can't wait to meet you.'

'Can I ask you, did you buy your skirt or make it yourself?' Anna-Marie fingered the blue linen appreciatively. 'It's lovely fabric.'

'This? I bought it at the market in

Bissington.' Helen smiled. 'I'm afraid I've never been good at making my own clothes. Why? Are you keen on sewing?'

'Yes, and fashion. I'd like to be a designer some day.'

'Too bad you'd have to pay someone to buy the stuff you dream up!' Flippie was back, ruffling Anna-Marie's hair as he passed her and helping himself to a cold beer.

'Stop it, Flip! And anyway, what do you know?'

'I know what I like. That orange thing you made with those weird patterns and beads all over it? It was a sight!'

'That was inspired by African prints, and everyone at school thought it was fabulous,' she replied indignantly. 'Even the teachers liked it. Miss Herbert asked me to make her one exactly the same, so there.'

Anna-Marie appealed to Helen.

'The African theme is very in this year. But this brother of mine thinks he's dressed smartly if he wears a pair of clean jeans! What does he know?'

Flippie grinned at Helen.

'Anna-Marie's trying to get out of doing a secretarial course at Hartley's Drift next term. Fancies herself as a dress designer, sipping cocktails on the balcony of her flat by the sea in Cape Town.'

'No, she doesn't,' Cora said with surprising firmness. 'Anna-Marie knows she can't go and live in Cape Town all by herself. She's going to get a good qualification and a good job close to home. Once she can operate a computer she might even get a job with Mr Lourens. He more or less said he'd take her on.'

'Ma! I don't want to work in that boring old lawyer's office! You can't make me do what I don't want to do!'

'Enough now, Anna-Marie.' Cora quelled her daughter with a look and turned to Helen.

'You're A Teacher?'

'So, Helen, tell us about yourself.'

Helen gave them an edited version of

her life. How her father had died when she and her sister were very young and how her mother had struggled to bring them up and run her herb centre at the same time. How her grandparents had been so much part of their lives when she and Angela were growing up, and how close she felt to her grandfather now he was alone.

She didn't mention Mark except to say her younger sister had recently married him, and she was surprised to find how easy it was to refer to him this way.

'I've been teaching the little ones for two years,' she ended. 'And I'm hoping to start at Great Hamwood Infants' School when I go back.'

'You're a teacher?' Adam stirred. 'Maybe you could give Tuleka some tips. She does her best but she's not trained at all.'

'Tuleka?'

'She's our cook. She's able to read and write, so I asked her to teach the labourers' children in her spare time. There are about four or five of them, all under ten. She just teaches them their alphabet and so on but they need more than that.'

'Don't they go to school?' Helen was horrified.

He shook his head.

'The nearest school's in town and there's no school bus. So they'd have a three-hour walk each way. This is the best we can do.'

'I'd be happy to help if I can.'

'Thanks, I'd appreciate that. I've tried to get the Hartley's Drift council to provide transport for them but they keep making excuses not to.' Adam was indignant. 'Those children ought to be in school.'

Jacob's Daughter

Helen sat back in the wicker chair and watched the sky darken over the *veldt* as the sun set, brilliant orange against the horizon. Bird calls she didn't recognise came from the gum trees as they settled for night and the air started to feel pleasantly cool after the heat of the day.

There was a fresh smell of damp earth and she became aware of a rotating sprinkler shooting great arcs of water over the lawn and the border of bright flowers.

Suddenly a single light bumped its way rapidly up the track towards the farm.

'There's Ouma!'

As Anna-Marie stood up, a scooter skidded to a halt next to the farm truck and the rider sounded the cheeky little hooter before climbing off rather stiffly. It was Amelia. She took off a purple helmet and shook free her long grey hair, revealing a thin, bony face and twinkling, deep-set brown eyes.

She clasped Helen in her arms and then looked at her intently.

'Helen, my dear child, welcome to Kasteelpoort.' She smiled. 'Better to be early than the late Miss McLeod, eh?

Flippie, pour your ouma a drink, I'm thirsty after that ride.'

She perched on a white wicker stool next to Cora, sitting upright and alert. Like a bird, Helen thought.

'Adam, did you notice that wretch Jacob de Wild has let his fences fall down again? He's not fit to care for animals. Those sheep of his will be all over the highway by tomorrow.'

'I'd better phone him and let him know,' Adam said rather unwillingly, unwinding his rangy form from where he'd been sitting in the shadows.

'If you phone him, Marita will keep you on the line till midnight!' Flippie laughed.

'You phone him, then.'

Adam abruptly sat down again.

'She's Jacob's daughter, isn't she?' Helen interjected. 'He mentioned her.'

'You'll meet her soon. She's always coming round here for some reason or another. Marita's in lo-ove with Ad-am!'

Flippie hurriedly left the verandah and headed for the telephone before his brother's cushion could find its mark.

'Marita's almost part of the family,' Cora explained 'She's a sweet girl. We've known her since the day she was born and she and Adam went to school together in Hartley's Drift.'

'But then she went off to college in Cape Town and worked there,' Anna-Marie muttered enviously. 'And now she's so glamorous. You should see her clothes. I don't know how she can bear to come back to the farm and just moulder away here.'

'She came back to be with her father, like any good daughter would.' Cora gave her a long look then turned to Helen.

'Her mother died two years ago, and Jacob was devastated. She's their only child and he really needed her. Marita seems happy enough and I don't think she'll ever go back to the city, do you, Adam?'

'You never know,' he replied shortly.

'No,' Amelia put in. 'With the de Wilds, you never know.'

Self-Sufficient

Helen was puzzled by the undercurrents every time the de Wilds were mentioned. Although a bit of a rough diamond, Jacob had seemed pleasant enough, and offering to purchase some land wasn't a crime, was it?

Cora obviously liked Marita, so what was the problem? But for someone who was supposed to be marrying Marita one day, Adam seemed surprisingly unconcerned about her.

'So, Helen. Tell me about your oupa. Is Bertie well?'

'Grandad?' No-one had ever called him Bertie! 'Oh, yes. He's fine. He's taken up growing vegetables organically and he writes a little newsletter about it every month.'

'I can't imagine Bertie in a garden!' Amelia gave a deep throaty chuckle. 'You know, when he came here all those years ago he couldn't tell a weed from a vegetable. My pa set him to work in the kitchen garden and he pulled out the whole season's crop of carrots.'

'I'll remind him of that.' Helen smiled. 'But these days he loves gardening and he's very knowledgeable about controlling insects without chemicals and that sort of thing. He even writes a column in the weekly paper.'

'He was a clever boy, your oupa. Very good with his hands. He fixed my pa's generator when he thought he'd have to buy a new one. Lasted for years after that — we only had to replace it about ten years ago.'

As if to remind them, the electric light dimmed briefly and then surged brightly again.

'All our light comes from the generator,' Flippie explained. 'When it's not working we have to use oil lamps and candles. There's a lamp in your room on the table, just in case.'

'I didn't realise you had to make your own electricity,' Helen remarked. 'What about water?'

'There's a stream coming down from the mountain but it dries up in summer. So we use borehole water. You'd have passed the windmills on the bottom fields as you came. We're luckier than some farms around here, we've got loads of water, more than enough.'

'So you're pretty self-sufficient? Grandad would love that!'

'All our own vegetables,' Amelia said proudly, 'and meat, of course. One thing about a farm, you'll never starve. Your oupa couldn't get over the big meals we had. Mind you, it was wartime and the poor boy hadn't seen a good steak for ages!'

'Speaking of food . . . ' Cora stood up. 'I can see Tuleka's ready with the supper. Shall we go inside? I think she has a treat for us tonight especially in honour of your visit, Helen.'

Life On The Farm . . .

'Another letter from Helen!'
Gwen McLeod opened it eagerly.

'Shall I read it out loud? It's addressed to both of us.'

'Yes, do.'

Albert helped himself to another cup of tea, trying not to sound too eager. He missed his older granddaughter and having her stay with him to sort his papers for the two months before she left for South Africa had made Helen's absence all the harder.

Gwen sat down in happy anticipation of the long letter.

'Dearest Mum and Grandad,

'I've been at Kasteelpoort for three days and all the Smits have been so welcoming that already I feel like one of the family. The farmhouse is enormous, with a verandah running round three sides and surrounded by big shady gum trees. The farm workers and their families live in small houses but I haven't been down there yet.

'There's an old slave bell near the barn that used to be rung to call the

slaves to work in the morning, so this house must be pretty old. Adam (he's the older son, tall, dark and rather serious. He seems to run things) refuses to use it and wakes the labourers by banging on a piece of metal hanging from a tree. This wakes the family as well so our day starts at 5 a.m.! He and Flippie, who's the same age as me, very tall, red-haired and great fun, head straight off to the lands in their 4x4 and we don't see them until about nine o'clock when they come back for breakfast.

'Mum, you cannot believe what they eat! Here's a typical breakfast for the brothers: first, a huge bowl of oats and creamy milk brought up from the dairy that morning, then eggs, bacon, fried sausage, grilled tomato and sometimes fried potatoes! Then toast, with lashings of farm butter, and finished off with gallons of coffee. Cora roasts the beans fresh every morning and the smell is irresistible.

'Cora and Anna-Marie have smaller versions of this breakfast but Cora never sits down for a minute so probably needs it. Anna-Marie has just turned eighteen, and she's also tall, with masses of curly red hair. A really pretty girl.

'So far I've stuck to warm home-made bread and Cora's delicious home-made jam, and a little bowl of stewed dried fruit, but any day now I'm going to give in and have a few great thick slices of farm-cured bacon . . .

'The boys go back to work then return for a huge cooked lunch, after which they disappear again with the sheep or whatever it is they do. Flippie says today they're dipping four hundred of them! He invited me along to watch this afternoon, but I'd promised to give Anna-Marie a lesson in make-up. Yes, me! Don't laugh, but for some reason she thinks I'm a fashion guru just because I come from overseas.

'I can't get used to having servants around to do the housework. There's a housemaid, and a washing maid and an ironing maid! They are all wives of the farm workers and don't speak much English, but Tuleka, who's in charge of the kitchen, loves to talk and has told me lots about the farm and the family. She's a marvellous cook, too.

'There are lots of buck up on the mountains and Adam says he'll take me up there some time in the pick-up. He and Flippie go hunting sometimes and there's a track all the way up to the top these days, Grandad; I won't have to climb, thank goodness!

'At first Cora treated me like a visitor but I made it clear I want to help, so she showed me her kitchen garden and I did some weeding. She's so kind and motherly but underneath pretty strong and determined, I think. She's very proud of her garden. It's enormous, with rows of every vegetable you can imagine — huge white pumpkins, butternut squash and delicious sweet potatoes.

'Grandad, you'd be so envious! Although you'd be upset at the way the gardener uses insecticides. He just laughs and says 'Bad bug, he eat everything!' and sprays the fruit trees, the leafy vegetables — the lot! I tried to tell him about tobacco dust for the insects but he didn't believe me.

'There's still so much to say but it will keep for my next letter.

'By the way, while I'm here I've agreed to help Tuleka with her classes — besides being the cook she also teaches five of the labourers' children in the afternoons. There's no school nearby and no school bus for them. Isn't that awful?

'Oh, before I stop, I must tell you about Amelia! She is such a lively, interesting person, Grandad. I can see why you liked her so much . . .

Strong Opinions

'How come we never heard much about this Amelia, Dad?' Gwen teased. 'Did Mum know about her?'

'Of course she did,' Albert said huffily. 'Amelia sent us a wedding present. That carved rhinoceros in the hall, you've seen that, haven't you? Mum was the one who kept her up to date with our family news every Christmas. We often talked of going out for a visit but we never got around to it.'

Cora continued reading.

'Amelia's moved to a flat in Hartley's Drift but often comes out here. She told me she worked hard all her life and when she turned seventy-five she decided it was time for a change. No more cheese-making and bottling jam for her! She's taking painting lessons and joined a writers' circle and a book club and Cora's worried because she's going off on holiday to

Cape Town *by herself next month.*

'Cora's a bit old-fashioned and thinks all big cities are dens of iniquity but Amelia's determined to attend lectures on palaeontology at the adult education centre there. Apparently there're some fossils on the farm and she's always wanted to know more about them. And she drives around on a purple scooter!'

Grandad snorted with laughter and shook his head at the picture Helen's description had conjured up as Gwen went on.

'She has strong opinions on everything from politics to the right way to dose sheep for blowfly (whatever that may be). I can see she must have been quite difficult as a mother-in-law and I think Cora might be a bit relieved that she's moved away! Amelia still tells Adam and Flippie how to run the farm but although they listen politely, I think they just do their own thing.'

'Doesn't sound as though Amelia's changed much.' Albert grinned. 'Always had her opinion on everything! But she was never my girlfriend. Not really.'

'Oh, Dad, come on, admit it! The two of you on the farm, both of you youngsters . . . it's not like you to be so backward in coming forward!'

Albert chuckled.

'Her dad kept a very sharp eye on the two of us. He had a neighbour's son marked out as her future husband and he made that very clear to me at the time.'

Was that a note of regret in her father-in-law's voice, Gwen wondered, finishing the letter.

'There is some sort of trouble to do with Kasteelpoort but I'm not sure what. The farmer next door wants to buy some land and they don't want to sell but I have a feeling they're struggling financially. If they were forced to sell I think it would break Cora's heart, and Adam's.

'*Must stop now, my services as a beautician are needed!*'

'That'll be a first for Helen!' Angela had come in halfway through the letter. 'I don't think she even owns any eyeliner. But it sounds as though she's having a great time.'

Over the Moon

Gwen glanced at Angela's parcels.

'It looks as though you are too, darling. I've never known anyone who loves shopping as much as you . . . What have you bought today? Are you still using up those gift vouchers you and Mark got for your wedding?'

Angela turned pink.

'Actually, Mum . . . and Grandad . . . I've got some news.'

Gwen caught the excitement in her daughter's voice and instinctively knew what was coming next.

'I'm pregnant!'

'Oh, darling, that's wonderful news. Wonderful!' Gwen wrapped her arms around Angela, her eyes filling with happy tears. 'Congratulations to you both!'

She wiped her eyes, smiling through her tears.

'Don't mind me, love, you know I always cry when I'm happy!'

'You and Mark both.' Angela grinned. 'He's over the moon at the idea of being a father. Keeps telling me to take it easy and put my feet up after tea. He's insisted on doing the washing-up ever since we heard.'

Gwen stroked her daughter's hair tenderly.

'How long have you known?'

'Since Tuesday.' She grinned. 'But I didn't want to phone, I wanted to tell you both properly. So, Grandad, how do you feel about being a great-grandfather?'

'It's great news, poppet.' Albert blew his nose loudly. 'But I don't feel a day older than a grandfather!'

'So, Mum, let me show you what I bought. I couldn't resist these . . . '

Angela emptied the carrier bags on to the table and Gwen admired the brightly-coloured baby suits and tiny soft shoes.

'I just had to buy these cute little red shoes with teddy bears on — and I thought this navy top and trousers were lovely. They'll do for a boy or a girl . . . '

'When you were a baby I knitted the most beautiful lacy pram set in pale lemon,' Gwen said wistfully. 'And Helen had the same, in pink. I've still got the pattern somewhere . . . '

'Mum, nobody dresses their babies in pastel shades these days!'

Gwen realised she'd have to revise her ideas of what to knit for the new arrival.

'Well, the doctor says I'm due about November, so by the time he's sitting up we'll need lots of little sweaters.'

Gwen smiled again.

'Helen will be back long before the

baby's born then . . . have you written to her yet?'

'We wanted to tell you and Grandad first, so I'm going to write tonight. Mark and I would like her to be godmother. Don't you think Helen would be a great godmother?'

Gwen was silent, wondering how her older daughter would take the news of Angela's baby. For all Helen's calm assurances that she was quite happy with the way things had turned out, she worried that this might reopen old hurts. Hurts, and perhaps resentments that Helen had never admitted to anyone, maybe not even to herself.

School Begins . . .

'Miss Helen, you like to come with me, meet the children?' Tuleka's round face beamed invitingly. 'Time for their school — you can be teacher today.'

'I'd love to try, but I don't know how

we'll get on if they don't speak English.'

Tuleka's comfortable bulk shook with laughter.

'Hey, Miss Helen, you teach them English, then our children become very clever!'

Helen smiled as she scooped up a notebook and pencil, realising that that would take months and she was only here for a week or two.

She and Tuleka skirted a small dam under some pepper trees, disturbing some sleepy white ducks on the grass banks as they walked to the labourers' quarters.

Several small, thatched huts were scattered against a low hill, each with a fenced garden where a few low vines straggled across the earth under wire netting.

'Pumpkin,' Tuleka explained, following her gaze. 'Must cover with wire or the goats eat them.'

Chickens scratched in the dirt and a thin dog lying in the shade of a thorn tree thumped its tail sleepily as they passed. A few yellow-eyed goats looked up and skittered away nervously. Women, some with babies strapped to their backs, sat outside chatting and greeted Tuleka cheerfully.

One of them said something in Xhosa and Tuleka answered, laughing.

'She say, you too thin, you need to eat more food! I tell her, you come from far away, but I'll make you fat quick-quick!'

Helen pulled a face.

'You're doing that already,' she complained good-naturedly. 'You cook too well!'

Tuleka's cooking made it impossible to refuse second helpings. Lunch that day had been an enormous dish of lamb chops casseroled in orange juice and cloves, served with baked pumpkin, sprinkled with cinnamon and sugar and delicious baby peas she'd picked herself from Cora's garden.

While she'd tucked in, Helen thought of the single cheese sandwich she used to pack for herself when she was teaching, and promised herself to get back to her normal fare as soon as she left the farm.

Tuleka grinned at the compliment, then clapped her hands and called. Five barefoot but brightly-dressed children appeared from behind one of the huts, each clutching a book. They stopped short, staring at Helen in alarm. Tuleka said something and they followed her meekly to the old tables and stools which constituted her school under a pepper tree.

She and Helen sat on upturned buckets and faced the children.

'Good afternoon, boys and girls,' Tuleka pronounced slowly.

'Good afternoon, teacher,' they chorused.

'They speak English?' Helen was amazed.

'No, that is all they say,' Tuleka answered, 'but I teach them English letters.'

She fired off something in Xhosa and the children stood up and recited in a sing-song voice, 'A-B-C . . . ' going right through the alphabet at the tops of their voices, then sat down smiling proudly.

Helen was nonplussed.

'But have they learned the sounds the letters make?' she asked hesitantly.

'No, just say the ABC.'

'Can they write anything?'

Tuleka took a book from a small girl and opened it. Wavery capital letters were scrawled across the page and Helen smiled encouragingly at the little girl who stared down at her feet, grinning with embarrassment.

'That's very good,' she said.

'Mister Adam, he give them all a pencil, but goat ate some of them,' Tuleka said dolefully. 'Now Mr Adam, he say I must buy pencil box. Next time I go to town, I buy.'

'Maybe I could teach them to read one or two words, just to start them off?'

'Yes.' Tuleka beamed. 'Today, Miss Helen, you are the teacher!'

Translate

Helen bit her lip and smiled at the expectant faces. Where on earth do I start, she wondered. something familiar, something they know. Then she took a book from one of the children and drew a picture of a dog. Underneath she wrote *d-o-g* and, pointing to each letter, said the phonetic sound.

'D-O-G,' the boy said hesitantly, then beamed hugely. '*Inja!* Dog!'

'He say dog in Xhosa,' Tuleka said. 'Ho, Miss Helen, you draw nice picture.'

The book was passed along the bench, each child slowly pronouncing the sounds and grinning in recognition, pointing to the dog lying in the shade.

Helen felt a small, teacherly thrill. She could see that suddenly, they'd seen the connection between the letters and an actual word. She drew a picture of a pig, and wrote the word underneath it.

'P-i-g,' she enunciated, pointing to

each letter as she did so. The children's lips moved silently in imitation and she could almost feel their concentration.

'Tuleka, how old are these children?'

'Kanyiso, he nine year old. Her, Wenla, she don't know, her mother never write it down but she think five years. That boy, Mondli, he same as Kanyiso. Him, Yena, he six years and Meena, she seven years.'

I'll never remember these names, Helen thought. I must make them little name badges to wear, and I must prepare some simple worksheets. And see if I can find some coloured crayons.

Her mind raced ahead, thinking of the problems of teaching in English to children who had never heard the language before.

'Tuleka, could you translate for me when I explain?' she asked. 'I'd love to give them some basic reading lessons while I'm here but if I can't speak Xhosa . . . '

'Yes, Miss Helen, they like to learn English very much.'

Their trusting brown eyes were fixed on her, waiting for the next fascinating thing this strange woman would show them. I wish I were staying here a bit longer, she thought, there's so much I could do with them.

Helen felt something nudge her back roughly and turned round in alarm. A goat, bolder than the rest, was bent on investigating her notebook as a snack.

'Shoo!' she cried, flapping the book and the children burst out laughing. 'Shoo! Shoo!' they imitated and the goat shambled off.

'Tuleka's keeping you busy, I see.'

Adam seemed to appear from nowhere, then she saw his pick-up parked behind the huts. He looked over her shoulder at her clumsy efforts at drawing and smiled.

'Looks as though you could do with a proper reading book for them.'

'And that's not all!' she burst out. 'We need a reading book for each child, and some crayons, and a lined book for writing in, and . . . ' She pictured her well-equipped classroom in Bissington.

'And some colourful charts and — we need a classroom, too. We can't shoo the goats away all the time.'

'Hang on, hang on,' he protested. 'Tuleka's not a qualified teacher and the idea was that she'd teach them their letters and a few simple sums until the council decided to provide transport for them.'

'Adam, some of them are already much older than they should be for starting school. Back home most of my class were reading already and they were only five years old. These children have so much catching up to do. I'd really like to try and help them.'

He looked down at her quizzically.

'If I bought all the right stuff, would you stay on a bit longer? Get them reading and ready to enter the school?'

'No, much as I'd love to, I couldn't. I've a tour of a game park up near Johannesburg already booked, starting seven days from now.'

Adam was silent.

'Well, if you change your mind, I

know the children would be very grateful and so would I. So would the rest of the family. We all love having you here.'

She shook her head.

'I wish I could, really, Adam, but I have to get back home. I'm expecting to start a new school next term.'

A Change Of Heart

The past week had been wonderful and staying on at the farm with the Smit family was a tempting idea, but she had an obligation to the school.

'I understand.'

Adam led her to the pick-up.

'By the way, here are a couple of letters for you that Ma picked up at Hartley's Drift.'

One, redirected by her mother, looked official and she opened it first. In three politely worded lines, the principal of Great Hamwood Infants' School regretted her application for the post had been unsuccessful, but wished her every success in her future career.

Numbly, Helen recognised Angela's exuberant scrawl on the other letter and tore it open.

She read the words *Baby . . . Mark and I are so thrilled . . . I know he'll make a wonderful daddy . . . Mum's already knitting . . . we want you to be the godmother . . .* then the handwriting blurred.

Mark and Angela were going to have a baby. They were going to be parents. She knew she should have been prepared for this, and she could tell how thrilled Angela was. So why did she have this hollow, desolate feeling instead of being pleased for them?

Maybe, deep down, I'm envious of my little sister's life, she thought wretchedly. She had a house, a husband and now a baby on the way. Angela sounds so happy and content while I don't even have a job waiting for me when I go home . . . She felt a sudden impatience with Angela, with her confidence that her sister would greet her announcement with unconditional joy, and her certainty that Helen would agree to be the godmother.

'News from home?' Adam queried, looking at the stamps.

'Yes.' Helen looked at the children and Tuleka in the shade of the pepper tree then turned to Adam decisively.

'If your mother wouldn't mind having me a bit longer, I can stay on after all, if you want me to,' she told him.

There was no reason to hurry home any longer.

3

Rewarding

Today was a colourful day at the 'School in the Shed', as Helen thought of it. She stood in front of her class, each child wearing a hat they'd made themselves, each one painted a different colour. Looking at the glowing faces, she pointed to the smallest girl, one of seven who'd come from Jacob de Wild's neighbouring farm the previous week to join the class.

'Tombi, what colour is Wenla's hat?' she asked.

'Wenla's hat is yellow,' Tombi said slowly.

'And — Meena? What colour is Yonke's hat?'

Meena took a deep breath, her face split by a wide smile.

'Yonke's hat is green.'

'And Kanyiso? What colour is my hat?'

That was a challenge, as she'd made herself a pointy, striped hat using every colour of the rainbow, but the little boy knocked over the small plastic chair in his rush to answer.

'All colour! Is red, is green, is blue, is black, is yell, is . . . '

'Yellow,' Helen corrected gently. 'Very good, Kanyiso.'

Helen was thrilled at the speed with which the children were learning the new words.

They're so rewarding to teach — like little sponges, she wrote to her mother. *They hang on to every word I say and remember things so well. I remember how nervous I was to start with, but I'm enjoying this class more than any I've ever taught.*

She looked around the old shed with satisfaction. Barely a month ago it had been full of old garden pots and broken farm equipment, all covered in a thick layer of dust and cobwebs, the light barely able to filter through the dirty windows.

Today it looked like a real classroom. Helen had whitewashed the walls and decorated them with colourful posters of animals and birds. Adam had fitted a makeshift ceiling so the sun didn't beat down directly through the tin roof and Anna-Marie had made some curtains out of old sheeting, hand-painting them with a pattern of fish in bright reds and greens.

Cora had offered a pile of the Smit family's old storybooks and Amelia had provided a beautiful model of a dinosaur which had pride of place on a cupboard.

One morning the children had all piled on to the back of the pick-up to buy supplies in Hartley's Drift. For most of them it was their first-ever visit to a town and they were round-eyed with the excitement of the shops and traffic.

Pencils, crayons, pots of paint, brushes, workbooks, posters, coloured paper . . . Helen had made a list, determined to equip her little school as best she could.

She'd bought the very simplest reading books and found some more on the old bookshelves in the farmhouse. Small plastic tables and chairs were arranged in a circle before her, and each child had a workbook and pencil in front of them.

Twelve pairs of solemn brown eyes watched their teacher intently; twelve hands were raised to answer her questions.

They still wore the little nametags Helen had made for them, but she was already able to identify all the children.

Tuleka had explained that every *Xhosa* name had a meaning.

'Kanyiso, it means 'shining light',' she'd told her.

Just right for Kanyiso, Helen thought. He's such a cheerful boy and certainly one of the brightest.

She'd illustrated his badge with a yellow sun. Vuyo meant happy, so she drew a smiling face. Mondii meant 'supporter of the family', so after a bit of thought, Helen drew a wall of bricks. When Tuleka explained this to him, the little boy smiled proudly and murmured something to her.

'Mondii, he say he build for his mother a big house one day,' Tuleka informed her.

For the first few days of her classes, Helen had begged Tuleka to stay and translate for her, but she'd soon realised that she needed to communicate with the children herself. So far it seemed to be working, although sometimes the children dissolved into giggles at her attempts to act out the words.

She glanced at the clock on the wall. Midday, which meant it was story-time. She opened a book and the children drew their chairs closer in readiness.

Helen read slowly and carefully, pointing to the words as she did so and holding the book up for them all to study the pictures.

She quite lost herself in the story and

was startled to hear someone approach. It was Cora.

'Oh, I don't mean to interrupt, Helen. If you're not finished . . . '

'It's quite all right. I think that's enough for today . . . '

Helen dismissed the children, making sure they packed everything into their bags. Still wearing their paper hats, they filed sedately past her then burst into a fast gallop outside the door. All except Meena, who'd won the coveted role of classroom monitor for the week and stayed behind for a few minutes to sweep the floor and wipe the little blackboard.

'A Breath Of Fresh Air'

Helen closed the door of the classroom and walked with Cora towards the vegetable garden, enjoying the dappled shade of the flowering gums and the buzz of the bees, loud in the midday sun.

'I can't tell you how happy I am that you're teaching the children, my dear.' Cora smiled. 'Tuleka says they're all really making progress. You're quite a breath of fresh air in our lives, although I know you must be regretting that teaching job you were hoping to get in England.'

'Oh, I don't really mind that at all,' Helen responded. 'Teaching here is far more of a challenge than Great Hamwood Infants! And staying with your family is a lot fuller than my life at home. There's always something happening on the farm.'

Helen had taken over the bottle-feeding of two orphan lambs kept in a pen next to the vegetables, and besides teaching each morning, she worked in the garden, helped Cora in the dairy and had generally immersed herself in the daily doings of the farm. She and Tuleka had become good friends, and most evenings before supper, Helen went into the kitchen to watch and learn from her.

'I wanted to pick some green beans for lunch,' Cora said, 'and we've got such a good crop this year I thought I might bottle some curried beans as well.'

'That'll be something new! I'll give you a hand.'

They started filling the basket between them, pulling off handfuls of crisp, green beans.

'My grandfather would love this huge garden,' Helen told Cora. 'I've never seen veggies so big and healthy.'

Cora smiled.

'You won't believe how it looked one year, after the locusts. Twenty years ago they didn't know how to control them, and we lost all the crops — even the grass in the fields. Those locusts swarmed so thickly you couldn't see the sky. It was as though it turned to night and we just prayed they wouldn't settle on our lands.

'But they did, and we could hear them chewing, millions of tiny little mouths biting at everything that was green and growing. And an hour later when they flew off, there was nothing left, just bare earth.'

'That must have been terrible. Like a scene from a horror film.'

'Adam can remember it, but Flippie was too young to understand. Anna-Marie hadn't been born then.'

Cora paused.

'That's another reason I'm so glad you've decided to stay with us, Helen. You're a good influence on Anna-Marie. She's so headstrong, with all that dreaming of being a dress designer! That's not for a country girl like her. Besides, she needs to train for a proper job. These days a girl can't expect to marry a rich farmer and just stay at home.'

'Is that what you did?'

Helen knew that staying on the farm was the last thing Anna-Marie wanted to do.

'Let's just say I married a good farmer, not a rich one. I was born across the mountains and I'd known Gerard since we were youngsters. I always knew we'd marry one day. But Anna-Marie must become a secretary and find a nice secure job in Hartley's Drift.'

'But she's really talented, Cora. She makes such beautiful clothes for herself and she's so creative. Perhaps if she went to college in Cape Town and . . . '

Cora's voice was abruptly cold and firm.

'Anna-Marie is much too young to leave home. I know what happens to girls in big cities like Cape Town. It sounds as though you might also be encouraging her in this nonsense. Ouma and Marita are bad enough, but I thought I could rely on you to talk some sense into her. Apparently not.'

Cora picked up the basket and walked back to the farmhouse, her lips set in an angry line. Helen's heart sank.

Talented

Helen hurried after her, alarmed at Cora's sudden anger, and caught up with her in the kitchen.

'I'm so sorry, Cora. I never wanted to offend you,' she apologised. 'I didn't say I was encouraging Anna-Marie to leave home against your wishes, I just meant . . . '

Cora seemed calmer now.

'We'll say no more about it. Just remember you're a sophisticated girl from overseas and Anna-Marie isn't. But she's a good child and will do what she knows is best for her. Now, my dear, would you ring the bell and call everyone for lunch?'

Helen loved banging the piece of metal hanging from the tree. It was the signal for the workers to stop for their midday meal and for the family to gather around the big dining-room table. Tuleka brought steaming bowls of vegetables and a huge casserole dish filled with what looked like a browned custard dotted with leaves.

Helen sniffed, mystified. It reminded her of curry.

'This is *bobotie*, Miss Helen, very

nice. Is mincemeat and curry spices and onions, with egg and milk on top and then I put over bay leaves and I bake it.'

'Another one for my recipe book!' Helen grinned. 'You must give me the recipe, Tuleka. It smells wonderful.'

'No, Miss Helen, you know I don't weigh. I just put in with my hand!'

'And the only thing to serve with *bobotie* is yellow rice and raisins,' Amelia said briskly.

She was leaving by coach for Cape Town that afternoon to attend a fortnight's course on palaeontology at an adult education centre and had come to say goodbye.

'I'm taking the photographs of those fossils near the river,' she said to Adam. 'I hope I can have them identified while I'm there. I'd love to take a few samples with me but they're too big to move. Besides, I know you're not supposed to do that unless you're an expert.'

'Which you no doubt will be when you come back, Ouma,' Flippie teased.

'You're so lucky, Ouma,' Anna-Marie mourned, looking pointedly at her mother. 'Out every night and seeing movies and visiting all those shops. I read in the paper there's an international fashion show at the convention centre there. All the big names will be showing, with famous models and everything.'

'Never mind, darling, one day the name Anna-Marie Smit will also be up there,' Amelia said, purposefully ignoring her daughter-in-law. 'You'll get your chance.'

'Ouma Amelia!' Cora warned.

'Well, she will,' Amelia continued defiantly. 'My granddaughter is a very talented girl. She's going to make the name of Smit famous one day with her designs, you mark my words.'

'One day when I'm old and doddery, if Ma has anything to do with it,' Anna-Marie muttered.

'Change the subject, this record's getting worn out,' Flippie put in, determined not to let things get too serious. 'Hey, Helen — fancy a ride up to the top of the mountain?'

'I'd love it!' Helen agreed immediately.

Protected Species

The Three Castles loomed over the farm, a solid and comforting backdrop. Sometimes covered in cloud, sometimes a hazy blue, the mountains with their rocky cliffs crowning the summits were well named, Helen thought — Drie Kasteels. The central peak was slightly higher than the other two and on a clear day a small beacon could be discerned against the horizon.

Surprise

After lunch, Helen picked up the sun-hat Anna-Marie had lent her and followed Flippie out, but to her surprise Adam was loading the back of the pick-up with feed bags.

'*I'm* taking Helen,' Flippie fumed. 'Didn't you hear?'

'The top camp needs more oats,' Adam answered equably. 'There's no point in making two trips. Besides, Helen might like to see the goats.'

'Your precious babies!' Flippie grunted. 'I'm sure Helen isn't interested in a bunch of kids.'

'No, I'd love to see them,' Helen said politely, thinking that she'd seen plenty of the scrawny animals near the huts.

Adam climbed up behind the driver's wheel and Flippie, his face like thunder, handed Helen up to sit between them.

'I hope you don't mind a rough ride,' Adam said, 'but the view from the top is pretty spectacular.'

'Beats walking to the top, I'm sure!' She smiled. 'My grandad climbed all three of the peaks while he was here. Apparently your gran tricked him into doing them. She told him it was a tradition!'

'That sounds like Ouma, all right.'

Adam grinned. 'Mind you, she used to climb up there quite often herself when she was younger. I think she was a bit of a tomboy.'

'She always complained that her father stopped her climbing because of the leopards,' Flippie added. 'The mountains are full of them. Man-eaters.'

'Leopards?' Helen swallowed. A dear little buck would be delightful, but a wild leopard?

'Flippie's joking. We haven't seen a leopard on these mountains since I was about ten,' Adam said regretfully. 'It's a pity, really. They didn't do much damage, just took the odd lamb or two. But in those days, most farmers round here liked to show off with a couple of leopard skins hanging on their walls. They shot the lot.'

'Jacob's got a leopardskin cover on his sofa,' Flippie put in. 'Had it specially made. He says it's worth a fortune.'

'They're protected game these days

and there's a huge fine for anyone caught shooting one. And a good thing, too,' Adam added firmly. 'Anyone lucky enough to have wild game on their farm should look after it, not shoot it.'

'We might see our zebras,' Flippie went on. 'Adam bought a couple ages ago and they've been breeding well. How many now, Ad, eight of them?'

'One of the young females is pregnant. She could be foaling round about now so we could get lucky and see her baby.'

They'd left the low-lying lands of the farm and were bumping up a rough track at an alarming angle. Wedged firmly between Adam at the wheel and Flippie, Helen braced herself firmly against the dashboard, gasping and laughing out loud as they dipped and swayed over the humps.

'This is fun!' she shouted above the noise of the motor.

'This is nothing, Helen.' Flippie grinned. 'Wait till we get on to the top.' She couldn't help noticing that Flippie had casually put his arm around her shoulders to steady her.

Adam brought the pick-up to an abrupt, dusty halt next to a fenced field that ran almost vertically down the mountain. Clustered around a small water trough were about a dozen white goats, some with small kids. They were plump, with long, silky white hair, and looked nothing like the bony, pencil-eating goats down at the huts.

'They're beautiful. What are they?' she asked him.

'Angoras. You get mohair from them and I'm experimenting to see how they do here.'

'Adam's convinced there's big money in mohair,' Flippie said caustically. 'Always trying something, is my brother. Remember the pineapples?'

Adam's lips tightened slightly but he smiled easily.

'So, that crop didn't work out. It was the wrong soil and they needed too much water. But these goats are looking good.' He pulled a silvery strand from where it had hooked on the barbed wire fence. 'Feel this.'

The strand of hair was smooth and rich under Helen's fingers and she could imagine herself wrapped in a warm swirling cloak of the soft shining stuff.

Adam offloaded the oats and tipped the contents into the feeding troughs, watching the goats gathering around greedily.

'Right, Helen, are you ready to go on to the summit?'

There was more?

'Of course,' she said calmly, but peering down the almost vertical slope she felt a flood of panic. What if they rolled off the edge?

'It's the kind of road these four by fours were built for,' Flippie said gleefully. 'Better than a rollercoaster!'

Helen swallowed, and shut her eyes tightly.

'It's a rather primitive track and it's pretty overgrown these days,' Adam said as he changed down to the lowest gear and the pick-up ground its way noisily uphill, crushing the small bushes that grew on the track. 'But don't worry, we're perfectly safe, I promise.'

Helen opened her eyes and laughed out loud with the thrill of it. The horizon jerked and leapt as they drove higher, the road falling away in a sheer drop on one side and the rocky crags looming above them on the other. Strangely, she just felt exhilarated and not frightened at all.

Adam seemed to have a masterly control of the enormous vehicle, and on her left, Flippie was whistling unconcernedly.

'This — is — hair-raising — but fantastic!' Helen gasped, wishing the bumpy ride could go on for ever. All too quickly, it seemed, they'd reached the summit, where the track ended in dense scrub.

All around them was the hot silence of the mountain top, broken only by the buzzing of unseen insects and the shrill cry of a black eagle skimming the wind beneath them.

'Great view, isn't it? Thought you'd like it,' Flippie said proudly.

'Like it? This is amazing,' Helen whispered. She turned to Adam. 'Thanks for bringing me up here. It's wonderful. And the ride was great, too. Like Flippie said, better than any ride at the fair.'

'Glad you enjoyed it.' He grinned.

'I can see the farm!' Helen delightedly spotted a small bent figure. 'There's your mum down there in the garden. And someone's hanging out the washing. They look like dolls from here.'

Delighted

Adam suddenly gripped her arm.

'Shh . . . look.' He pointed down the mountain slope to a smooth patch of green. Well-camouflaged by the dappled shade of a thorn tree, two zebras and a long-legged foal were peering nervously up at them. As they watched, a second foal stood up on wobbly legs and started to nurse, butting its mother with its head.

'She's had twins! That's lucky. Zebras very rarely have twins.'

Adam was obviously delighted.

'I'd like to build up a fair-sized herd. There used to be lots of Cape Mountain zebra here, but they disappeared after some bad droughts about twenty years ago.'

'Your mum mentioned those.' Helen nodded. 'Is that the de Wilds' farm?'

She pointed down to a wide scattering of farm buildings with a big red-roofed homestead in the centre, the whole settlement ringed with trees. A small, ant-like sports car, followed by a puff of white dust, sped off from the farmhouse.

'Yes.' Adam pursed his lips and turned away.

'Hey, that's Marita! I bet she's on her way over to ours.' Flippie was irrepressible. 'Looks like she's in a hurry to see you, Adam. We'd better get back. We wouldn't want to keep your lady waiting . . .'

'She probably wants to meet you, Helen,' Adam said, ignoring his brother's remark. 'She'll have heard about you from her father.'

'I'm looking forward to meeting her, too,' Helen remarked. 'Anna-Marie can't stop talking about her.'

She smiled at Adam as she said the words, although, truthfully, she would have preferred to stay on top of the mountain, listening to the hum of the insects and watching the zebra foals.

A Bone Of Contention

'Hello, Mum.' Angela Milne put her head around the door of the herb centre her mother, Gwen, owned and ran almost single-handedly. 'I thought we'd find you still here. Any chance of a cuppa for two thirsty shoppers?'

'Of course, dear.' Gwen put down the punnets of marjoram she had just pricked out.

'Make that three thirsty people. I'm

nearly done. You know where the kettle is.' She hugged Mark. 'I didn't expect to see you two in the middle of the week!'

'Wednesday's early closing for the Leighton office,' he explained. 'That's to make up for having to work on a Saturday morning. I had the weekends free before.'

'Suits me!' Angela called from the tiny kitchen behind the workroom. 'I can have a nice lie-in without feeling guilty.'

Gwen smiled at her son-in-law.

'Sit down, Mark, and tell me all about your job. Is everything going all right?'

'Fine, Gwen.' After five years of calling her Mrs McLeod, Mark had finally made the leap to her first name. 'They're a really nice crowd. Helpful, too.'

'Is the work very different from what you did before?'

'A bit. I've got my own office and I'm sort of in charge of the software department. It's only seven people, though.'

'Oh, he's the boss, he's just too modest to tell you!' Angela ruffled her husband's hair as she brought the tea. 'He works far too hard. I hardly see him.'

'You know I can't leave early,' Mark said evenly. 'There's loads of work coming in. I can hardly walk out if half of them are working till eight o'clock. I have to be the last to leave.'

'But eight o'clock? That's a very long day, Mark.' Gwen was sympathetic, but not Angela.

'Tell me about it! I've given up cooking him a nice tea as it's always dried up by the time he comes home.'

She glared at Mark, who shifted uncomfortably.

'Come on, Angie, don't be like that. You've got to understand that for the time being — '

'What I don't understand is why you can't all just be a bit more efficient and come home at a reasonable time!' she burst out. 'I get lonely. I haven't any friends there and I shouldn't be all on my own for so long if I'm expecting. It's not right.' She turned to Gwen. 'You tell him, Mum.' There were tears threatening in her big blue eyes.

Gwen bit her lip. This wasn't a discussion she wanted to be part of, and she wished Angela wouldn't quarrel with Mark in front of her.

'I'm sure things will work out after a bit, dear,' she soothed. 'You must expect Mark to take time to settle in to his new position. After all, he's in charge now. And I'm sure once you've made some friends there you'll be able to pop in for tea and that will make the day seem shorter.'

Selfish

Privately, she wondered why her younger daughter didn't look for temporary work for a few months. It wasn't good for her to sit moping at home, and there was no reason why she shouldn't carry on working a while longer.

Mark stood up and wrapped his arms

around his wife, kissing the top of her head.

'I'll try to get home earlier, sweetie,' he said helplessly. 'I'll do my best. I know it's not easy for you.'

'Promise?' Angela sniffed and wiped her eyes. 'I know I'm being a wimp, but blame my hormones! Sorry for snarling at you, darling.'

Gwen smiled in relief, but she felt the stirrings of concern, wondering how many of those sorts of outbursts Mark had to put up with, hormones or not. It wasn't like Angela to be so selfish. She was usually so sunny and optimistic. She just hoped that Mark would understand.

'How's Grandad?' Angela asked, her sharp words forgotten. 'I haven't seen him for quite a while.'

'I'm a bit worried about him, to tell the truth,' Gwen admitted. 'I think he's doing too much. He's over eighty, you know, and he just won't slow down. I thought he was looking tired last weekend, but he said he'd been out delivering those newsletters of his and forgot to eat lunch.'

'Well, you can't stop Grandad,' Angela said cheerfully. 'He's got more energy than I have.'

'Next week he's off on some protest about that chemical plant near the bird sanctuary,' Gwen fretted. 'I've decided to go along, just in case. You never know how those things will turn out.'

'Helen should be here to keep an eye on him,' Angela said. 'He misses her. And so do I. But she seems to want to stay on over there for ever.'

'Not for ever,' Gwen said mildly. 'She'll probably just stay until the end of the year. She's so interested in teaching those African children. It must be quite a challenge, but you know your sister, she loves to get involved. Anyway, I'm sure she'll be home for Christmas.'

'I thought she'd be back in time for the baby,' Angela said crossly. 'I wanted her to make matching curtains and a cot cover for the nursery.'

'Why not make them yourself?' Gwen

asked reasonably. 'You can sew perfectly well.'

'Not as well as she can. I suppose I'll just have to go out and buy them and hang the expense!'

'But, Angie, you know we agreed to stick to a budget . . . ' Mark began. Then he grinned suddenly. 'Oh, what the heck, I can see you've made your mind up!'

He glanced ruefully at Gwen and gave a crooked grin.

'Born to shop, my wife was.'

No, she wasn't, Gwen thought. They'd just bought that big house and Angela wasn't earning. Someone needs to talk to this young lady, and I suppose it'll have to be me.

But she wasn't looking forward to it.

Animated

Shaded by the riotous pink carpet of bougainvillea which trailed down the side of the verandah, Helen sat on an old wicker chair observing Marita, who was perched nonchalantly on the arm of Adam's chair.

She was tall, striking rather than beautiful, with smooth tanned skin and masses of dark hair swept back into a French roll, from which curly tendrils escaped. Her brown eyes sparkled with fun and her whole face was animated and expressive. Helen couldn't help liking her.

'So there I was, with this traffic cop frowning at me and taking out his book and I thought, oh, no, another ticket and my pa will explode!' Marita waved her slender hands around in mock horror.

'So I opened the door and let him see a bit of leg, and said, 'Oh, please, officer, give me another chance! I promise I won't speed again, but my little dog is having puppies and I must be there to hold her paw!' And of course he gave me a nice smile and said OK, just this once, and maybe he could come and see the puppies one day if I gave him my address — so I gave him yours, Ouma Amelia!'

Her laughter was infectious and Amelia joined in.

'I'll offer him a cup of coffee if he ever appears on my doorstep!' she promised, patting Marita's hand affectionately. 'You get away with murder, my dear!'

'Honestly, Marita, all traffic cops aren't as dim as that.' Adam was smiling at her. 'You'll try your crazy excuses once too often.'

'There's always another story where that one came from!' She grinned. 'So, Helen, I hear you've started a school for the kids. How's it going?'

'Well, I think. The children really seem to enjoy the lessons and most of them can write their names and even read a few words.'

'My pa says since you've started teaching he can't find any kids to open the gates or clean his truck, because they're always in school!'

'It's only three hours a morning,'

Helen protested. 'I hope he won't stop them coming.'

'No, I wouldn't let him. I told him it was a good idea. The workers are so pleased you're doing something for them.'

'Thank Adam,' Helen said. 'If he hadn't helped out and paid for the equipment, I'd never have got any-where.'

'Yes, he's a star, isn't he?' Marita turned to Adam and kissed him playfully on the cheek. She leaned lightly against him and continued. 'I've got a lot of my old picture books somewhere. Could you use them?'

'All contributions gratefully received.' Helen smiled. 'Perhaps you'd like to sit in on the lessons some time? You could give me a hand helping them with their writing.'

'Me? Teaching just isn't my thing, I'm afraid. But I'm sure you're good at it. You look the patient sort.'

Her friendly grin took the sting out of this remark.

'Adam,' she went on, 'there's a dance at the centre in Hartley's Drift next Saturday and I want you to come with me. They've got a decent disco for a change, up from Cape Town.'

'Oh? I hadn't heard about that one.'

'It's in aid of the children's home. Come on, you can't say no. I'll drive us.'

'Well . . . ' Adam hesitated.

'That's great!' Flippie put in. 'We can all go! Helen and I could come, too.'

'You And Flippie?'

Helen smiled weakly. 'But I haven't brought any — er — party clothes.'

'Don't worry about that, dear,' Amelia said. 'The dances are great fun and I'm sure Anna-Marie can run you up something to wear in no time. Right, my sweet?'

''Course, I'd love to.' Anna-Marie grinned. 'I'll design something fabulous for you, Helen. We can go to town

122

tomorrow to find some material.'

'So we'll all go. Adam and me, Flippie and Helen, and Anna-Marie.' Marita couldn't have made the pairing-off more obvious. She winked at the teenager.

'There'll be loads of gorgeous guys there, Anna-Marie, all dying to dance with you!'

'I know, and they're all farmers,' she grumbled. 'Not one of them knows how to dance.'

'Hey, my footwork's fantastic!' Flippie protested.

'Yeah, for someone with two left feet you're not bad.'

'We'll go in our pick-up, then,' Adam said. 'We can't all fit into your sports car, Marita.'

'Don't sound so relieved! I'll take you for a drive on your own one day.' She smiled at him. 'I promise not to exceed the speed limit.'

Cora bustled out on to the *stoep*, car keys in hand.

'Ouma Amelia, if you want to catch

that coach, we should really get going.'

Adam threw Flippie a look.

'It's time we went back to work, too. Goodbye, Ouma, look after yourself and have fun.'

'I will, I promise!' Amelia was flushed with excitement. 'It's five years since I was last in Cape Town. I'm definitely going to enjoy myself!'

The boys loaded her luggage into the boot and watched as the car disappeared down the farm road.

The three girls sank back on to their chairs, Helen fanning herself in the heat.

'So . . . you and Flippie, eh?' Marita smiled at Helen. 'He's such a cute guy.'

'No, I mean, I like him, of course, but it's not me and Flippie. Not like that.'

'Well, he certainly fancies you, anyone can see that.'

Marita turned to Anna-Marie.

'Guess what? My dad's going to buy me a little flat in Cape Town, just so I can spend some weekends there. Isn't that sweet of him? And if you came, I could show you the hot spots around town. We'd have a ball!'

'Ma would never let me.' Anna-Marie sighed.

'She'll change her mind if you just keep on at her,' Marita said languidly. 'My dad always does what I want, in the end.'

'Well, Ma's not like that. You know how she feels about big cities.'

'But Cape Town's hardly a den of iniquity. It's got great beaches and the mountain and the shops along the waterfront are fabulous. If you went to college there you could stay in my flat . . . Think about it,' Marita finished.

Helen said nothing, watching the emotions flit across Anna-Marie's expressive face as Marita spoke. Envy . . . longing . . . determination.

If Marita goes on encouraging her there'll be trouble, she thought. Poor Anna-Marie, she's so desperate to become a dress designer!

'It does sound fantastic.' Anna-Marie

sighed. 'And I'll get there sooner than Ma thinks, see if I don't.'

A Party Atmosphere

'Dad? Are you ready?' Gwen knocked again and then opened Albert's front door. She picked up the post from the mat and went through to the dining-room, where the table was buried under piles of old newspaper cuttings and letters, surrounding an old upright typewriter. She knew her father-in-law was busy with some sort of book he was writing, but she wondered how he could find anything in such a muddle.

There were boxes of old photographs and in one she recognised a much younger Albert, standing next to a tractor in what was obviously a foreign background. Kasteelpoort?

'Ah, there you are!' Albert was wearing an old sheepskin jacket and carrying a rolled-up flag. 'Just finished making this. What do you think?' He unfurled it proudly and waved it about.

Hands Off Meredale Marshes! its slogan read.

'Great, Dad, very eye-catching. Now I've brought some hot chocolate and biscuits in case this protest goes on a bit long. You never think of your own comfort.'

'Probably won't have time to drink anything,' Albert said briskly. 'The lads are planning quite a do today. We've got the TV people coming, so we really need to make folk sit up and take notice.'

When they arrived, the entrance to the bird sanctuary was teeming with people, many of whom recognised Albert and greeted him cheerfully. There was almost a party atmosphere and Gwen could see that most people wore protest badges from other demonstrations as well as a *Save Our Meredale Marshes* button.

'You go and park the car down the lane, Gwennie. I'll see you around here,' Albert said, and was immediately swept up in the crowd.

He's in his element, Gwen thought fondly as she drove off. He's a real old battler, is Albert McLeod.

The protest had been well advertised and she had to drive a long way down the lane before she found a spot to park. Then she took the basket of tea things and an extra sweater for her father-in-law off the back seat and locked the car.

TV Cameras

Walking back up the lane, she noticed someone had erected a makeshift platform near the gate and Albert and several others were standing on it. One of them was addressing the crowd through a loud-hailer and Albert had unrolled his banner and was waving it aloft for the benefit of the TV cameras opposite.

'Do we want our water to be polluted so that some multinational company can make a profit?' the speaker shouted.

The crowd answered him good-naturedly.

'NO, WE DON'T!'

'Do we want our endangered birds killed by poisons in the water?' he shouted again.

'NO, WE DON'T!'

Honestly, Gwen thought as she drew closer. It's like some sort of football match sing-along.

'And do we want a concrete disaster to be built in this famous beauty spot?'

'NO, WE DON'T!'

Just then, several youngsters tried to climb on to the platform. Gwen saw them scrambling up and someone else trying to stop them, then suddenly the whole wooden structure disappeared before her eyes with a loud, splintering crash.

All the people on the stage, as well as Albert, were thrown to the ground as it collapsed. Horrified, Gwen rushed up to the edge of the crowd, but she could see nothing over their heads. She could only hear the yells of those on the ground.

'Albert!' she shouted, pushing frantically through the press of people.

If something had happened to him, she'd never forgive herself for letting him attend this protest. Why hadn't she thought it through properly and tried to prevent him from coming here? She could only pray he'd be all right . . .

4

On Camera!

Gwen frantically pushed her way through the crowd of protesters milling around the broken platform.

'Let me through!' she shouted, and with a strength she didn't know she possessed, she used her elbows and made her way to the front.

'Sorry . . . excuse me . . . let me pass, please . . . '

Trembling, she reached the front and was hugely relieved to see Albert sitting up, rubbing his ankle but still clutching his banner. Next to him, a young lad was lying against the splintered remains of the platform. His leg was folded at an awkward ankle and he was sobbing with pain. Two men carrying a first-aid box hurried forward and cleared the people who were ineffectually trying to help.

'Albert! Are you all right?' Gwen crouched down next to him. Her father-in-law's face was white with shock but he managed a little smile.

'I'm fine, love. Just wrenched my ankle. This poor lad caught the worst of it.' He patted the boy's shoulder. 'Don't worry, Kevin, they'll get you off to hospital and sorted in no time, right, boys?'

'What about you, Mr McLeod?' One of the men felt Albert's ankle gently. 'Should be at home watching it on telly, not jumping around like this at your age!'

'If everyone felt like that about important issues, young man, nobody would get anything done.' Albert snorted. 'I'm right as rain. Help me up, Gwenny.'

She grimaced ruefully at the first-aid man, who smiled back.

'Right old battler, aren't you?' he murmured. 'Come on then, let's see if you can put some weight on that ankle.'

Together, they helped Albert to his feet. He leaned heavily on Gwen's shoulder and hobbled away from the crowd, insisting he was all right.

'I'm taking you home right now,' Gwen said firmly. 'Let's find you a seat while I get the car.'

Albert sank gratefully on to a log without an argument.

'I'll wait here,' he said. 'I'll be fine. I just need to rest this ankle.'

Gwen hurried down the lane to where she'd parked the car. When she drove back, she was amazed to see a camera pointed at Albert, who was talking animatedly to a young girl holding a microphone.

'These marshes are the largest feeding grounds for wading birds in this part of the country,' he was saying. 'We've recently spotted the Gadwall duck, which is very rare around here, nesting in the reeds. We simply cannot allow the interests of big business to destroy our British bird life. Don't you agree, my dear?'

Albert gave the girl from the television a charming smile.

'If you'd like to sign our petition it's on the table.'

The reporter turned to face the camera.

'And that was Battling Albert McLeod on behalf of all the birds of Meredale Marshes . . . '

'You'll find petition forms at all the good shops in Bissington High Street,' Albert interjected loudly, off-camera.

Gwen grinned. There was just no stopping her father-in-law!

'Battling Albert. I like that!' He climbed slowly into the car. 'Well, after all that excitement, I could do with a cup of your hot chocolate now, Gwen!'

'You're Taking Mark's Side!'

'Mum! I've just seen Grandad on television!' Angela's excited voice on the phone broke into Gwen's thoughts that evening. 'He looked so well! I bet everyone watching went straight off and signed his petition.'

'I worry sometimes that your grandad's doing too much,' Gwen fretted. 'When I got him home he wouldn't even put his foot up. He insisted on making phone calls and getting excited about the protest all over again.'

'Can't stop him, can you? He loves getting involved.'

'I was wondering if you could spare a day to go over and visit him, dear? He was happy putting his papers in order when Helen was here, and if we could interest him in that again, perhaps he'd be prepared to stay in one place and have a good rest.'

'Mmm.' Angela didn't sound very enthusiastic. 'Sorting through those old papers sounds like a real waste of time. Maybe I could take him out for a drive or something?'

Gwen couldn't hide her annoyance.

'Angela, the idea is to get him to stay quietly indoors for a bit. And Helen said his old cuttings and letters were fascinating. Get him to tell you about his time in South Africa, and during the war. He's full of stories.'

'Oh, OK, I'll phone him when I have time. Did I tell you, I've met this really nice girl next door? Her name's Maeve Anderson and she's expecting, too.'

'That's nice. Someone to talk to.'

'She's at home all day and she asked me over on Monday for coffee. You should just see their house, Mum. Her husband's quite a bit older than she is; he runs a big plastics company. They seem to have loads of money. She's got the most beautiful furniture, and she's getting their nursery all fitted out.'

Gwen ignored the note of envy in Angela's voice.

'Speaking of the nursery, how's the sewing getting on?' she enquired briskly. 'Did you buy the material for the curtains and cot cover?'

'No. I'm hopeless at sewing, Mum. I'm going to buy them ready-made.'

'Angela, love . . . '

Gwen didn't want to interfere, but

136

felt she had to say something.

'I know you've had a lot of expenses with moving house. There's nothing wrong with home-made things and you've got a perfectly good sewing-machine. Curtains are so easy, after all, just straight seams.'

'You're taking Mark's side again!' Angela was instantly indignant. 'Don't you want your first grandchild to have nice things? I want our baby to have a pretty nursery like I saw in a magazine. And I want to buy one of those special baby cupboards with the bath built in and . . . '

'But those cost a fortune . . . your dad and I didn't have the money for special baby furniture but you didn't suffer, did you?'

'Of course not, Mum, but that was years ago! There's no need for our baby to do without anything. Mark's got a good job, after all. We can afford whatever we want.'

'I'm just saying that you'd have more fun if you did things yourself.' Gwen sighed. 'And Mark didn't sound very happy about you spending money unnecessarily. But if you made things yourself, you'd have a wonderful feeling of accomplishment. I could help you to measure your windows for curtains, if you like.'

But Angela had made up her mind.

'Stop nagging, Mum. Maeve's taking me shopping tomorrow. She knows all the best baby shops and she has some great ideas for our nursery. Mark won't mind when he sees how nice everything's going to look. Maeve's got wonderful taste.'

Gwen was pleased that Angela had found a friend, but wondered wryly if having this wealthy neighbour around was going to be such a good thing.

A Good Night Out

Cora insisted they drove to the dance in her spacious old sedan, with its cracked leather upholstery and rusty patches.

'We can't possibly cram into the pick-up with all of us dressed up to the nines! What are you thinking of, Adam?' she'd protested indignantly to her son when he'd suggested it.

'You're absolutely right, Ma.' He'd grinned, the appreciative look he'd given Helen making her glow.

She was delighted with the dress Anna-Marie had made for her — a simple black-and-white design which was cropped just on the knee. It showed off her newly-acquired tan and brought out the colour of her eyes. Her hair was swept off her face and held in a matching scrunchie.

'This would cost a fortune in a shop, Anna-Marie,' Helen had said as she tried the dress on that afternoon. 'And you just ran it up in a morning without a pattern! You really are what my mum would call clever with a needle. I hope you can persuade your mother to let you do this professionally.'

'I will, don't worry.'

Anna-Marie had made herself a

brown dress and had stencilled black and white designs along the hemline, giving it a fashionably ethnic look. Cora didn't seem to notice that her daughter looked a good ten years older than she was, with her copper-coloured curls tamed into a French roll, and black jet earrings.

'I hope the Venters will be there,' Cora said as she settled herself comfortably on the front seat. 'I want to speak to Louise about buying some of her goslings. She's making good money with those geese of hers. I'd like to try those next year.'

Helen slid on to the wide back seat, annoyed to see that Flippie immediately climbed in and sat next to her, his arm across the back of the seat behind her.

'I'll be the thorn between two rosebuds.'

He grinned and Anna-Marie winked at Helen. Oh, dear, she thought, annoyed. Flippie never misses a chance to get close, and everyone obviously thinks there's something between us. Even Adam.

Stunning

They had to drive all the way down to the main highway and then up Jacob's farm road to pick up Marita. It was the first time Helen had seen Jacob de Wild's farm, but it was too dark to make out more than a big freshly-painted barn and a paved courtyard in front of the farmhouse. The verandah of the big house was brightly lit and as Adam drew up, the door opened. Jacob stood framed in the light, smiling genially.

'Hello, boys. Good evening, Helen. Oh, good evening, Cora, I didn't know you were going along, too?'

Cora nodded shortly but didn't reply. Adam was civil enough as he bade him good evening.

'Still no rain . . . ' Jacob continued. 'Another couple of weeks and we'll have to start worrying, I reckon. How're those Angora goats of yours?'

'They're all right,' Adam replied curtly.

'Another of your mad ideas, but I guess you young ones have to learn from your own mistakes,' Jacob said without rancour. 'Ah, here she is.'

Marita waltzed up behind her father and planted a kiss on his cheek.

''Bye, Dad, have a nice evening. Don't wait up for me.'

She spun round on the verandah for their approval, her halter-neck dress a shimmer of red silk. Her cascade of dark curls framed her carefully made-up face. She looked stunning.

'Well, girls, what d'you think?'

But it wasn't their opinion she wanted, Helen thought.

Adam looked at her and smiled.

'That's a pretty dress, Marita. Make it yourself, did you?'

'You're joking, of course!' Marita waited while Flippie climbed out and held the door open for her. 'This came from the smartest shop in Cape Town. Anna-Marie, when you visit, I'll take you there. The clothes are to die for!'

Anna-Marie was awe-struck.

'You do look beautiful.'

She glared at her brother.

'How can you even think her dress is home-made? Anyone can see it's got class.'

Privately, Helen thought that, given the same expensive material, Anna-Marie could easily have turned out something just as good.

A Surprise Appearance

The community centre was packed. Tables with grandmothers, parents and small children sitting round them were placed against the walls, with a makeshift bar — currently three deep in people — at the end of the room. The music from the band on the platform competed with the babble of conversation and roars of laughter which erupted every now and then.

Helen was intrigued by the variety of fashions.

Some of the men, obviously farmers,

had started the evening in suits, although their jackets and ties had already been discarded in the heat, while others were in jeans and T-shirts. Their partners were dressed up, some with practical, short hairstyles or stiff perms and others with their hair gelled into trendy spikes.

She looked at the posters on the walls which showed the centre was used for a host of small-town events — baby shows, Miss Teen Queen of Hartley's Drift, handicraft exhibitions and a cake sale in aid of the orphanage.

Climbing ropes and wooden bars attached to the wall were part of the gym training for the local high school and there was still a painted backdrop on the stage from the last amateur dramatics production.

'Let's get that free table over there,' Flippie said. 'You girls sit while Adam and I get some drinks.'

Cora screwed her eyes up in the dim light.

'Oh, there's Louise Venter. I'll just go

over and say hello.'

The girls sat down and Marita looked around her, tapping her foot in time to the music.

'The whole of Hartley's Drift is here, by the looks of things,' she said happily. 'Watch out, Anna-Marie, here comes your number one fan!'

A hugely tall, sunburned young man came and stood in front of Anna-Marie, shyly mumbling something.

'OK, Willem,' Anna-Marie said resignedly as she stood up. 'But mind my toes, all right?'

He led her on to the crowded floor and Helen watched in amusement as he swayed awkwardly in front of Anna-Marie, unable to match her energetic rhythm.

'That's Willem Lourens — his dad's the lawyer here,' Marita told Helen. 'He's mad about Anna-Marie but she's not interested. Don't blame her, really. He doesn't have much to say for himself.'

'Who, Willem?' Cora came up behind

them. 'He's a lovely boy and I wish Anna-Marie would be a bit nicer to him.'

'Any luck with the goslings?' Helen asked, moving her chair to make room for Cora's.

'Yes, Louise is going to let me have a dozen. Oh.' Cora's voice changed. 'Marita, I didn't know your father was coming.'

Jacob de Wild made his way across the crowded hall to their table, smiling and nodding to people as he passed.

'I didn't, either,' Marita said in surprise.

'Hello, again.' Jacob smiled at them. 'May I?'

Without waiting for an answer, he sat down.

'Enjoying your holiday, Miss McLeod?' he asked genially. 'I hear they've got you hard at work on the farm these days.'

'The school? Oh, that's hardly work, I'm enjoying it so much.' Helen smiled. 'And thank you for sending your workers' children over as well. They're all doing really well.'

'That's good, I suppose,' he said doubtfully.

'These children are really keen to learn,' Helen said spiritedly. 'If they went to a proper school in town they could become anything. You might well have a future doctor or a lawyer on your farm!'

'That's all well and good, but I need them on the farm as soon as they're big enough to be useful. Well, Cora . . . ' He turned to her. 'When I saw you were coming along tonight, I thought you might need a partner to keep you company. So here I am.'

Cora managed a smile, but Helen could see the older woman was discomfited.

'I'm quite happy just watching the fun,' she said equably. 'My dancing days are over, I think.'

'Nonsense! That's a good band they've got here tonight. You're not just going to sit and watch, are you?' He stood up and proffered his hand. 'I

147

remember how you used to enjoy yourself at these dances. Come on, let's show these youngsters a thing or two!'

Cora hesitated but rose to her feet, and Helen could see she didn't want to cause a scene by refusing.

'Just one dance, then,' she said unwillingly, and with a triumphant smile Jacob led her into the throng on the floor. Helen wished she knew the cause of the tension between the two families.

'Here we are, ladies.'

With a flourish, Flippie deposited several cans of beer and some glasses on the table.

'Nice and cold.'

Well Suited

Helen bit her lip. She disliked the taste of beer but hadn't thought to tell Flippie and didn't want to hurt his feelings.

'Or would you rather have this?'

Adam handed her a tall glass of iced mango juice.

She accepted it gratefully and took a long sip.

'Our beer's an acquired taste,' Adam said quietly. 'It's pretty strong stuff.' He looked as though he was about to say something else but Marita stood up abruptly.

'About time, Adam,' she said. 'Come on, let's dance.'

She took his hand and led him off to the floor, leaving Flippie looking apologetic.

'Sorry, I should have asked what you preferred,' he mumbled, reddening.

'Don't worry, Flippie,' Helen said. 'I must be the only one here who doesn't like beer. I've just never got to like the taste of it.'

They sat in silence and sipped their drinks, watching Adam and Marita.

'Poor old Adam hasn't a chance.' Flippie smiled. 'Marita's made up her mind that he's the one for her.'

Helen felt her throat go dry, but he

was stating the obvious. Adam and Marita seemed so well suited, she thought, both of them tall and good looking. Marita threw her head back and was laughing up at Adam, and she saw his hands tighten on her back as he held her closer then spun her around. Helen had no doubt that Marita would get whatever she set her heart on.

'Feel like dancing?' Flippie asked. 'I mean, Helen, would you do me the honour . . . ?'

She smiled.

'I'd be delighted.'

Helen had never particularly enjoyed dancing, but everyone in the crowded hall just seemed to be bobbing up and down in time to the music in such a variety of dancing styles that it was obvious anything went.

Helen watched Flippie and copied him, amazed to discover she was loving it.

When the music finally stopped, they went back to their table, panting and laughing. They found another couple had drawn up chairs and were chatting to Adam and Marita above the noise.

Adam stood up to make the introductions.

'Helen, this is Paul Wilson and his wife, Dawn. I was at school with Paul but he's living in Cape Town these days,' he said by way of explanation. 'He and Dawn have been doing an adventure trail up country in their pick-up and it's sheer luck that they came here this evening.'

'Tell Me More'

'We're on our way home and Paul wanted to show me what a country dance is all about,' Dawn added. 'But we've just had our bones shaken and rattled for two days and I'm ready for a nice comfy bed at the hotel.'

'Adventure trail? What's that?' Flippie was immediately interested.

'A farmer I know up near Graaf-Reinet has opened his mountain track to the public,' Paul explained. 'There were about five four by fours doing the trail. Really hair-raising stuff, but great fun. A pity it's such a long way from Cape Town or Dawn and I would be up there more often.'

'Speak for yourself.' His wife smiled. 'I'm going to take weeks to get rid of these bruises!'

'You mean people pay good money to drive up a bad road?' Flippie interjected.

'Sure! It's the kind of thing those big babies were built for. All that power under the hood, all those special tyres, and Dawn just uses it to go shopping! But now we've joined this adventure trails club, we'll be doing more of these weekends. Won't we?' Paul grinned at his wife.

'I guess so,' she said. 'We had a good time, especially in the evening. The farmer laid on a big *braai* for us with music, and we met some nice folk from all over the country. A really fun weekend.'

'A *braai*?' Helen queried. 'What's that?'

'A barbecue,' Dawn supplied. 'Lashing of chops and sausage and steak cooked on a fire with jacket potatoes baked in the coals.'

'And lots of beer to wash it down.' Paul grinned.

Flippie was intrigued.

'That four by four trail sounds a great idea . . . Tell me more.' He leaned forward, his eyes alight with interest.

'Sounds a bit daft to me,' Adam said dismissively before turning to Helen. 'Would you like to dance?'

Helen's heart leapt and she accepted with a smile.

'I can see why some folk from the city would pay for that sort of adventure,' Helen remarked, as they threaded their way through the tables to the dance floor. 'I loved that ride up the track with you and Flippie to see the goats.'

'Some people have more money than sense,' Adam said sourly, then his expression changed with the tempo. 'Oh, they're playing something slow. We can actually talk to each other.'

He took Helen in his arms and she leaned against him, giving herself up to the magical moment of dancing with Adam. She knew she shouldn't let herself enjoy this too much, because it was clear from Marita's words and actions that Adam was spoken for.

She could tell that Marita was watching them intently as they spun around the floor, but she was overwhelmed by Adam's strength and closeness against her body.

She didn't want to talk at all, she just wished the music would go on and on.

'I'm glad you're here, Helen. With us on the farm, I mean.'

'So am I,' she said softly. 'I'm loving every minute of my stay.' She was so close to him she could feel his chest reverberating as he spoke.

'You make a difference to all of us,' he continued. 'I've sometimes thought you must have been born on a farm to fit in the way you do. Sure you haven't got farming ancestors?'

'Not at all!' She laughed. 'Although my mum runs a herb centre, she's really just got a big garden and buys in quite a lot of her stock. My grandad's really keen on organic farming but he's only got a small patch to practise on. He mostly just writes about it.'

'Do you ever get homesick? For your family in England?'

'Not really. Maybe I've just been too busy to think about them too much . . . Of course, I know I'm not here for ever,' she added, feeling suddenly disloyal. 'I'll see them all again at Christmas.'

'That's only eight months away.'

Helen's heart leapt. Unlike Flippie, Adam had kept her at arms' length, always friendly but never too close. That could be because he and Marita were planning to marry, or it could be because Flippie had made it obvious that he liked her. But the hollow note in Adam's voice gave her hope that he considered her something more than another sister.

'A lot can happen in that time,' she said lightly. 'I'm sure you'll all be tired of me by then!'

'No, not at all. I think you're very good for Anna-Marie, and my ma loves having you around. And I . . . '

And I?

Then she saw Adam's mouth tighten.

'What's Jacob de Wild doing here?' he said coldly and stopped in his tracks.

Helen turned and looked at Cora and Jacob, sitting alone at a table in the corner. Cora appeared to be listening intently to what Jacob had to say, and as they watched, Jacob put his big hand over hers and patted it.

'He just came up to our table and said he'd decided to come this evening after all,' she replied. 'I don't think your mum wanted to dance with him but he's a hard person to refuse.'

'I don't know how she can bring herself to speak to that man,' Adam said grimly. 'He's definitely after something, and I'm surprised Ma can't see it, after what he's done to us.'

'What did he do?' Helen was mystified.

'Old history,' Adam said shortly. 'There's nothing anyone can do about it now.'

He watched his mother as she got up and shook Jacob's hand, then walked back to the table alone to join the rest of her family.

Adam looked at her enquiringly, but Cora shook her head.

'We'll talk about it tomorrow,' she said quietly.

'Give Me Time'

Cora was pouring the coffee after breakfast the next day.

'All right, Ma,' Adam said abruptly, 'what was all that about with Jacob de Wild last night?'

Helen immediately rose from her seat.

'I'll go,' she said. 'I've got lessons to prepare . . . '

'No, dear, you stay,' Cora said wearily. 'You're practically part of the family anyway.'

She turned to Adam.

'Jacob's made me another offer for the bottom fields. He knows our situation at the bank and he's offered a very good price.'

'We can't consider selling that land, Ma. That would be the end of our water. We may as well sell the whole farm if we let those fields go.'

'Adam, you know how I feel about the farm. But you also know what a debt we have. Even with a good wool cheque we'll have to use most of it to pay off the overdraft.'

Although Cora had never mentioned it after the night she arrived, Helen had noticed little signs that money was tight on the farm. Cora's battered old car was at least fifteen years old, the curtains in the farmhouse were faded and the carpets were almost threadbare in places. Anna-Marie made all her mother's clothes as well as her own and

Cora had never mentioned taking a holiday away from the farm.

'I know you're doing your best with those Angora goats but they're not going to be making money for a couple of years yet. We have to raise the cash somehow and I just don't see how else we're going to do it. If we sold off those fields we'd still have the borehole near the huts. That would keep us going.'

'That borehole isn't reliable, Ma. Remember when it dried up during the drought two years ago? And this summer it's hardly giving any water. You absolutely cannot sell those fields.'

Adam stood up and pushed his chair away from the table.

'Pa would be furious if he knew you were thinking of doing that. I'm going to think of something to get us right with the bank. Just promise me you won't sell to Jacob, no matter how much he offers. Don't even discuss it with him.'

He strode out of the room, white-lipped, and a moment later they heard the truck roaring out of the farmyard.

'Adam just can't face facts,' Anna-Marie said casually. 'If we sold the whole farm, Ma, would we have some spare money? Maybe we could all move to town and I could go to college.'

Cora looked at her, stunned.

'How can you even think we'd sell the farm?' she asked faintly.

'This is our home.'

'I know, Ma, but other people move on. Other people get a life.' Anna-Marie looked sulky. 'I'm going to leave one day soon, anyway. So as far as I'm concerned you could sell this place and go and live in Hartley's Drift, like Ouma.'

'I can't believe you really think that, Anna-Marie,' Cora said, deeply hurt. 'Kasteelpoort is your inheritance, yours and your brothers'. You'll come to your senses when you're a bit older and wiser.'

Anna-Marie snorted under her breath and scowled.

Flippie cleared his throat.

'Ma, I've been thinking,' he blurted out. 'What if we made an adventure trail here on the farm? We could get people to come here instead of going all the way up to Graaf-Reinet.'

His mother looked at him in surprise. 'An adventure trail . . . ?'

Flippie explained what he'd learned the evening before.

'There's good money to be made,' he added enthusiastically. 'Adam's mates paid a lot for the privilege of crashing their four by four over some farmer's rough track. Why shouldn't we do it, too?'

'It *could* work,' Cora said slowly. 'We've already got that gravel road right up to the top of the mountain. Would that be long enough?'

'It's about seven kilometres. But don't forget it's also connected to that old wagon track Oupa made ages ago.'

In Charge

Flippie turned to Helen. 'Years ago, when Oupa ran the farm, the farmer on the other side of the mountain made a rough road so he could take a short-cut through Kasteelpoort to get to town. Adam and I used to ride our horses over it when we were kids, but no-one's used it for years.'

'You'd have to do a lot of clearing,' Cora objected. 'You can hardly see the track for the bushes on it.'

'Just thorn trees, Ma, they're easy enough to chop down,' Flippie reasoned. 'I took the four by four up early this morning and had a look. The track's still there. A few days of clearing with the men should do it. I reckon there would be about three hours' seriously rough driving if we linked the tracks together.'

'I think that's a marvellous idea,' Helen said warmly. 'It sounds like the sort of thing Paul was talking about. The bumpier the better!'

'Have you discussed this with Adam?' Cora asked. Helen could tell she was interested.

'No. He'll probably think of lots of reasons why it can't be done. The main one will be because *I've* thought of it.'

Flippie sounded bitter. 'Adam likes to be boss. As I expect you've noticed.'

'Now, son,' Cora said firmly, 'don't start on about Adam. He's your older brother. He needs to be consulted about this.'

Helen had a sudden insight into how difficult it must be to be the younger brother of someone like Adam She remembered hearing them quarrel on her first night on the farm. Adam, always so sure of himself and always in charge, was the one his mother relied on for help and advice.

'Flippie, I really don't think he'd shoot your idea down in flames,' she said carefully. 'He heard how Paul enjoyed his trip, and there are adventure trail clubs starting up all over the country. There could be a lot of people who'd be keen to come and drive these mountains.'

'I'm going to get all the figures together and show them to you, Ma. As far as you're concerned, it's always Adam's ideas and Adam's decisions.

You seem to forget I'm not a kid any more.'

'A business plan will impress him,' Helen said quickly. 'And you sound pretty organised.'

'I am . . . and I know we could make a successful adventure trail. I think we could make good money with a venture like this.'

'And what about people staying here on the farm?' Helen put in. 'Remember, Dawn said they'd slept over on the farm and the farmer had made a — what did she call it? A *braai*?'

'Staying over?' Cora mused. 'Well, we've plenty of spare rooms here.'

'City people would love to sleep here,' Helen told her. 'How many of them will have had the chance to stay on a real farm? With all your lovely old antique furniture and your feather mattresses . . . they'd love it!'

'We could do bed and breakfast!' Anna-Marie suddenly enthused. 'People could come the night before and we could give them a good farm breakfast and then they could go off and drive around the mountains and then come back here and we'd have a big party for them!'

'And a *braai* for them here on the *stoep*!' Flippie grinned. 'With lamb chops and some of your home-made sausage, Ma, and Tuleka's hot bread. We could charge a fortune!'

'Don't let's get carried away now.' Cora smiled. 'Do your homework, Flippie, work out how much it will cost to clear that track, and let's talk about this again when you've got something on paper.'

'I'll do that right away.'

Friendly

He pushed his chair away from the breakfast table, looking pleased with the way things had gone.

'Anna-Marie, would you like to give me a hand? We'd have to work out the cost of feeding these customers and a whole lot more besides.'

'Sure,' she answered. 'Oh, here's Marita!'

A bright red sports car braked to a stop and Marita leapt lightly out.

'Hi, all,' she said. 'Am I too late for a cup of coffee?'

'Never too late, Marita.' Cora smiled. 'I'll just fetch another cup.'

Marita sat down on the chair Adam had recently vacated.

'Enjoy the dance last night?' she enquired, with an edge in her voice.

'Yes, thanks,' Helen said. 'I loved the way whole families just mixed in and danced together.'

'Yes, people around here like a good party. But Adam was just being friendly when he asked you to dance last night.'

'Well, yes, of course he was,' Helen agreed faintly.

'And Flippie was pretty upset when he saw you two dancing like that.'

'Like what?' Helen was stunned.

'Close. Listen, Helen, I like you but I think we need to get something sorted right now. I saw the way you were dancing with Adam and I get the feeling you might have ideas about him. So get one thing straight. Adam's mine, all right?'

5

A Long Walk

The Smit family had just finished lunch and Cora rang the bell for Tuleka, who came to clear the table.

'Thank you, Tuleka. That was delicious, as usual,' Helen enthused. 'How did you do that chicken?'

'That was Malay curry, Miss Helen. Not too hot to burn your tongue. I put in lots of coriander and cumin and a little bit of ginger. Also cinnamon and cloves and . . . '

'Stop!' Helen laughed. 'I'll get the proper recipe from you in the kitchen.'

Tuleka shook her head.

'No book, Miss Helen. Is just one spoon this, one pinch that.'

Cora was sifting through the post she'd collected in town that morning.

'Ouma seems to have had a good

time in Cape Town,' she said, reading from a postcard. 'And she's coming back tomorrow. The course was wonderful, apparently. She's met all sorts of people who are just as interested in old bones as she is.'

'Amelia's amazing, isn't she?' Helen helped herself to iced water from the frosted jug on the table. 'I can't think of anyone who has so many interests. I wouldn't recognise a fossil if it jumped up and bit me! What do they look like?'

'Exactly like big white stones,' Adam said. 'Ouma spotted them a few years ago. She's convinced they're the bones of prehistoric creatures — dinosaurs of some sort.'

'She was walking down by the river,' Cora added. 'Or what used to be the river. It's been dry for years now. A lot of fossils have been discovered in the Karoo, but no-one has ever really looked for them here on Kasteelpoort.'

'Some of them are embedded in the rock,' Flippie put in. 'I can't see how anyone could ever get them out. So all she could do was take a lot of photos.'

'She says she's shown them to her lecturer,' Cora said, reading from the card. 'He's quite excited and told her he wants to come and study them one day.'

'Would you like to take a look, Helen?' Adam asked casually. 'I've got to go down to the bottom lands anyway to check the fences.'

'They're dead boring,' Flippie warned.

'Thanks, I'd love to.' She smiled at Flippie apologetically. 'I've never seen a fossil.'

Half an hour later, Helen was almost regretting that she'd agreed to go. It had been a long walk from the farmhouse and the midday sun beat down relentlessly through her sun-hat. She could feel the baking heat of the riverbed stones through her thin sandals as she jumped from rock to rock.

'Here's one,' Adam said, stopping abruptly. 'You can see it's the shape of a bone if you look closely.'

Helen squatted down.

'*This* is a bone?'

It was bleached white in the sun, but she wouldn't have recognised the long white lump as anything but a river stone.

'Amelia must have pretty good eyesight.'

'She's sharp, all right. Ouma reckons there're a lot more buried in the bank somewhere. They'd be easier to get out.'

Business Plan

They wandered slowly along the gully, with Adam pointing out more specimens, and gradually Helen started to be able to tell a rock from a fossil.

Something greyish-white was poking from the hard white soil that had once been the riverbank. Helen squatted and scraped away the dirt, suddenly convinced this was a weathered joint from some animal that died millions of years ago.

She felt a thrill of discovery run through her.

'Wait, Adam!' she called. 'I think I've found something. Let's see what this is!' But she was unable to dig any further without a tool of some sort.

'I need a trowel,' she said ruefully. 'It's held fast by all these little pebbles.'

'Here. Use my knife.' Adam produced a pocket knife and she determinedly scratched the surrounding gravel, but had to give up in frustration.

'I don't want to ruin your blade,' she said finally. 'It's pretty big. Besides, I might damage it. I've seen pictures of people using special tools and even paintbrushes to dig these things out.'

'I'd think a bulldozer would be more effective.' Adam grinned. 'But I'm only a farmer — what do I know? Anyway, if Ouma's professor comes to have a look, you could watch the experts in action.'

'I'd love to help them.'

She looked around, trying to imagine huge, long-dead animals stalking the dusty landscape. What on earth had they found to eat? Why had they died here so long ago?

'Anyway, you'd have to be really keen on dinosaurs to poke around in this heat!' Adam said, taking her hand. 'Hey, what have you done to your poor fingers?'

They were scratched and roughened. In her excitement at finding the fossil she hadn't felt anything, but now she sucked her fingertips, grimacing in pain.

'It's nothing,' she said, embarrassed. But he took out a clean handkerchief and dabbed them tenderly.

'You daft girl. Take a break now. There's some shade over there.'

Grateful for the rest, she sank down on to the coarse grass below a spindly tree, its branches spiked with pairs of long white thorns, and reached up to break off a pair which were at least ten centimetres long.

'Watch out, those are sharp,' he cautioned. 'Mimosa thorns.'

'These are what the children use for

horns when they make those little clay oxen,' she exclaimed in delight. 'Kany-iso's so clever. He made me one last week, and a little goat. I hope they'll survive the trip home. I want to take them back for Angela's baby.'

'I doubt they will, they're just made out of mud. Flippie and I used to make those, too, when we were small, but they just crumbled to sand after a while.'

'I could bake them in the oven. That would harden them, like pottery.'

'You're full of good ideas.' He smiled at her lazily. 'So tell me, what do you think of Flippie's adventure trail?'

Impressed

It was hard to imagine anyone wanting to get into a four by four and drive up the mountain in this heat, but Flippie's enthusiasm had been infectious.

'I think it could work,' she answered. 'Your friend Paul said there were lots of folk interested in doing these trails.

Look how far he and Dawn drove just to find one — we'd be a lot closer for people from Cape Town.'

'I'm not sure about having people to stay with us,' Adam mused. 'Strangers coming up here every weekend, taking over the house.'

'But they'd be out most of the day, wouldn't they? We'd just have to give them breakfast and supper at night. Tuleka could make them a packed lunch for while they're driving on the mountain.'

'Maybe you're right. I was quite impressed with young Flip,' he conceded. 'He showed me a proper business plan this morning, with everything figured out — costs of clearing the track, costs of preparing their rooms with sheets and towels, costs of feeding them. He's pretty serious about it.'

The cost of feeding them. Helen swallowed. How could she have been so blind?

'Adam,' she blurted out. 'I didn't realise, when your mother was talking about finances, that I must be costing you money just by being here. All the meals I'm eating, plus everything you spent on setting up the school . . . and I'm not contributing anything! I've been incredibly selfish. What must you all think of me? Maybe I should leave. I must have outstayed my welcome already . . . '

Adam turned to her in amazement.

'Helen, how can you even think that? Your meals don't cost us anything — we all have to eat! And you more than contribute to things here. You help Ma in the garden, you're teaching the children. And just by staying here you seem to have magically turned Anna-Marie into a young lady.'

'But Flippie working out the cost of everything, it suddenly made me realise . . . ' she finished helplessly.

'That's what a business plan is all about. It's about making money from business. *You're* like part of the family.'

'Oh, well, perhaps I could pay a bit towards my board and lodging?'

'Don't be ridiculous.' He put his hand firmly over hers. 'We should be paying you a teacher's salary! So let's call it quits, OK?'

'All right,' she said, slightly mollified.

Old Friends

Helen leaned against the tree and gazed at the silhouette of the Three Castles shimmering in the heat. She could just make out the thread-like track winding up to the summit of the tallest peak. In the distance she could see the cluster of huts under the pepper trees where the farm workers lived.

Somewhere in the fields behind a windmill pump sucked noisily up and down and sheep bleated to each other. There was a buzzing in her ears and she closed her eyes for a minute.

The next thing she knew, Adam was tickling her forehead with a feathery piece of grass.

'Come on, sleepyhead,' he whispered,

his face so close to hers she could see the flecks of gold in his deep brown eyes. 'Time to go back for tea.'

Helen looked up at him drowsily, then realised she must have drifted off.

'Have I been asleep?'

The thought that Adam had been watching her while she slept made her heart skip a beat. He continued to look down at her with a strange expression, then bent slowly forward and kissed her gently on the lips.

'Sorry,' he said, 'but I've been wanting to do that all afternoon.'

'Oh,' Helen could only whisper. *Me, too.* But she said nothing more, her mind in a whirl as she gazed up at him. So Adam had felt it as well, this attraction she'd sensed since the first moment she saw him? Then, unable to stop herself, she blurted out the last thing she wanted to say.

'What about Marita?'

Adam sat up abruptly.

'Marita and I are old friends, that's all.'

Marita doesn't think so. She felt the words on the tip of her tongue, but realised she'd ruined the moment and sat up, furious with herself.

'How long did I sleep?'

'About an hour.' He spoke quite normally, as though he hadn't just turned her world upside down. 'I don't blame you, it's the heat. But I spent the time thinking deep and meaningful financial thoughts.'

'And?'

'And I think we should have a go at Flippie's adventure trail.'

Congratulations?

He pulled Helen to her feet and they started back towards the house, his grip warm and firm as he helped her over the rocks.

'I don't suppose it's going to make a huge difference to our debt with the bank,' he continued, 'but every little bit helps.'

179

'Anna-Marie has all sorts of ideas for entertaining the visitors when they stay over. She wants to let them feed the lambs and maybe offer them horse rides. And your mother's already moving furniture around in those three spare rooms down the passage. Tuleka's thrilled — she said she loves cooking for lots of people.'

'Sounds like everyone's decided already, then.' Adam grinned. 'Well, this trail will be Flippie's baby. He can take care of all the problems.'

'And put all the profits in the bank!' she agreed.

He smiled at that. He didn't let go of her hand as they walked across the fields, but he kept the conversation to farm matters and Helen was beginning to wonder if his kiss had been part of a dream. But as they mounted the steps up to the verandah, he turned to her.

'Helen, I've been wanting to tell you for ages . . . '

But Helen never found out what he intended to say.

'Hello, Helen,' Marita said coolly, from the depths of the old cane chair. 'You two look very pleased with yourselves. Adam, did you forget we were going into town to choose a ring?'

Helen looked at Adam, stunned. How could she have been so stupid as to think she and Adam were getting closer when all the time . . .

'Should I be saying congratulations to the two of you?' she asked evenly.

Marita burst out laughing.

'Not that kind of ring! Although maybe one day, eh, Adam?'

She got up and put her arm playfully around his waist.

'No, Adam promised to help me choose a ring for my pa. It's his sixtieth birthday and I want to buy him one of those big signet rings and have it engraved.'

'Sorry, Marita, it slipped my mind,' Adam confessed. 'But there's still time to go to town. Helen, would you like to come?'

One glance at Marita's face was

enough to help her decide.

'No thanks,' she said. 'I think I'll go and help Tuleka with the tea.'

'I'll drive us, Adam,' Marita said, pleased. 'It's time you had a ride in my baby.'

'Are you sure I'll fit into that thing?' He sounded dismayed. 'Won't you let me take you in the pick-up?'

'No way. Don't be such a coward!'

Time To Think

They clattered down the steps, arguing good-humouredly, and Helen went into the cool depths of the house towards the kitchen. She desperately needed time to think.

Amelia returned the following day, brimming with talk about her course.

She seemed to have been particularly impressed with Professor Philips, who led the course.

'Such a knowledgeable man!' she told them. 'He's retired from the university but still leads expeditions to look at fossil finds. He's very interested in coming here, Cora, so I told him there would always be a room for him if he wanted to stay.'

'Of course,' Cora murmured.

'Never mind the old bones, Ouma, did you get to see any of the shops?' Anna-Marie asked eagerly. 'Did you go to one of those big malls?'

'Yes, my dear, Professor Philips took me to lunch at one of them.'

'And the shops?'

'Very smart. Too smart for my taste and too expensive! Some of them only sold one thing. Only shoes, or only glassware, or only toys. Ridiculous.'

'Has Flippie told you about his adventure trail idea, Ouma?'

Cora had thrown herself into the plan wholeheartedly and had taken down all the curtains in the spare rooms to wash them, ready for any guests who might arrive.

'Yes, I think it's a wonderful scheme and he seems to have it all worked out.

That boy's got a good head on his shoulders.'

Amelia nodded her grey curls approvingly and her long jet earrings tinkled in harmony.

'He's taken a team of the men up there this morning to start clearing the old track,' Cora told her, delighted that, for once, her two sons were in agreement over a project and that Flippie was handling his side of things with such determination.

'Flippie reckons he'll get it ready in a week or so,' Anna-Marie put in. 'Then we can advertise it in the Cape Town papers. It's going to be great! All those new people coming here to the farm . . . '

'We won't get crowds of people to start with,' Cora cautioned. 'Maybe one or two. But they'll tell their friends.'

Further Plans . . .

Helen and Anna-Marie were invited along for the inaugural ride up to the top of the mountain on the newly cleared track. They sat at the back, which made Helen feel quite carsick as they rocked and rolled violently up the bumpy road in first gear.

'This isn't my idea of a great adventure,' she muttered to Anna-Marie, who was whooping with glee and urging Flippie to drive even faster.

'Well, do you think they'll get their money's worth?' Flippie asked cheerfully. 'You can see for over a hundred miles from here, I reckon.'

'Definitely.' Helen smiled. 'We just have to get them to come!'

'Let's put an advert in the Cape Town papers,' Anna-Marie said. 'There're two, one in the morning and one in the afternoon.'

'Both, then,' Flippie decided immediately. 'We'll write the wording tonight and post them off tomorrow. We should be able to make the weekend papers. Total saturation of our market area.'

'You've been reading too many business articles!' His sister grinned.

'Just be sure you mention the gorgeous young hostess who'll be there to welcome them with an iced drink on the *stoep*!'

'You'll be too busy working, my girl,' Flippie said in mock seriousness. 'This is a family business, don't forget.'

'Well, let's hope the generator keeps working over the weekends.' Anna-Marie sniffed. 'It's broken down so often lately. These sophisticated people from Cape Town won't be happy with cold baths.'

★   ★   ★

That evening, a round-table discussion continued noisily for over an hour before Flippie was satisfied with the wording of his advertisement.

'Right,' he said at last when he'd read it out. 'I've put in our phone number and our box number.'

'Well done, son,' Cora said. 'I'll write it out neatly and whoever's going into town tomorrow can drop it off at the post.'

'Marita said she'd be going,' Anna-Marie said. 'She's got to collect the ring she bought for her father's birthday. She's had it engraved with his initials.'

'Jacob's birthday?' Amelia raised her eyebrows. 'Oh, of course, he must be turning sixty.'

'I remember his fiftieth, when he threw that huge party,' Cora said. 'That was quite an evening, eh, Ouma? When you taught everyone how to do the tango?'

She turned to Helen.

'His wife Aletta was still alive then and she arranged this enormous surprise party for him, with a band from town and the whole garden decorated with balloons and candles. They had more than a hundred people there. We all had such fun . . . ' Her voice trailed off sadly. 'Jacob's changed a lot since those days.'

'Marita hasn't mentioned any party this time,' Flippie said. 'Not that we'd go even if he had one.'

'Anyway,' Anna-Marie said briskly,

'I'll walk across first thing tomorrow and ask her to post it.'

★　★　★

Gwen was packing her overnight bag to spend the weekend with Angela and Mark when the phone rang. It was Albert.

'Just phoned to chat,' he said. 'I had a nice long letter from Helen this week. She seems to be enjoying herself.'

'Yes,' Gwen agreed warmly. 'It was the best thing she ever did, going off to South Africa like that. And she's got you to thank for it.'

'I knew she'd like it. She's doing a good job with that teaching, too, by the sound of it.'

'Albert, I can't talk now, I've got a train to catch. I'm off to Leighton for the weekend.'

'Are you now? Well, give Angela and Mark my best. It's been a long time since I saw her. You tell that young woman she'd better come and visit her grandad before I forget what she looks like!'

'I'll do that.' Gwen smiled.

That's not like Angela, she thought. She knows her grandad loves to see her, especially now that Helen's not around. And she's not working; she could easily come over and visit for the morning.

But it sounded as though Angela's mornings were all taken up with her new friend. Once Gwen had arrived and been proudly shown Angela's new house, Maeve Anderson was all she could talk about.

'You'll like her, Mum,' Angela enthused. 'I've asked her over for tea so you can meet her. She's such fun! And she has her own car, of course, so we go all over the place together.'

They were having lunch in Angela's neat little back garden, which was bright with daffodils and anemones.

'It's all Mark's work,' Angela commented when her mother complimented her on the show. 'He's mad about his garden. When he gets home this evening, he'll be straight into it, mucking about until dark. He's even growing veggies now, just like Grandad.'

'That's lovely. And it must save you quite a bit on your housekeeping, having homegrown vegetables?'

'I suppose so. But he'd rather be out there weeding his garden than inside talking to me.'

Angela sounded petulant, but Gwen wouldn't hear any criticism of Mark.

'It's very nice that he has such an interest. And he has to make use of the daylight hours while he can, I expect.'

Gwen hadn't been able to resist knitting little cardigans and booties for her expected grandchild and had come laden with hand-made clothes as well as a pretty little crocheted baby blanket in lemon and white.

But she'd been disappointed and a little hurt by Angela's reaction.

'These will all do for a boy or a girl,' she'd said happily, watching Angela unwrap the gifts. 'Look, I found these lovely little teddy bear buttons.'

'Maeve says she's not buying hand-knitted things for their baby,' Angela said dubiously. 'She says all that fluffy wool can cause allergies.'

'For heaven's sake, what nonsense!' Gwen snorted. 'You and Helen had nothing but hand-knitted things and you're both perfectly fine.'

'It's False Economy'

Maeve's opinions seemed to hold sway over Angela and Gwen doubted that she was going to admire this young woman quite as much as her daughter hoped. She changed the subject tactfully.

'You were lucky to find such a nice, sunny house. And the baby's room is really beautiful.'

Angela had made the nursery very pretty, with pastel-painted walls and bright animal print curtains. There was a tufted Peter Rabbit rug on the floor and a very smart white cupboard for the baby clothes that opened up to reveal a baby bath. Gwen recognised it as the cupboard Angela had been enthusing over some time ago and wondered if Mark had agreed to this expense.

Angela flushed, pleased by her mother's words of praise. Being pregnant suited her, now that she was over the early months of suffering morning sickness, and she had that special glow that expectant mothers have.

'I've seen the most wonderful pram,' Angela said. 'That's the next thing on the list. It's got absolutely eveything and will be really comfortable for the baby.'

'Oh, that reminds me . . . Remember Mrs Watson from round the corner? Her daughter Marion's wanting to sell her old pram and I thought I might buy it for you. It's still in very good condition.'

'Second-hand?' Angela wrinkled her nose. 'Mum, I don't want to buy second-hand stuff for our baby.'

'But, Angela — '

Her daughter hurried on before Gwen could utter another word.

'Mum, it's false economy to buy used things. We're sure to have another baby one day and by then that old pram would probably be falling to pieces!'

Gwen was about to say that prams didn't fall apart that easily, but she could see Angela's mind was made up so, difficult though it was, she kept her counsel.

★ ★ ★

Maeve breezed in to tea that afternoon, all bright laughter and full of fun. She was beautifully dressed and had just had her glossy brown hair cut in a new style and streaked with golden highlights.

'Felt like a change,' she said airily, when Angela admired it. 'I don't want to let myself get dowdy just because I'm stuck at home. Do you think Peter will like it?' She twirled around to show off, knowing she looked good.

'I think I'll book us a table somewhere nice for this evening just to celebrate my new look. Would you and Mark like to come? And bring your mum, of course!'

Thankfully, Angela refused. Gwen was looking forward to an evening with just the three of them. She could see why her daughter was attracted to Maeve; she was charming and self-assured and had definite opinions on everything from furnishings to food.

'Nice cake,' she said, once they were sitting over their tea. 'Did you get it from Homebakes?'

'I thought you'd made this yourself, love?' Gwen raised her eyebrows. 'It's lovely. Tastes just like home-made . . . '

'I haven't time for baking, Mum.' Angela flushed. 'But Maeve discovered this good little place where you can buy real home-made stuff. I always go there.'

'I'm so glad Angela and Mark live next door, Mrs McLeod.' Maeve smiled. 'I don't know what I'd do without your daughter around to cheer me up. We have loads of fun together, don't we, Angela?'

Angela smiled in agreement.

'Did you tell your mum what we're doing next week?' Without waiting for an answer, Maeve babbled on. 'We're off to the races! Peter's company has a box there and we're going to get all dressed up and have a day out, just the two of us.'

'Horse racing?' Gwen was stunned. 'Isn't that — I mean, do you bet on the horses?'

'Of course! No fun without the chance of winning a bit.'

Or losing a lot, Gwen thought grimly.

When Maeve had left, Gwen was in the kitchen washing the tea things and wondering whether to come straight out and say what she felt or to be more tactful, when Angela turned to her with a worried look.

'Mum, do you think you could lend me some money? Just for a week or two until Mark gets paid?'

Gwen nearly choked.

'What for? So you can lose it on some horse races?'

'No.' Angela was nearly in tears. 'I knew you'd disapprove of that and I'm going to try and make some excuse not to go. But I owe for the gas and I haven't paid the phone bill from last month.'

She looked so wretched that Gwen felt a rush of sympathy for her.

'Does Mark know about this?'

'No, of course not! I can't tell him, he'd be furious. He just wouldn't understand. Mark's so careful with everything. He just can't see that sometimes I need to buy extra things for the baby.'

A Clean Slate

'Come and sit down, love.' Gwen faced her daughter squarely over the dining table.

'You're in a pickle, but don't make the baby your excuse for not managing your money. You're not working any more and that was your choice. But a lot of women go on working until a month or two before the baby's born.'

'Mark said I needn't work any more,' Angela grumbled.

'Well, you've only one income now and you can't go spending money the way you're doing. I don't mean to criticise, but you paid a painter to decorate the nursery — you could have done that yourself very easily if Mark didn't have time.'

Angela wiped her eyes.

'I'm not buying anything we don't need, Mum. Everything's just so expensive.'

'I'm just saying this baby doesn't need the newest and the best of everything if you can't really afford it. Maeve can; she's married to a man who runs his own company and obviously they have a lot more money than you two. I know it must be hard to see her spending so much money and you'd like to do the same, but if you can't, you can't. My grandchild's not going to suffer if he has to sleep in a second-hand cot!'

Angela gave a watery smile.

'I suppose you're right, but I still need some money, Mum.'

Gwen looked at her levelly.

'Darling, the worst is that you're hiding this from Mark. You can't keep secrets like this from him. He's got a right to know if you're in debt, and if he's disappointed, I wouldn't blame him in the least.'

'He will be. He'll be so angry,' Angie said shakily. 'We've already had a big argument about money, Mum.'

'You can't start having problems like this and not sharing them. So here's what I'll do. When you've told Mark about the money you owe, then I'll happily give it to you. Not lend, *give*. That way you can start with a clean slate.'

Angela bit her lip.

'All right,' she said finally. 'I'll tell him. Thanks, Mum. But I'll wait until next week, OK? I don't want him making a scene while you're here.'

Gwen couldn't imagine quiet Mark making a scene.

'I'll send you the money as soon as you've discussed it,' she said. 'You'll feel much better about everything once you've told him, you'll see.'

But Angela didn't look convinced.

No Clue . . .

'Do you think we might get a call from someone by tonight?'

After supper on Sunday Flippie was tense, unable to sit still while he waited for a response to the advertisement that had been placed in the Cape Town weekend papers.

'Maybe people will only read it this evening,' he mused. 'They'll probably phone tomorrow to book.'

'Relax, Flip,' Adam said easily. 'It

takes time. Give it a week at least. Then maybe place another advert if you don't hear from anyone.'

He and Helen were playing Scrabble in the dining-room. The nights had started to be cooler, although the days were still very hot, and for the first time since her arrival, Helen had a sweater draped over her shoulders.

'You're a demon,' Adam said ruefully as Helen triumphantly laid another five high-scoring tiles on the board. 'You're about a hundred ahead. I think I should admit defeat and make us all some coffee.'

'Good idea, but let me help you.'

Helen joined him in the kitchen, taking mugs from the cupboard and laying them on a tray while waiting for the enormous black kettle to boil on the coal stove.

She hadn't found herself alone with Adam since the afternoon they'd gone to look at the fossils, and she was determined to wait for him to be the one to say anything. But he seemed to have forgotten entirely about the fact that he'd kissed her and talked about everything except the one subject that mattered most to Helen.

He leaned against the big kitchen table, watching her with his arms folded across his chest. The dim light from the ceiling threw his strong features into relief and his deep-set eyes became pools of shadow in which she could read no clue as to what he was thinking.

That kiss probably didn't mean a thing, she thought bitterly. I'm silly even to think it did. It doesn't matter that he said Marita's just a friend — Flippie's right, she'll make sure that she and Adam end up together. She made that perfectly plain to me.

Adam carried the tray through to the others and she handed round the big bowl of buttermilk rusks for dipping into the coffee, then claimed she needed an early night and went to bed. She forced herself to plan the next morning's lessons and put Adam Smit out of her mind.

'Don't Tell Adam'

The following morning, as Helen was waiting for the children to tidy their tables before going home for the day, she was surprised to see Marita's little sports car pull up in a cloud of dust in front of the school-room.

'Hi!' Marita called brightly. 'I dug out some of my old books as I promised and thought I'd bring them across.'

'That's nice of you. Kanyiso, can you and Yena help bring the boxes inside?'

Marita's books were in beautiful condition and the children crowded round, fingering them cautiously.

'These are lovely.' Helen smiled. 'What do we say to Marita, class?'

'Thank you, Miss Marita,' they chorused, beaming.

Helen was delighted with the children's progress and would have liked to show Marita their schoolbooks, but she didn't look as though she meant to stay long.

'I'd like to start a little library,' Helen

confided. 'I thought I could let them each take a book home to read for themselves and bring it back the next week. That would get them into the habit of reading for pleasure — even if it's just looking at the pictures.'

'I never managed to get into the reading habit.' Marita laughed. 'Some of those books are still brand new. But if you want them to take the books home, just remember the goats!'

'Oh, yes, of course. Well, maybe they'd better keep the books here, after all.'

'Are you nearly done here? I'll give you a lift back to the house.'

'Heavens, that's not necessary.' Helen smiled. 'I can walk.'

'It's too hot. I'll wait for you.'

Helen dismissed the class and watched as they left. Then she shut the door and climbed in beside Marita, who gunned the little car around the gum trees and headed for the farmhouse over the bumpy track. On one of the bigger bumps, the glove compartment flew open and some papers cascaded down on to Helen's lap.

Amongst them were two envelopes, addressed in Flippie's scrawl to the Cape Town newspapers.

Helen gasped.

Marita glanced down and pulled a face.

'Oh, darn. I quite forgot to post those. Never mind, I'll do it this afternoon. I'm going into town again.'

Helen was stunned at how casual she sounded. Hadn't Marita known how much this meant to Flippie?

'Flippie was expecting those adverts to be in last weekend's papers,' she said faintly. 'He was waiting for a reply all of Sunday.'

'Whoops! Well, my name will be mud, then!' Marita giggled. 'I'm such a scatterbrain!'

She came to a halt next to the verandah of the farmhouse.

'Coming in for a bite of lunch, Marita?' Cora called.

'No thanks, can't stop, I'm on my way to town,' Marita shouted back, idling the car. Then, before Helen could get out, she clutched her arm and spoke in a low, urgent voice.

'Listen, Helen, I'm really sorry about forgetting the advert. I'm not exactly famous for my good memory. But I'll post the letters the minute I get to town, so they'll probably be in time for this weekend. So, er, . . . don't tell Adam, all right?'

'I won't,' Helen promised.

A Bad Liar

As Marita roared off down the drive, she stuck her head out the window.

'Don't worry, Helen, I'll make sure not to forget this time! Bye!'

Flippie came out of the house.

'What was that about? What did Marita forget?'

'Nothing . . . just something she promised to bring for the children at school.'

'Helen, you're a really bad liar. She

forgot to post our advertisement, didn't she?'

'Yes,' she admitted, wishing Flippie hadn't been so quick to guess the truth. 'But she's going to make sure they're in for this weekend.'

'I knew we shouldn't have trusted her.' Flippie was furious. 'Don't tell me she just forgot! She's probably working hand in glove with her father, making sure this idea doesn't get off the ground. Jacob would be only too pleased; he's just waiting for us to admit defeat and sell up to him. And Marita's doing her bit to make sure that we fail.'

'Marita's doing what?' Adam's voice cut coolly across his brother's tirade. 'Stop thinking the worst of Marita. She's always been our friend and she's a hundred per cent behind this idea.'

'Don't be so blind!' Flippie countered. 'She and Jacob are working together to get us off the farm!'

'You're being ridiculous.'

Helen watched wretchedly as a

full-scale argument erupted between the brothers. Just because she couldn't lie convincingly, she'd really dropped Marita in it. And she'd never believe Helen hadn't done it on purpose . . .

6

Marita Saves The Day

Helen spent a sleepless night, anxious about the trouble she might have caused between Adam and Flippie after she let slip that Marita forgot to post the all-important advertisement. But she needn't have worried.

First thing the following morning there was a cheerful toot from her car and Marita came skipping up the verandah steps, all vivacious smiles and apologies. Adam had already left to see to his Angora goats, but everyone else was still finishing their coffee at the breakfast table.

'Flippie, my angel, will you forgive me?'

She planted a quick kiss on his cheek before he could even stand up.

'I don't know if Helen mentioned it, but I forgot to post your adverts last week. Well, I mailed them yesterday so they'll be in this weekend for sure. But even better, I've found your first adventure trail customer!'

Flippie struggled to his feet, his annoyance with Marita giving way to a huge grin.

'What? How did you do that? Who is it?'

'Well . . . ' She sank into the chair recently vacated by Adam.

'Oh, thanks, Cora, I'd love some coffee. Well, I was just filling up with petrol and this great big four by four came growling up next to me and a very nice man jumped out and asked if he was on the right road for Doringwater.

'So I told him where the turn-off was, and asked him what on earth he wanted to do in that back-of-beyond dustbowl, and he said he was from 'Go For It' magazine and he was going to test-drive a new adventure trail they've started up there.'

'And . . . ?'

All Systems Go

She studied her nails absently for a few moments, then smiled sweetly up at him.

'*And* I told him about yours, and mentioned casually that it was much longer and a lot more exciting than the one at Doringwater, plus a whole lot closer to Cape Town and that seemed to impress him.'

'Longer and more exciting?' Anna-Marie queried. 'How do you know?'

'It's got to be.' Marita grinned. 'Anyway, his name's Marcus Retief, I have his mobile number and he promised to look in this weekend and try it out when he's finished up at Doringwater.'

'Wow, couldn't be better Marita! I owe you one.'

Flippie's mind was racing ahead.

'I'll phone him to confirm he's coming. Ma, is the big bedroom off the verandah ready for occupation? And could Tuleka make something really special for supper on Saturday night? Or maybe we should have a *braai* outside. No, depends on the weather, I suppose.'

'Ask him if he's a vegetarian,' Helen put in. 'Or if he has any special dietary requirements.'

'Good thinking, that'll impress him.'

Flippie took out the notebook he'd taken to carrying and wrote it down.

'Looks like it's all systems go then.' Anna-Marie smiled 'So . . . this Marcus. What's he like, Marita?'

'Much too old for you darling,' Marita said firmly. 'He's at least thirty. But he's gorgeous.'

Progress

In the schoolroom, Helen watched as Meena and Wenla carefully glued their coloured paper creations together, their tongues sticking out in concentration. The smaller ones were learning to use scissors, cutting out triangles and circles to make patterns.

'Go on wall?' Wenla asked, her bright

eyes gleaming hopefully.

'Of course, Wenla, it's beautiful.'

The schoolroom was bright with the children's artwork. All the drawings and paintings formed a colourful frieze around the room, after Helen had learned the hard way that pieces of paper taken back to the huts often became goat food.

She'd made some shelves out of planks and bricks to display the picture books Marita had given them, and the older children were sitting on the floor, reading.

Helen was thrilled with the progress the children had made, nine-year-old Kanyiso particularly. He's really bright, she thought, watching his lips move as he read to himself. It's almost as if he was waiting to be shown how to read and now he's catching up on all the years he's missed. He ought to be at a proper school — they all should.

Helen had written to the council in Hartley's Drift, telling them about her efforts on the farm and repeating how important a school bus was, and received a non-committal reply that they 'would look into the matter'.

'Don't hold your breath,' Adam said, reading the letter. 'That's what they told me last year.'

'I think I'll go and speak to them,' she decided. 'These children deserve proper schooling, and access to all the equipment they need.'

'Even so, you've taught them a lot.'

'Some things they don't need me to teach. Have you heard them singing?'

'No, but I know what you mean.' Adam grinned. 'They say if you put three Africans together you'll have a choir.'

Helen had noticed the children often broke into song quite naturally as they left the classroom, and the lovely harmony wafted back to her as she returned to the farmhouse. Their natural love of song made most of the English schoolroom favourites sound a bit flat and silly, although they all enjoyed doing the animal noises for 'Old MacDonald's Farm'.

Adam often popped in to listen to the lessons for a few minutes, so when the schoolroom door opened, Helen didn't glance up from the reading she was doing with Mondli. When he'd finished, smiling in relief, he was rewarded with clapping from the back of the room.

It was Marita.

'Well done, Mondli,' she said. 'Can I sit and watch for a bit, Helen?'

'Of course,' Helen said, although she wondered why Marita was showing an interest.

As the children were getting ready to leave, Marita came to the front of the room.

'Do you mind if I ask the children something?'

'Not at all.' Helen smiled, mystified.

Marita broke into a stream of rapid Xhosa which completely baffled Helen. Everyone on the farm spoke the language fluently, but try as she might, Helen had only learned a few words and she couldn't follow what was being said.

The children were smiling and nodding, and when she'd finished, Marita looked satisfied.

'Sorry,' she said. 'That was a bit rude of me. I was asking them if they'd like to come and sing for my father on his birthday next Wednesday. It's his sixtieth and he loves to hear the children singing.'

'I'm sure they'd love to. Are you having a party for Jacob?' Helen remembered Cora saying what a wonderful celebration he'd had for his fiftieth.

'No, he doesn't want any fuss this time.' Marita looked a bit downcast. 'He isn't his usual self these days. He seems a bit depressed. So I'm just making him a big cake with sixty candles and inviting . . . ' She hesitated. 'Actually, I wanted to invite Cora. Do you think she'd come? She and my pa used to get on so well in the old days.'

'I honestly couldn't say,' Helen demurred. 'I know there's ill feeling between this family and your dad, but I

215

don't know what caused it. But Cora sometimes talks about the times when your folks were family friends.'

'When we were kids, Cora and Gerard were really close to us,' Marita told her. 'Always having a *braai* with my ma and pa. We'd have tennis parties on that old court behind our house. It's all grown over with weeds now. Pa doesn't play any more and he never sees anyone. Since my ma died he's sort of cut himself off from everything.'

'At least he has you there.'

'Not for ever.' She sighed. 'I might go back to Cape Town one of these days. I don't think I can take much more of farm life, it's too boring. Unless something exciting happens.'

She means unless Adam proposes, Helen thought.

Paying Guest

Marcus Retief had confirmed his visit for Saturday morning and Flippie had given him directions to Kasteelpoort. Adam had taken himself off to the barn after breakfast to fix a broken pump, but everyone else was in a state of barely suppressed excitement, even Tuleka.

She'd been marinating a haunch of venison in red wine for a few days, but was waiting for Flippie's decision about a *braai*. In case they decided to eat outside, Tuleka had spiced lamb chops and slices of rump steak, and had taken pink ropes of home-made sausage from the freezer ready to be grilled over the fire.

'There's enough meat here to feed an army, Tuleka!' Helen laughed. 'It's only one extra man.'

'He must be happy with the food, Miss Helen. He mustn't say he go away hungry.'

'I'm sure there's no chance of that here!'

Tuleka giggled as Anna-Marie burst into the kitchen.

'Come and meet him.'

Their first guest had stepped out of

the biggest, dirtiest four by four Helen had ever seen, with metal jerry-cans strapped to the front and back, two spare tyres and a folding tent attached to the top. He was explaining these to Flippie, who was admiring his vehicle.

'I do a lot of travelling in the bush,' he was saying. 'I sleep on top so the lions don't get me. Last time I was up in the Northern Cape three big ones were prowling around all night but I was quite safe. Ah — ' He broke off, seeing the girls. 'Marcus Retief. Call me Marcus.'

His grip was warm and firm and he looked at Helen and Anna-Marie appreciatively as they introduced themselves. Marcus suited his vehicle; he was large, deeply sunburnt and slightly dishevelled in his khaki shorts and bush shirt. He looked as if he'd be a good man to travel with through uncharted territory.

'Are you ladies the resident trail guides by any chance?'

'No fear!' Helen said, but Anna-Marie smiled shyly.

'I'll go up with you, if you like. It's such fun.'

'Why don't you go, too, Helen?' Cora urged. She clearly didn't want Anna-Marie to go off all on her own with this larger-than-life stranger.

'If there's room for me,' Helen said unwillingly, remembering her last uncomfortable ride up with Flippie.

'Sure, there's plenty of room for three up front,' Marcus said pleasantly. 'How long does this one take, top to bottom?'

'You can drive it in three hours,' Flippie said, 'but longer if you stop at the top for lunch.'

'Lunch sounds a good idea. I think I've some biscuits in my truck somewhere . . . '

'Heavens, Marcus, we can't let you go all the way up there with only biscuits for lunch! I'll see what we can rustle up. Anna-Marie, offer our guest some coffee and rusks.'

Cora headed off to the kitchen.

Exciting

Marcus was charming and full of stories about the magazine assignments he'd done and the remote areas he'd visited.

'I never travel without my camera,' he said, producing a small digital one from his top pocket. 'Never know what I might find!'

'There's not much wildlife up in those mountains,' Flippie said. 'Just lots of buck and some zebra. There used to be leopards but we haven't seen them for years.'

Helen thought they should know something about the competition.

'So, Marcus, what was the trail at Doringwater like?'

'Not bad. A bit too well-made, if you know what I mean. It all felt rather tame, but the view from the mountain-top was pretty good. And a very nice young couple, the Roberts, run the farm. Not such great food, but I had a good visit.'

'So will you give them a good write-up?' Helen persisted.

'Probably. I like to encourage new enterprises. I'm glad I've found out about your adventure trail. I can do them both in the same article, and compare them.'

Is that a good thing or a bad thing, Helen wondered . . .

'We can promise you this trail isn't too well-made.' Flippie grinned. 'You want exciting, you'll get exciting!'

Cora returned with a basket filled with a flask of coffee, cold chicken, salad, ham sandwiches and slices of *melktert*, a thick custard tart with feather-light flaky pastry. It was one of Tuleka's specialities.

'He won't be able to complain about the food,' Cora said to Adam as she waved the three of them off as they left the farmyard. 'We'll beat Doringwater in that department, at least!'

'I hope he's a careful driver,' Adam mused. 'He mustn't take any chances with the girls on board.'

'They'll be fine,' Flippie said. 'He knows what he's doing.'

An Anxious Wait . . .

But by five o'clock they still hadn't returned. 'Six hours,' Cora fretted. 'Even if they took an hour for lunch they should have been back by now.'

She and Adam scanned the mountainside for the glint of the setting sun on a window to tell them that the four by four was on its way down, but could see no sign of movement.

'I'm going up to find them,' Adam said abruptly. 'They could be in trouble up there.'

'Do you think they've had an accident? What if Marcus turned that huge truck over and they're lying pinned underneath?' Cora was white with anxiety.

'Don't fuss, Ma,' Flippie said easily. 'He's probably taking pictures or something.'

'I'm getting the tractor out,' Adam said, ignoring him. 'Helen didn't really want to go anyway and she's probably getting cold by now. And Anna-Marie,' he added hastily. 'Coming, Flip? Bring some tow rope.'

'Oh, all right. But I'm sure they're fine — just enjoying the view.'

Just then the phone rang and Cora unwillingly tore her eyes away from the mountain and went to answer it. When she came out she was smiling with relief.

'That was Marcus,' she said. 'He had his mobile with him. Apparently he's had engine trouble and now they're stuck. He needs to be towed.'

Flippie scowled.

'What sort of a write-up will he give us if he breaks down? What if the track's too rough and he's broken something on the pickup?'

'It didn't sound as though he'd broken anything,' Cora said comfortingly. 'His engine just kept cutting out. He said he thought it was a blocked fuel pump.'

'Why didn't he phone sooner?' Adam demanded.

'He couldn't get any reception where

he broke down. The poor man had to walk up to the very top of the mountain before his phone would work.'

Once her two sons had chugged out of the barn on the tractor, Cora headed for the kitchen where Tuleka was preparing a huge spread of vegetables and salads.

'They're going to be back later than we thought, Tuleka,' she said. 'Better start the venison. I'm sure they won't feel like standing around a fire tonight.'

A Great Success

It was well after eight o'clock and pitch dark by the time the rumble of the tractor signalled the return of the party. Cora had been too jumpy to enjoy her usual glass of wine and hurried out into the dark to meet them.

'Oh, thank heavens,' she exclaimed. 'You must be freezing! Come inside and have a hot shower.'

'We're starving, Ma.' Anna-Marie

grinned. 'But it was great. And, Ma, you'll never guess! Tell them, Marcus!'

'We sighted a leopard, near the top.' Marcus grinned. 'A female, I think, and I've got a great shot of her.'

They crowded around his digital camera and Cora marvelled as he switched it on. A tiny picture the size of a postage stamp showed the leopard in the middle of the track, snarling slightly.

'That's incredible.' Adam was impressed. 'I wonder if she's got cubs?'

'Better keep an eye on your goats, Adam,' Flippie said. 'If she's feeding them she'll be hungry and the Angora kids might be in trouble.'

Helen was numb with cold and hugely relieved to be back, although seeing the leopard so close had made the ride worth the discomfort. She hadn't enjoyed herself nearly as much as Anna-Marie, who'd whooped and shrieked in delight and clutched Marcus's arm over the rougher bits of terrain.

'Are you all right?' Adam asked softly.

'Nothing a hot bath won't fix.' Helen

smiled weakly. 'So, Marcus, what did you think of the trail?'

'Terrific!' Marcus grinned. 'Definitely not for the faint-hearted, though. I can see this one becoming popular with the Cape Town crowd. Glad I drove it before the rest of the mob discover it.'

'He seemed to aim for the roughest parts of the road.' Anna-Marie groaned in mock complaint. 'I thought you were a wild driver, Flippie, but this man! Phew! I thought we were going to take off after some of those bumps.'

'Bumps are there to be driven over,' Marcus said cheerfully. 'We had an excellent drive up there. I'll take your offer of a hot shower, Mrs Smit.'

While they were waiting for the others to warm up and change their clothes, Flippie relaxed.

'He really liked it. When we got there, he couldn't stop raving about the view and the fact it was rough enough to give him some thrills!'

'What about his truck?' Cora asked anxiously. 'Can you fix it?'

'Sure, Adam and I will take a look tomorrow. I think it's the carburettor.'

He sniffed the air appreciatively.

'Supper smells good, Ma. Now we'll knock him for six with Tuleka's superb cooking!'

Flippie rubbed his hands in great good humour.

'I have a good feeling about this visit. We owe Marita for this — big time.'

'She's Headed For Trouble . . . '

'More cottage pie, Dad?' Gwen had invited Albert round for a spot of lunch and a chat. She'd hardly seen him recently as the Meredale Marshes protest was gaining momentum and the committee had voted for Albert and two others to go to London and present a petition to the Minister of the Environment.

On his return, Albert had been in great demand, speaking and writing and handing out pamphlets. He was doing altogether too much, in Gwen's opinion.

'Are you eating properly, Albert?' she asked, spooning another helping on to his plate. 'There's nothing wrong with your appetite, but I expect it's just baked beans and bacon sandwiches at your house.'

'Not at all,' the old man said smugly. 'I had a meeting with three councillors yesterday. A right bunch of ninnies they were, too. Wouldn't say boo to a goose! But they gave me a slap-up lunch at the Royal Crown afterwards. It didn't match your pie, though, Gwenny.'

'Flattery will get you the rest of this to take home and heat up for tomorrow.' She smiled.

They were enjoying a cup of herbal tea in Gwen's bright little sitting-room and Albert eyed her shrewdly.

'Is anything the matter, Gwen? You don't look your usual cheerful self. The girls all right?'

'It's Angela.' She sighed. 'I can't help thinking she's heading for trouble, but I don't know what to do.'

She poured out all of her worries while Albert listened without comment.

She told him how Angela had taken up with that unsuitable neighbour Maeve and was overspending without Mark knowing. How she made no attempt to economise and seemed to think it was beneath her to buy anything but the best.

'She's spending all that money but she hasn't paid their gas or their phone bill. I offered to help her out, on condition she told Mark the pickle she'd got herself into. But so far she hasn't done so. Not that she's told me, anyway.'

'I can't understand why she stopped working,' Albert mused. 'Healthy girl like her, she could be earning a bit of money and keeping herself out of mischief.'

'My thoughts exactly.' Gwen nodded. 'I know she had a bit of morning sickness to start with but she's right as rain now, full of energy. Mind you, she's starting to show a bit, but that shouldn't stop her getting something as an office temp for a few months.'

'Does she want to work?'

'It certainly doesn't look like it,' Gwen said grimly. 'She's too taken up with having a good time with that Maeve, who's a bit older and a lot richer than she is.'

'Well, she's young, she must make a few mistakes. Tell her next time she comes over on the bus to come and see me . . . I might have an idea that'll help her out. And, anyway, she owes me a visit.'

'Maybe you can talk some sense into her . . . ' Gwen grinned. 'Read her the riot act, Albert!'

'Not at all.' Albert shook his head. 'I'm not good at that. Maybe I'll just give her a call and invite her over to tea . . . '

Bad Feeling

'It's Jacob's birthday today,' Cora announced.

'So it is.' Amelia nodded. 'Well, he's not as young as he used to be. Turning sixty, isn't he?'

'What if he is?' Flippie asked. 'It's nothing to do with us.'

'Well, actually, the school children are all going to sing for him this afternoon,' Helen said. 'Marita invited them. Her father loves singing, apparently.'

'And I'm going to have tea with him.'

Dead silence greeted Cora's quiet announcement. Then Flippie exploded.

'Ma! How can you? How can you even set foot in his house after the way he's treated you — treated us?'

'Jacob is a lonely man and I'm going to have a cup of tea with him on his birthday,' his mother said firmly. 'We've been neighbours for thirty years! I can't wipe out all the good years we had when your pa was alive, no matter what he's done since then.'

What did he do? Helen was dying to ask but she'd been too often rebuffed when she'd tried find out the cause of the bad feeling between the two families.

'Well, you're a true Christian at heart, my dear,' Amelia said briskly. 'I couldn't bring myself to speak civilly to the fellow, let alone eat birthday cake with him.'

Adam shook his head

'How can you be sure he hasn't asked you over to twist your arm about selling him the land? I don't think you should go, Ma. You know how persistent Jacob de Wild can be. You might end up feeling sorry for him!'

'It was Marita who invited me, not Jacob.' A little stiffly, Cora got to her feet. 'I have no intention of talking about selling the land, as he knows what my answer would be. Now, Helen, tell me when you and the children are ready and we'll walk over together, shall we?'

Helen looked uncomfortably from Adam to his mother.

'They're all coming back here at three o'clock to get dressed,' she said.

'Then we'll go. Marita wanted us there at four o'clock.'

★   ★   ★

Schoolwork had been forgotten that morning as everyone concentrated on the concert that afternoon. Tuleka had been consulted about the songs and she'd rehearsed three with the children, all in Xhosa. Helen could only stand and listen, thinking how beautiful their voices were, pure and unaffected and joining in a harmony which would have been the envy of any English music teacher.

'This one is especially for important old man,' Tuleka explained. 'They sing how great he is and how great is his family. This other one they sing is a church song about how God made the mountains and the rivers. And the last song is about flowers.'

Flowers. That gave Helen an idea.

'Let's all make something special to wear for Mr Jacob's birthday,' she told the class. 'We'll make big bright flower hats for you to wear when you sing.'

The rest of the morning was spent cutting and pasting and at the end of it, every child had made a hat out of coloured paper petals. Helen fetched a mirror from the farmhouse and when they saw their faces ringed with petals they beamed with pleasure.

Good Friends

Cora, who had changed into a smart frock for the occasion, was most impressed when she saw them ready for the party. She said something to them in Xhosa and they burst out laughing.

'I told them they looked like a garden full of flowers and if they weren't careful, the goats would come and eat them!'

She straightened the shoulders of her dress, then grinned at Helen.

'Right, let's be off to Jacob's tea

before my family try and lock me in my bedroom!'

I've got to ask her, Helen thought. This mystery is driving me mad!

As they walked across the fields to the boundary fence between the two farms, she couldn't contain her curiosity.

'Cora, what did Jacob do to make you all hate him so much?'

'Hate?' Cora smiled. 'That's a very strong word. I certainly don't hate Jacob. I know Adam and Flippie resent what he did, but I can't bring myself to dislike the man, just his actions.'

'Even Marita doesn't seem exactly sure what it's all about.'

'Well, all right, I'll tell you. But talking about it won't change anything.' Cora sighed.

'As you know we were always good friends. When Gerard was alive, he and Jacob got on so well and Aletta and I were in and out of each other's houses. And the children played together, especially Adam and Marita. And when

Gerard died, the de Wilds were so kind, always around to help.'

'So what happened to change things?'

'He Pulled Strings . . . '

'Gerard died at a very bad time.' Cora sighed. 'We'd had that awful drought for three years and owed the bank a great deal of money. But all the sheep farmers in the country owe money to the bank and we all pay it back when the wool cheque comes in. It's like a cycle, and no-one's too worried about owing the bank.

'But the problem was Gerard had decided to try something new apart from sheep. He had this big idea that he could go in for trucking, and that he'd make money by transporting livestock for farmers selling off their animals. So he borrowed the money for an enormous truck and fitted it out for carrying cattle. And the first time he drove it, he had an accident. He turned it over and it rolled down the side of a mountain pass.'

'Was he hurt?'

'No, by some miracle he walked away with just a few bruises. And luckily there were no animals inside it. But the truck was a complete write-off and he hadn't been able to afford insurance for it. So there we were, with no truck and all the payments still owing on it, plus the huge debt to the bank. Then the wool cheque that year was much less than usual so we couldn't meet even a fraction of our debt.'

Cora was silent for a time and she seemed to be struggling to speak.

'Don't tell me if you don't want to,' Helen said gently. 'It sounds as if you had a terrible time.'

'Then Gerard died, falling off his horse,' Cora said. 'The doctor thought he might have had a heart attack while he was riding. It couldn't have happened at a worse time. Three days after his funeral, the bank foreclosed. They gave us thirty days to come up with the money. And of course, we couldn't, so they sold off a big part of the farm. In fact . . . this bit we're walking on now used to be part of Kasteelpoort.'

They'd crossed the boundary fence some time back and were approaching Jacob's big white farmhouse, the children chattering and laughing in a long line behind them.

'And Jacob bought the land?'

'Yes. But the thing was, he got it for a song. The sale of the land should have cleared our debt and left plenty over to re-stock with sheep but the bank didn't put the land up for auction as they usually did. Jacob bought it without telling anyone and we found out later that the new bank manager was his cousin. He must have pulled some strings.'

'That was pretty treacherous of him.'

Helen's impression of Jacob as a big friendly bear had changed somewhat with Cora's explanation.

'We thought so. I couldn't believe it when I heard what he'd paid for the land. You know, I always felt something happened to Jacob when Aletta died. He would never have done anything so underhand, so ... so unfriendly, if she'd still been alive.'

'So that's why everyone is so against him.'

'Yes. I couldn't bring myself to speak to him for months and I'm afraid Adam and Flippie can't forgive him. But not Marita, of course, she's a lovely girl and she's not to blame for her father's actions.'

'No, of course not.'

'Even after all these years, we've never really managed to get completely clear of debt. That truck's been a big millstone around our necks because the interest we owed just kept increasing. But we made the final payment last Christmas, so things can only improve. And don't worry, my dear ... '

They'd reached the house and Marita came out on to the verandah to welcome them.

'The farm's a constant worry but I'm

sure we'll muddle through.' Cora sighed. 'What with Adam's goats and Flippie's trail ... they'll make sure Jacob doesn't get his hands on any more of our farm. So let's just go inside and enjoy a nice cup of tea with him.'

All the same, Helen thought, I'm going to stick close to Cora this afternoon and not give Jacob a chance to get too friendly. He's not the sort of man to give up easily, and who knows if that famous de Wild charm won't wear her down in the end?

7

An Awkward Situation

'So, Helen, how was Jacob's tea party?' Flippie asked.

The day before, she'd found an old table in the barn which would make a perfect nature table for the children, and Flippie had offered to help her paint it a cheerful bright green.

Now they were taking a break and admiring their handiwork. The air around them held the spicy smell of pepper and Helen reached up and picked a swag of pink peppercorns from the graceful branches above, crushing them in her fingers and inhaling the aromatic smell with delight.

'Very nice, I thought,' she said. 'Marita went to a lot of trouble to provide a gorgeous tea and an enormous birthday cake. And the children sang like angels.'

'I bet Jacob spent the afternoon trying to persuade Ma to sell him more of our land.'

'Not at all. Actually, he was awfully nice. He's got a cracking sense of humour. He and your mum seemed to get on really well and chatted about the old days. You've got some paint on your cheek, did you know? Let me wipe it off.'

'Ma might get taken in by that old so-and-so, but Adam and I wouldn't trust him an inch.'

Flippie stood still, looking down at her intently while she cleaned his cheek, then gripped her upraised hand.

'Helen, listen, I — '

With a wretched feeling she knew what he was about to say but couldn't stop him. For a long time, Flippie had been taking every opportunity to be alone with her and she was starting to find the situation a bit awkward.

He was great fun to be with, but she would never be able to see him as anything more than the younger brother she never had.

'I really like you a lot, Helen. Do you think you and I — I mean, could you ever feel the same about me?'

He was scarlet with embarrassment.

'I already like you, Flippie. You know that you're my favourite red-haired guy!'

But Flippie wasn't going to be put off by her light-hearted answer.

'You know what I mean, Helen. I love you. I mean, I'd like us to get — you know — serious. About each other.'

She bit her lip.

'Flip, I can't. I just don't feel the same way you do. I like you as . . . as a brother.'

A very young, immature brother at that, she thought, feeling desperately sorry for him at that moment. He groaned.

'That's just about the worst thing any girl can say to a guy!'

'I'm sorry, but it's true. I really, really like you. But I'm not in love with you and I won't ever be.'

He was silent, kicking the dirt at the foot of the tree.

'It's because of Adam, isn't it?' he asked sulkily. 'You're in love with him.'

'No, Flippie, I'm not in love with either of you.'

'That's good, because you have to face facts. He's going to marry Marita one of these days.'

Helen flushed as she remembered that kiss by the dry riverbed. Everyone assumes he's going to marry Marita, she thought, except Adam himself. Or did he?

But she said nothing and started cleaning the brushes, searching for a way to change the subject.

'It Wouldn't Work'

'Flip, what would you do if you weren't a farmer?' she asked suddenly.

'Me? I've never thought, really. I guess I'll always farm; it's all I know.

Although . . . I wouldn't mind being in business of some kind. Sort of making my own life, if you know what I mean?'

He drew his hand through his hair, choosing his words carefully.

'On the farm, no matter how hard you try, things are out of your control. There's either a drought or the price of wool goes down or the stock gets sick and dies and there's nothing you can do . . . ' His voice trailed off and he cheered up. 'But this adventure trail could be a big thing.'

'That's true. It's more like a real business venture.' She smiled. 'Little things like drought and locusts aren't going to stop people wanting a thrill!'

'Sure!' Flippie grinned back. 'We've got two couples from Cape Town booked to come here next weekend, did Anna-Marie tell you? And Marcus wants to come back, too.'

'That's wonderful. Can we find beds for all of them?'

'I guess Ma and Anna-Marie will sort all that out.'

She pushed down the lid of the paint tin and picked up the newspapers they'd laid around the table while they painted.

'Thanks for all your help, Flip.'

'My pleasure. Um — are we OK, then, Helen? You're not going to start avoiding me or anything?'

'Of course not!' Impulsively she gave him a quick hug and kissed his cheek. 'I'm just very flattered!'

'If I were a businessman and moved to a big town, would you change your mind?' he asked seriously.

'Heavens, no!' Helen laughed. 'Exactly the opposite. I love the farm. But it's got nothing to do with where you'd live or what you'd do. Flip. It just wouldn't work between us.'

'Well, I'm warning you, I'm not going to give up. I'm happy if you just like me, and I don't mind how long I have to wait for your like to turn to love.'

Honestly, he sounds like a bad pop song, she thought, suddenly irritated.

'Don't wait, Flip. Nothing's going to

change. See you back at the house. I just want to check the stationery supplies.'

She watched as Flippie mooched off, his hands in his pockets, then turned with relief into the schoolroom.

Preparations . . .

As the weekend drew closer, Anna-Marie threw herself into a frenzy of planning and arranging for the expected visitors. The whole adventure trail, with the promise of exotic guests from the city, had filled her with excited energy and she seemed much less discontented with life on the farm.

'Helen, I could move in with you just for Friday and Saturday night, if that's all right with you,' she said. 'Then we'll get Ouma's old yellow-wood double bed out of the loft and put it in my room, so we'll have enough space for everyone.'

'And where will Marcus sleep?'

'Marita's offered to put him up at Blouberg. They've got loads of room. Come and see, I've made a new cover for that old eiderdown Ma's had for donkeys' years.'

'Wow, this is gorgeous, Anna-Marie!'

Helen fingered the new cover — a clever patchwork of pastel shades, the seams concealed by a lattice-work of old cream lace and edged with a deep flounce.

'It looks almost Victorian. And it's so dainty . . . ' she breathed.

'That's just the effect I wanted! All that lace came from one of Ouma's old tablecloths. And Ma found some ancient mushroom-coloured velvet curtains, very faded, but they look stunning. I'm going to use that china washbasin with roses painted on it and fill it with leaves and whatever roses I can find. I'll call it the Victoria Room. What do you think?'

'I think it's brilliant,' Helen said truthfully. 'And maybe if we keep getting visitors you could redecorate the other rooms with a theme, like the African Room, or . . . '

'Or the Jungle Room, and I could paint creepers and trees all over the walls . . . well, maybe not.' Anna-Marie grinned. 'Flippie's looking for some good music in case the *braai* on Saturday night turns into a bit of a party.'

'If they're not completely dead beat by the time they've driven the trail!' Helen laughed.

'A nice hot bath waiting and they'll feel loads better,' the girl said confidently. 'People who live in cities don't go to bed when the sun goes down.'

'Anna-Marie, my dear . . . ' Amelia was sitting in her cane chair on the *stoep*, painting. 'I'm nearly finished this still-life. Some of the roses look a bit odd but overall I think it's quite pretty.'

'It's perfect, Ouma,' Anna-Marie enthused. 'I'm going to replace that old picture of Ma's with this. It'll go beautifully with the whole old roses theme.'

'By the way, don't forget Professor Philips, my tutor in Cape Town,' Amelia reminded her granddaughter, sitting back and looking critically at her painting.

'I need to know when there'll be a room free for him, because he might stay for a few days. He won't want to rush off if he finds some interesting fossils.'

'Actually, Ouma, I've been thinking we should turn the old dairy into a little flat of some sort,' Cora put in. 'We're going to need more space and that big room already has a tap and an electric point. I'm sure Adam and a couple of the men could make it ensuite. And it would need a ceiling, but that's no problem.'

Helen loved the way things got done on the farm. If anything was needed, Adam and a few of his farm workers just did it. Or made it. Or mended it . . . Tractors and pumps got fixed, a bridge over the dry riverbed was rebuilt and a road constructed, without any

250

long-drawn-out planning.

Helen had no doubt that Adam could turn his hand to plumbing a new shower.

He and Grandad would get on well, she thought. They're both practical types.

'We must talk to Tuleka about the menu,' Cora went on. 'She's delighted we're getting a crowd, but we need to choose food that everyone will like.'

'That's your department, Ma.' Anna-Marie smiled. 'I'm going to take a look at the other bedroom and see how I can jazz it up a bit.'

Cora and Helen went off to the kitchen to consult with the cook. Even if they came back cold, tired and aching from their trail-driving adventure, Cora intended her guests to be well fed!

'What's All This About?'

Angela had just checked that the macaroni cheese in the oven was browning nicely when she heard Mark's key in the lock.

'Hello, gorgeous!' He threw down his briefcase and wrapped her in his arms. 'Mmm, you smell good!'

'Are you sure you're not just smelling good home cooking?' She grinned, snuggling up. 'You're home nice and early for a change.'

'Yes, for some reason we got through everything today without a hitch. And how's Baby Milne?' Mark patted her nicely rounded tummy. 'Behaving himself?'

Angela nodded happily.

'Been doing his stretching exercises again.'

The baby's movements were a real thrill and Mark never tired of placing his hand over her bump whenever she could feel the kicking.

'Boy or girl, I think we've got a professional soccer player here!' She laughed.

'I'll just go and take a shower and then how about having supper outside?'

'Great idea. We haven't had a long evening together for ages. I wish you'd come home at this time every day.'

Angela cheerfully busied herself with a tray, listening for the sound of the shower, and was just wondering if Mark would like a beer with his supper when he came back into the kitchen, his face like thunder.

'What's all this about, Angela?'

He had the gas bill in his hand as well as her credit card statement and the two letters of demand from the baby shop.

Tears

Angela groaned inwardly. Earlier that afternoon she'd been adding up what she owed and had forgotten to put the bills away at the back of the drawer. The total was so alarming that she had just made herself a cup of tea and wandered into the garden and tried to forget it altogether.

'I thought you paid the gas last month?' Mark persisted.

'Um . . . well, I paid some of it.' She flushed. 'But then I had to pay for the baby cupboard so I gave some of it to the furniture shop.'

'And is that paid in full?'

'No, I still owe a bit . . . '

'How much?' Mark's voice wasn't raised in anger but Angela was suddenly close to tears.

'A hundred and forty pounds,' she whispered.

He ran his finger down the credit card statement.

'And what's this one for Topkidz? A hundred and ninety pounds?'

'It's those nice little winter suits I bought with Maeve. You said you liked them,' she added defensively.

'Bought? I thought you told me they were a gift from her?'

Had she? Oh, dear.

'And this?' he went on relentlessly. 'Brighter Babies Books? Fifty-five pounds? I don't believe this!'

Angela began to feel less guilty and more rattled. Surely he should realise that this was an investment for their baby's future?

'Everyone knows you should read to your baby from an early age,' she countered. 'Maeve said those books were scientifically proven to increase their brain power.'

'What's wrong with 'The Three Little Pigs'?' Mark growled. 'And books about child psychology? Come on! I'd have to laugh if I wasn't so — so . . . '

'Angry? I know you are. I'm sorry, darling.' Angela searched his face for some sign that he would forgive her again.

'No . . . disappointed,' he said flatly.

Spoiled . . .

This was worse than anger. She could cope with a row — she'd expected it — but not this look of sadness on her husband's face.

'Angie, you've been lying and hiding stuff from me. What's happening here? We're supposed to be a team.'

She stared at him, unable to answer.

'You know exactly how much I earn. You know what we can afford, what we agreed to spend. Where do you think all this money's going to come from? Do I just say, OK, we'll be in debt for the rest of our lives because my wife has an uncontrollable shopping habit?'

'I haven't,' she whispered, tears running down her cheeks. 'I won't buy another thing.'

'I've heard that before. And what about these letters of demand? Do you realise that if you don't pay these by the end of next week we'll be handed over to a debt collector? And our name will go on to a national list of bad debtors?'

'I didn't know that,' she said weakly.

'Well, just what were you planning to do about these? Ignore them?'

'No.' She took a deep, wobbly breath. 'I've got a part-time job. Starting tomorrow. I'll get an advance on my wages and pay everything off.'

'And who on earth do you think will give you an advance the day you start work?'

'My grandad.'

Angela hadn't given a thought to her grandfather's offer all week. But if sorting through his dreary old papers would get her out of this mess, she'd just have to do it.

'You're going to work for Albert?' Mark was surprised and relieved. 'Like Helen did? That's a great idea — if you don't get bored and stop halfway through the job.'

'I wouldn't just stop for no reason,' she said indignantly. 'What do you think I am?'

'I'm not sure any more,' Mark said evenly.

Although they were polite to each other during supper, their lovely evening outside in the garden was spoiled and Mark went to bed early, claiming he was tired. Angela switched on the television and sat in front of it for an hour without watching.

She felt wretched and wanted desperately to make it up with Mark. It was all very well for her mother to say, 'Never let the sun go down on your anger', but it wasn't her anger the sun had witnessed, it was Mark's and there wasn't anything she could do about it.

She went upstairs, trying to be as quiet as she could, but as she crept into bed she could tell that Mark was still awake.

'I'm sorry,' she said in a small voice. 'Please don't be cross any more.'

'I'm not, silly. Come here.'

So everything was all right and by the time they fell asleep, they were friends again.

But one thing's for sure, she thought as she turned over and closed her eyes. Boring or not, I'll stick it out with Grandad's mouldy old papers to prove I'm not the airhead Mark seems to think I've become.

★ ★ ★

Albert took off his wet boots and hung up his jacket, enjoying the unaccustomed warmth that greeted him as he stepped from his little hall into the sitting-room.

It was two o'clock and Angela had already left to catch the bus to Leighton. But in the three days she'd been working for him, she'd made sure the fire was banked, his lunch-time soup was keeping warm on the stove and his post and phone messages were ready for his attention by his armchair.

Picking up the notebook and skimming down the list of phone numbers that had been neatly recorded next to each message, Albert wondered how he'd ever managed without her.

Apart from answering the phone, she'd piled his old papers, photographs and news cuttings neatly on the dining-room table and was busy sorting everything into the right sequence, entering the categories on to her laptop computer.

The War Years . . .

She'd tried to explain her system, which Albert had to admit was a lot quicker than Helen's had been.

'Amazing,' Albert had said enthusiastically, not really understanding.

'I've got one file called 'War Years' and all the cuttings you've got and your letters. I'm busy sorting those by date before I enter them. Was this your ship?'

She smoothed out a rumpled newspaper cutting of *HMS Howe* with the caption *Miracle Rescue At Sea Now Revealed*.

'Yes, wasn't she a beauty?'

'What was the miracle rescue all about?'

Albert scanned the photograph, then looked at Angela over the newspaper.

'One of the young lads fell overboard while we were sailing down the coast off West Africa. No-one saw him fall and he was only missed after a few hours. So our captain turned round and sailed back for miles, searching for him.

Found him, too.' He smiled at the memory.

'Spotting him in the water was like finding a needle in a haystack. It really was a miracle. Although after the story came out the captain was hauled over the coals by the top brass.'

'Why?' Angela was puzzled. 'Surely he deserved a medal?'

'Well, during the war, all captains had standing orders never to turn back and search in a case like that. But Captain McCall wasn't the sort to leave one of his men to drown.'

Albert's voice trailed off and he stood, lost in thought. Angela placed the cutting on the 'War Years' pile with a pleased little smile.

'This is more fun than I thought it would be, Grandad,' she said. 'One day you must tell me about your time at sea.'

'Well, I intend to write it all down when we have everything ship-shape.' Albert rubbed his hands together, looking expectantly at his granddaughter.

'And perhaps you can help me when I get to that stage, too?'

'Just as long as you get to it before the baby arrives,' Angela mused. 'I think I'll have this lot sorted in a week or so and then maybe you can start dictating what you want to say.'

'Er . . . well, there might be more up in the attic,' Albert confessed. 'But if you can get through these, I'll be very grateful.'

'Those Old Bones . . . '

He helped himself to a bowl of soup, poked the fire and sat down, stretching his legs towards the warmth. Then he turned his attention to the pile of post, smiling as he recognised Amelia's upright handwriting on the first envelope.

My dear Albert, he read.
I don't know if Helen is keeping you up to date with the recent

goings-on at Kasteelpoort but there are some exciting changes here since I last wrote.

Of course you will have heard about the school she started. Did you know it is in the old shed — yes, the very place where my pa made you sleep all those years ago!

But not content with just teaching them the three Rs, she's starting to give the children dancing lessons. She's also encouraged them to form a small choir and her pupils have sung at our neighbour's birthday party as well as the retirement home in Hartley's Drift. They are delightful to hear and Helen's talking of entering them in the Eisteddfod in Cape Town. She is so full of energy and enthusiasm — a lovely girl. You must be so proud of her. We are all fond of her and she has made an especially big impression on my two grandsons, I think!

Helen hasn't mentioned anything about that to me, Albert thought. But it would do her good to have a bit of male attention again. I wonder what those boys are like? If there's anything going on she might have told Gwen, though. Or Angela.

Her arrival here seems to have sparked off all sorts of happenings. Adam and Flippie have begun an adventure trail and every weekend we have visitors from Cape Town or Stellenbosch roaring up the mountains in their four-wheel drives. Adam turned an old storeroom into a little self-contained flat so this and the spare rooms in the house are now occupied by paying visitors every weekend.

If this carries on it seems likely the family will make quite a nice little income — myself included!

Before I was married, I loved to paint — I don't know if you remember that? My pa thought it was a silly waste of time so I never pursued it until I moved to town and joined a painting group.

Well, the first weekend Cora entertained a party from the city, one of the visitors admired a painting of mine, of two zebra. I didn't really want to sell it but she offered me far too much money so I accepted. Cora now has a little gallery of my wildlife pictures in the dining-room and so far I've sold four paintings! I'm the only one of my painting group to have sold anything and am beginning to feel like a real artist.

Albert reached for his bowl of soup, looking at the painting of the three mountains on the wall. Of course I remember. But she must have forgotten she gave me that keepsake . . . Smiling to himself, he read on.

Now for the really exciting news. Do you remember those old bones you and I discovered down by the river and how we joked they could be dinosaur fossils? Well, indeed that is what they are and over the years I've spent a lot of time digging around there. I mentioned them to a Professor Philips from the university and he came up to the farm last week.

He's very excited by what he saw and will be bringing a party of his palaeontology students up for a fortnight to start an official 'dig'. He was even talking of a TV interview (nothing new for you, I know, but certainly for us at Kasteelpoort!) because these are a totally new find, although of course on the farm we've known about them for a long time.

I am delighted that they have proved to be interesting and glad that some knowledgeable youngsters will take over the hard work of unearthing them. I have to confess that I'm beginning to find all that digging for bones quite tiring, although I wouldn't admit that to anyone here.

Do you sometimes find your family

have started treating you as if you're a precious piece of china because of your advancing years? Annoying, isn't it?

He grinned, knowing exactly what Amelia meant. Gwen worried about him, fussing with extra jackets and dry shoes whenever she could, and after he'd twisted his ankle at the last protest meeting, she had taken to phoning him for no reason just to make sure he was all right. He knew she meant well, but just because he didn't rush around like a ten-year-old didn't mean he was getting doddery!

Cora is always begging me to stop driving my scooter, but I'm a careful driver and so far I still feel perfectly safe on my trusty two-wheeled steed. I have no intention of becoming dependent on anyone else to get around. And from what Helen tells me, you're still full of beans, too.

She's very keen that you should

join her for a holiday on the farm before she returns to the UK. Any chance of that in the near future? I would so love to see you again.
Warm regards,
Amelia.

Albert's Hobby-Horse

Join Helen on the farm for a holiday? Why not? Amelia had asked him many times before but suddenly, the more he thought of seeing Amelia again, the better he liked the idea. Albert felt her letter needed an immediate reply. He got up and searched for notepaper and a pen.

Dear Amelia.

Then he couldn't think what to say. Although he'd run a small newspaper many years before, and enjoyed writing a stinging rebuke to some member of parliament or local councillor, ordinary correspondence had never been Albert's forte. And lately he'd preferred action to words.

In the end, he kept it short.

Glad to hear from you and that things are going well on the farm. That trail sounds like a good idea. Helen tells us she is enjoying herself and I am pleased she has been such a help to you. She has certainly been away longer than we expected and we will all be glad to see her home again before Christmas.

I will give your kind invitation some serious thought. I remember those old bones — who would have thought they were the real thing? Always imagined they were the remains of old cattle although you insisted they were too big for that, and you were right.

Then he decided to add a bit of his own news.

You seem to have many interests to keep you occupied. I also keep myself pretty busy. Since I retired I've been setting up a centre for the sale of organic vegetables from local farmers, getting permission for the weekly market and making sure everything on sale will be properly organic. I firmly believe that you are what you eat and if more people thought the same way I am convinced there would be less ill-health in the world.

Stop it, now. Don't get on to your hobby-horse, you silly old man, he thought crossly. He knew some people's eyes glazed over in boredom when he got into his stride about food additives and harmful chemical sprays.

I can understand how you feel when your family makes a fuss. Mine are the same, although I am perfectly able to look after myself and still drive my own car and do all my own cooking.

Suddenly he remembered that Gwen had lately taken to stocking his freezer with small dishes of stew and cottage pie, which he just had to re-heat, and felt a stab of guilt at this claim. He hadn't actually made more than a cup of tea in his kitchen in quite a while, he realised. Even the soup he was enjoying had been made by Angela, but he didn't want Amelia to think he was a helpless sort.

I suppose I'm slowing down a little, too, but as I'll be eighty next birthday, that's to be expected.

He definitely wouldn't mention the pains in his chest. It was probably indigestion, anyway.

My regards to you and your family, Albert.

I'll ask Angela to pop this in the post tomorrow, he thought. His easy chair next to the fire looked inviting and he decided to go through the rest of his post in comfort before answering all those calls. But his head drooped on to his chest and in five minutes Albert was fast asleep.

The Guests

Cora looked at the cheerful crowd chatting on the *stoep* and smiled in relief. So far, everything about this fourth weekend of adventure trail visitors had gone perfectly.

The three couples, who had started off as strangers to each other the night before, had made fast friends over breakfast on Saturday morning, which Tuleka had served on the *stoep* in the shade of the bougainvillea.

To Cora's surprise, Marcus the travel writer had appeared on the Friday evening, saying he was just passing so thought he'd stay over for the weekend.

This was his third visit to the adventure trail and the second time he'd begged a room from Marita, who seemed quite happy to put him up at short notice. Privately, Cora thought this was a bit thoughtless and inconsiderate of Marcus, but he was on top form this evening, regaling everyone with stories from his travels through Africa.

That morning the three couples had gone off with a packed lunch of cold venison pie and salads, cherry cake and crunchy oat cookies as well as beer and home-made lemonade packed into a cool box. They'd returned without incident, gleeful at their various hair-raising experiences which they were now sharing at the top of their voices.

Marita had come over for the evening, looking very fetching in a black halter-neck dress. She was standing with Marcus, and obviously enjoying being part of his attentive audience.

' . . . Thought we'd had it for a moment there, what an angle! But we pulled out of that one OK.'

' . . . Reminds me of a trip I did up to Namibia . . . '

' . . . Looked for the leopard that's supposed to be up there but no luck. Lots of buck though, and zebra — and what a view!'

Suspicious

The sound of happy laughter greeted Marcus's every anecdote, bringing a smile to Cora's lips. She wondered if the leopard was amongst the rocks on Kasteelpoort, or had moved on, perhaps to Jacob's part of the mountain. As a precaution, Adam had herded his precious Angora goats down to a lower camp, but the buck and zebra would have to take their chances.

And the leopard would have to take its chance with Jacob, who'd been a keen hunter all his life and had regarded leopards as fair game because they took his lambs.

'Ma, I've got the coals just about ready. Where's the meat?'

Adam had put himself in charge of

the fire while Flippie mixed with the guests. Her younger son was in his element and so was Anna-Marie, laughing and talking. In particular, Richard Warren, a middle-aged man, was engaging her in conversation. His attractive wife Margie was off talking to the rest of the crowd.

Cora, annoyed with herself for being suspicious, couldn't help calling across to her daughter.

'Anna-Marie, could you help fetch the meat from the kitchen?'

'In a minute, Ma.' Anna-Marie turned back to Richard.

All Cora knew about the man was that he owned a factory in Cape Town and their arrival the evening before had been delayed by some work-related problem. He looked pleasant enough and seemed to find Anna-Marie very interesting. Cora bristled. He was a married man and she was a young girl just out of school!

'Anna-Marie!' she said peremptorily.

'Let me fetch it, Cora.'

Fascinated

Helen had been standing with Adam next to the fire, pleased to have him to herself for a while. She couldn't help noticing that Marita seemed fascinated by the travel writer, standing closer than necessary and hanging on his every word.

So much for claiming Adam as her own, she thought indignantly. She wondered if Adam had noticed, and if he had, did he care?

Helen knew Anna-Marie had wanted to talk to Richard Warren ever since he'd casually mentioned that he owned a clothing factory with a big staff of designers.

'I'll bring the salads out,' she said to Cora. 'Leave Anna-Marie to chat to Richard. They're discussing clothes, if I'm not mistaken.'

'Clothes? What sort of man talks about clothes?' Cora said scathingly.

'One who manufactures them.' Helen smiled. 'Wild horses won't drag Anna-Marie away from him until she has finished picking his brains about the fashion scene in Cape Town.'

Cora clicked her tongue, unconvinced.

A Veritable Feast!

In the kitchen, big trays of home-made sausages, ostrich steaks and lamb chops were laid out, seasoned and ready to go on the fire, as well as skewers threaded with small pieces of chicken, baby onions and dried apricots, which had been marinating in a mixture of garlic, fruit juice and wine all afternoon.

'*Sosaties*,' Tuleka explained. 'Cook very quick. Tell Mr Adam he must only cook two minutes or they burn.'

She and Cora had been hard at work all afternoon to produce a splendid array of salads. Fresh cold asparagus, tiny deep crimson beetroots as big as a marble, baby ears of corn and a huge dish of sweet-and-sour bean salad were ready for the guests.

She took bowls of lightly curried potato salad from the fridge, along with cauliflower and bacon salad, an exotic-looking rice mixture and a huge platter of tossed greens.

'And Mr Adam, he's making baked potatoes in the fire, yes?' Tuleka beamed. 'All very nice. And don't forget, Miss Cora, here is the bread.'

'There's enough here for fifty people, Tuleka!' Helen giggled in disbelief. 'We'll have to serve them the leftovers for breakfast!'

But she was wrong. Conversation almost came to a stop as their visitors helped themselves again and again until the plates and bowls were empty.

'I have never, ever, eaten so much,' Margie Warren groaned. 'But what delicious food! Where did you buy those baby beetroot, Mrs Smit? Were they grown locally?'

'I grow them here,' Cora answered with a smile. 'Everything was from our kitchen garden, except for the rice.'

'Really? That's amazing . . . Would

you show me your garden? Tomorrow, perhaps?'

'Of course, I'd be pleased to. But it's just vegetables,' Cora added doubtfully.

'And the fruit trees, don't forget,' Helen prompted. 'The cherries are wonderful right now. There're so many of them they're weighing down the branches.'

'Those I have to see!' Margie beamed.

As if on cue, Tuleka appeared with a tray of desserts. There was home-made ice-cream, a bowl of dark red cherries swimming in a thick brandied syrup and a gooseberry fool with a big jug of thick yellow cream.

She looked indignant at the muted cries of protest.

'You eat!' she told the guests firmly. 'You enjoy it!'

No-one could resist this final, delicious indulgence and soon the sound of spoons scraping the last from the pudding bowls satisfied Tuleka that her efforts had been properly appreciated.

Cora was making a pot of coffee in the kitchen when she heard the music start up outside. When she returned, everyone was dancing.

'Come on, Ma!' Flippie laughed, putting down his beer. 'Do me the honour!'

'Oh, you! Silly boy.' But she smiled and joined him with the others. 'You're not dancing with Helen . . . ? Oh.' Her eyes followed his, to where Adam and Helen were dancing dreamily on the edge of the crowd. Helen's eyes were closed and they were swaying together, hardly moving.

Her first thought was, poor Flippie.

Although he'd never said a word to her, she'd seen how her younger son looked at Helen and she'd been pleased to think a romance might be developing there. Helen had fitted in so well from the very first day and after all these months she'd come to think of her almost as a second daughter.

And where was Marita, if she wasn't in Adam's arms where she belonged?

Over there, dancing with that noisy fellow Marcus, looking as if she was enjoying every moment.

Cora frowned. What was Marita thinking of? Surely she and Adam had an understanding that went back to their schooldays?

But even as she watched, Marita said something to her partner and broke away from him, skipped over to Adam and tapped him lightly on the shoulder.

'Beautiful Silence'

'My turn,' Marita said sweetly, and left Helen standing as she whirled him away. Adam grinned ruefully and waved at Helen over Marita's shoulder as she sat down next to Amelia.

Marcus started towards her, obviously meaning to ask her to dance, but Cora quickly pushed Flippie forward.

'Go on, Flip, what are you waiting for?'

Flippie strode across and cut in front

of Marcus to offer Helen his arm.

'My turn, Miss McLeod!' He laughed and Cora was relieved to see Helen take his hand willingly, smiling and chatting to him. I'm sure she likes him really, Cora thought. They'd be well suited and he's more her age.

She went over to Amelia and sat down.

'A lovely evening,' Amelia stated, looking around the room. 'Everyone's enjoying themselves. Who's that rather good-looking man Marita was dancing with? Is that the travel writer?'

'Marcus Retief,' Cora said shortly. 'But — '

Just then the lights went out, the music stopped and the *stoep* was plunged into darkness.

'Oh, heavens, the generator's gone again.' Cora grimaced. 'Of all times to break down . . . Adam! Flippie!'

A calm, confident voice rang out, to Cora's relief.

'Don't worry, everyone, we'll get the lights on again in a minute,' Flippie assured the guests. 'Just take a seat and enjoy the stars.'

He and Adam disappeared down the steps and melted into the darkness.

In the sudden silence the guests fumbled their way to the cane chairs and sat down, listening to the night noises coming from around them.

Out in the garden, frogs called and unseen insects clicked and chirruped. The occasional bleating of a sheep and the thump of the windmill far away came faintly over the night breezes, and above them, the night sky was unbelievably black and deep, lit only by a wide swathe of stars from the Milky Way.

'Isn't this lovely?' Margie Warren whispered to her husband. 'Have you ever heard such beautiful silence?'

Beautiful silence or not, Helen realised they'd soon want a light and went to the kitchen, feeling along the shelf for the store of candles kept there, ready in their tin holders. Then she felt her way to all the bedrooms and left two or three in each room and some in the bathroom, ready lit.

Flippie and Adam would probably have the generator working again in no time, but it would never do to have the guests complaining.

Cora was already in the kitchen, filling huge pots of water on the coal stove by candlelight.

'If the boys don't get it going, there won't be hot water for their baths,' she said, clearly worried at this possibility. 'We'll have to carry buckets.'

'I'm sure they'll think it's all very rural and romantic,' Helen comforted her, picking up a jug. 'The candlelight is so soft and mysterious. The guests will love it.'

'In the meantime I'll take the paraffin lamps out on to the *stoep*,' Cora said. 'Just hold thumbs they're successful.'

Stunned

Helen stayed in the kitchen, enjoying the quiet and watching the flickering

284

shadows of the drying herbs hung from the rafters. Tuleka had left the next morning's bread rising overnight in a big bowl, ready to be baked, and the metal containers for the fresh milk from the dairy were waiting at the door.

Helen enjoyed a sense of the quiet rhythm of life on the farm, especially in the kitchen, and she lifted the cloth and sniffed the bread dough appreciatively. No other bread could taste as good as this.

'Oh, there you are.' Flippie came in noisily, closing the door behind him. 'No luck with the generator, I'm afraid. We'll have to go into town and fetch a part but tomorrow's Sunday. So we'll be without electricity until Monday.'

'I don't think anyone will be too worried,' she said. 'But that's the end of the dancing, I suppose.'

'That's a pity. You and I were just getting started.'

'Flippie!' she warned. 'We were not getting started — with anything. A dance is all it was.'

But Flippie came up and put his arms around her, holding her fast.

'You don't mean that, Helen?' he pleaded. 'Can't you at least try to give us a chance?'

'Flippie, I've told you how I feel. Why can't you just leave it at that?'

'Because I love you,' he mumbled foolishly.

Without waiting for her reply, he bent and kissed her on the mouth, hugging her to him tightly as she tried to squirm away.

The kitchen door opened and over Flippie's shoulder, Helen saw Adam's stunned expression in the candlelight.

'Sorry, didn't mean to interrupt,' he said evenly. 'Helen, there's a call for you from England. It's your mother and she says your grandfather's been taken to hospital. He's had a heart attack.'

8

'How's Grandad?'

'Mum, what time is Helen's train arriving? Are you going to bring her straight to the hospital?'

Angela spoke in a low voice so as not to wake Albert.

She looks tired, Gwen thought, and no wonder. She's been a pillar of strength since Albert's collapse, but she should go home and take a break now. He's out of danger and she needs her rest.

'She gets in this evening at six,' Gwen said. 'I'll pick her up from the station and I'm sure she'll want to see Grandad straight away, but not for long. She'll be exhausted.'

'I can't wait to see her!'

'I know, love, but I was going to suggest you go home this afternoon. Helen could pop in here for a few minutes and then I'll take her home for a good long sleep. We could all get together tomorrow.'

Gwen looked down at the sleeping Albert and smoothed back his wispy white hair with a smile.

'He's so much better, we really don't have to be here all the time, dear. The doctor says he's made an excellent recovery.'

Albert was already complaining about the fuss everyone was making, which the nurse said was a good sign.

Gwen only hoped Helen wouldn't feel she'd been brought back under false pretences, but Albert's condition had been serious and Gwen knew that Helen wouldn't have forgiven her if she hadn't let her know about it — six thousand miles away or not.

'Come on, let's go. You off to Leighton and me back home to make up Helen's bed.'

'I'll phone her this evening, then,' Angela agreed somewhat unwillingly. 'And I'll be round first thing tomorrow.'

'Why not come for a late breakfast?' her mother suggested.

'That's a good idea. Thanks, Mum.'

Gwen couldn't resist straightening Albert's blankets and fluffing his pillow before she and Angela left the ward together, arm in arm. The bus to Leighton stopped just outside the hospital grounds and Gwen waited until her daughter was safely on board before turning for home.

But when Helen stepped off the train, and embraced her mother with tears in her eyes, Gwen's doubts about letting her know about Albert's condition evaporated.

'Oh, Mum, it's so lovely to be home! It's great to see you! But how's Grandad?'

'It's lovely to see you, too, darling, and he's much better.' Gwen hugged her hard. 'Although he gave us all a scare. They're still keeping him in bed, though.'

'But is he going to be all right?' Helen persisted anxiously.

'The doctor says he'll be fine. He's going to have to take things a bit easier, but at his age, he needs to slow down a bit!'

'Can I visit him this evening?'

'He knows you're coming and I wouldn't dare keep you away! But not for too long, darling. You'll both need your rest.'

Gwen had a good look at Helen for the first time and thought how well she appeared. Her new tan suited her and her blonde hair, tied back with a jaunty bandanna, was streaked with gold from the African sun.

But there was something more, a new confidence in her manner. She's grown up a lot, her mother thought.

★　★　★

Albert was propped up against the pillows when they walked in, and he looked as if he was asleep.

'Hello, Grandad,' Helen said softly, taking his hand in hers.

His blue eyes opened slowly and he gave a wide grin.

'Helen, sweetheart,' he said in a soft voice. 'My, don't you look a sight for sore eyes. But you shouldn't have come back! I told Gwen she was making a silly fuss . . . '

'I wanted to come, Grandad. Aren't you pleased to see me?' she asked in mock offence.

'Of course I am! And I see you've put on a bit of weight — it suits you.

'I remember those farm breakfasts.' Albert chuckled softly. 'They made very good porridge when I was there.'

'They still do, with lashings of creamy milk and honey, although Amelia still eats it with salt. She says you taught her the proper way to enjoy porridge.'

'Ah, she learned something after all!' Albert's eyes twinkled. 'So, you enjoyed yourself at Kasteelpoort?'

'Grandad, I've loads to tell you and photos to show you but all that will keep.' She yawned. 'I'm just so glad to see you're getting better. Right now all I want to do is go home and sleep . . . '

'That's more than thirty hours she's been on the go,' Gwen said. 'I'm taking her off home for some nice hot soup and then bed. You need your rest, too, Albert. We'll be round to see you in the morning.'

When Angela phoned later that evening, Helen was fast asleep.

'She went out like a light,' Gwen told her. 'So you didn't miss anything. But I'm sure she'll have lots to tell us at breakfast.'

Moody

Cora gave the spongy, fragrant bread dough a final punch, then wrapped it in an old towel and placed it in a warm corner near the coal stove for the evening, ready to be baked at first light.

It still didn't seem quite right to sell it, but when Flippie had seen her giving Margie Warren two warm crusty loaves after she'd said how much she enjoyed it, he was quick to see another way to make some money.

'Ma, don't give it away,' he'd said. 'Folk will snap it up! And the vegetables, too. Everyone went home with bunches of those little beetroots and you wouldn't let them pay you. That's crazy.'

'But we still have so many left!' Cora protested. 'And people love getting something fresh from the garden.'

'That's just the point. We're running a business here, Ma,' he said seriously. 'And they're happy to pay for fresh organic vegetables.'

'I suppose you're right, son. Helen always said we should open a little farm stall and sell our produce on the main road to passing traffic. But that would never work.'

Cora could almost hear Flippie's mind clicking into gear.

'That's a brilliant idea! Good for Helen. We could build a little shelter right next to the gate and pick fresh food every morning.'

'But who'd stand there and sell it

all?' Gwen argued. 'None of us have the time.'

'What about a couple of the men's wives? I bet they'd be glad of a job.'

'But they can't speak English. It's just not practical . . . What about handling the money?'

'Ma, those women probably know more about handling money than you do! We could ask Tuleka.'

Cora wasn't convinced, but Tuleka was delighted with the idea.

'Kanyiso's mother, Tombi, she very clever. She like that job,' she said immediately. 'She the wife of Silas Tractor. And Tandiswa, she's very clever also. She the wife of Amos Milkman.'

Cora remembered how Helen had laughed at the way Tuleka had identified the farm workers, but she knew the African surnames were usually too difficult for stiff English tongues.

It all seemed so easy, suddenly. Cora wondered why she'd objected when Helen had suggested it. Two days later, Flippie and Silas had erected a sturdy little shelter next to the fence on the main tarred road. Anna-Marie had painted a colourful, eye-catching sign, using no words, just pictures of vegetables and fruit.

For some reason, Adam and Flippie weren't talking to each other and her older son had taken no interest in the farm stall. So she was surprised one evening, when she was in the kitchen bottling pickled onions, that Adam broached the subject.

'It might be sensible to put a sign some way back along the road saying *Farm stall ahead*, so people can get ready to slow down.'

'You're right,' Cora said thoughtfully. 'Everyone drives along the highway at such a speed they'd be past the stall before they know it. Why don't you suggest the sign to Flippie?'

'You tell him,' he said shortly. ''Night, Ma.'

'Good idea,' Flippie said, when Cora relayed Adam's suggestion. 'And I must go into town and buy some plastic bags.

And start collecting old cardboard boxes for customers who buy a lot.'

Flippie's clever at thinking ahead for this new project, Cora thought fondly, as she switched off the kitchen light and made her way to her bedroom. He's becoming a real businessman! Having something to think about besides the farm really seems to suit him.

But she worried about Adam.

Since Helen's unexpected departure he'd been moody and silent, coming in for meals and disappearing afterwards without speaking. Probably brooding about Marita, she thought. She's hardly been round at all the past fortnight.

Cora frowned in annoyance when she considered how flighty the girl had become. Maybe I should say something to Adam, she thought. Tell him it's time he settled things with Marita before she takes it into her head to go off and live in Cape Town!

Then she remembered Adam's cold, withdrawn expression at the supper table and realised he probably wouldn't discuss anything with her — certainly not his future plans with Marita.

Another Life . . .

Helen looked out at the icy autumn rain and shivered, although the house was warm enough. Had Bissington always been this cold and grey?

With Gwen at her herb centre, Helen knew she should be doing a bit of housework, or the shopping she'd offered to do . . . or start looking for another teaching job for the following term.

But she was filled with an overwhelming feeling of emptiness and couldn't bring herself to get up from the window seat, go downstairs and press on with all the things that needed her attention.

What would I be doing back on the farm right now, she wondered, looking at her watch. Eleven o'clock. We're an hour behind over here, so it's midday there. Anna-Maria would be reading the children a story before they start packing away their books and getting ready to go home. I wonder how she's getting on? It was good of her to take over like that, but I know she's not all that keen on teaching. I can't see her being very patient with the little ones.

She pictured her schoolroom with the shelves of books, the art table with the paints and brushes, the posters of wild animals on the walls, and the children all sitting working, their alert little faces grinning at her as she tried to explain something by using a mixture of English and Xhosa.

She could almost hear the rumble and jostling as the cows came past the schoolroom on their way from the milking shed. The sound of the four by four skidding to a halt under the pepper trees and Adam putting his head around the door to ask if she'd like a lift up to the house for lunch . . .

Stop that, she thought. That was another life. You're home now.

Helen went downstairs, picking up the post from the mat, and saw with a pang that, again, there was nothing for her from South Africa. It takes ages for letters to get here, she reasoned. And they're all busy, anyway.

She washed the breakfast things, then phoned her grandfather and invited herself round that afternoon.

Albert's voice wasn't as strong as it had been, and Helen noticed he took longer to get things done, but apart from that he seemed well and the doctor was pleased with his progress. He'd been home from hospital for ten days and had refused point-blank to come and stay with Gwen for a few weeks, saying he needed to be near his telephone.

'That wretched conference on sustainable energy could get along quite well without him,' Gwen observed. 'But he seems to think he's indispensable!'

'Mum, apart from the fact he has a strong constitution, the reason Grandad has recovered so quickly is because he likes to be busy and involved in something,' Helen pointed out. 'He's going to be up on the platform at that conference, one of the invited speakers.'

'*If* the doctor says he can,' Gwen said firmly.

Gwen was determined not to leave Albert on his own for long, so when Angela left for the day, Helen had taken to popping in to see him every afternoon. Then Gwen would go round for a while in the evening.

Regrets?

Helen arrived at his cottage just as Angela was shutting the front door behind her.

'Hi, Helen, I'm so glad to run into you,' she said hastily. 'Try to persuade Grandad to have a little nap this afternoon. And don't let him talk on the phone too much. It tires him out, although he won't admit it. Switch it to answer-phone and let them leave a message. I'll call them back in the morning.'

'You've turned into the perfect secretary!' Helen teased.

'Seems like it.' Angela smiled. 'I never dreamed he was so involved with so many groups. Oh, there's the bus. I must dash.'

Angela and Mark's baby was expected the following week but she hadn't slowed down much. Takes after Grandad, Helen thought, watching as she clambered safely aboard, then letting herself into the house.

'Grandad? Are you here?'

Albert was sitting in his comfy chair by the fire, his eyes closed. Helen smiled and tiptoed out.

She put a pint of milk in the fridge and got busy preparing some mince for a pasta dish he could put in the microwave that evening.

Then she wandered through to the dining-room, where Albert's photos had been sorted into boxes. She picked up the one marked *1939–40* and shuffled through black and white pictures of young men in uniform, some of them just boys. Halfway through she came across photos taken at Kasteelpoort and she looked at the pictures of the farm and a young Albert and Amelia with a stab of recognition.

'Ah! Didn't know you were here, love.' Albert walked slowly over to greet her.

'I'll make us some tea, Grandad. I bought some shortbread at the bakery.'

The phone rang twice while she was in the kitchen and she heard her grandfather answering cheerfully and at length.

'Enough!' she said, carrying the tray through. 'I'm switching to answerphone and giving you some peace.'

They sat on opposite sides of the fire and Helen poured the tea silently, her thoughts far away as she stared into the flames.

'How do you feel about being back home?' Albert asked suddenly. 'Missing the life over there?'

'Oh!' Helen started. Was it so obvious? 'Not really. Well, a bit. I suppose I'm missing the people, really. Cora and Anna-Marie . . . my pupils . . . and everyone.'

'Hmm.' Albert looked at her shrewdly. 'And the boys, too, I believe. Adam and what's his name — Flippie?'

'Them, too,' she admitted.

'So which one is it?' He was teasing.

'Adam. But there's nothing between us really, Grandad.'

Except that kiss. And when we danced.

'We just got on really well.'

She still quailed when she remembered Adam's face in the candlelight when he saw her in Flippie's arms the night before she left.

'I know you were brought back home well before you intended, love. I still wish Gwen hadn't made such a fuss.'

'Oh, Grandad, I'd have been furious if she hadn't!' Helen smiled. 'I intended to be home by Christmas, anyway. I just made my stay a couple of months shorter, that's all.'

'I know what it's like, coming home

after a long time away,' Albert said slowly. 'Everything seems a bit smaller and greyer, doesn't it?'

'Yes,' she said in surprise.

'To tell the truth, I found settling down after the war very difficult. I always wanted to go back to South Africa, you know. Loved the place. Loved the farm.'

'And did you love Amelia?'

'Yes, I did.' He smiled. 'Or I thought I did. But there was a war on, and we were both very young. Besides, her father would have taken his whip to me if he'd thought I had any intentions towards his daughter!'

'Then you came home and met Granny?'

'Yes, at a dance one night soon after I was demobbed. Fred Evans was her brother and he'd been with me on the *Howe*, and he introduced us.'

'So, no regrets about Amelia?'

'No regrets. Your gran and I were very happy all those years. We had a good life. But you . . . ' He paused.

'You're free to go where you want, do what you like. There's no stopping you young folk today.'

'I suppose so.'

Helen tried to picture the reaction of the Smit family if she wrote and said she'd be coming back. Cora and Anna-Marie, she knew, would welcome her with open arms. Flippie, too, of course. And the children.

But Adam? He's probably back with Marita, she thought bleakly. Everyone expects it, and even though Marita's been flirting with Marcus, she's probably still planning to marry Adam. And there's family pressure on both sides.

'So, would you like to return to the farm?' Albert persisted. 'Or are you going to find a teaching post here?'

She was silent, then raised her eyes to meet Albert's.

'I'd go back like a shot,' she said truthfully. 'But I don't think it's the right thing to do. Besides, I can't afford the air fare. I need to find a job.'

Letters From Africa . . .

Three days later Helen was woken by the click of the letter-box and a loud thump on the hall carpet.

'Helen, post for you,' Gwen called.

Helen ran downstairs, smiling. There was a pile of letters and postcards and one extra fat envelope, all with air stickers and stamps featuring brightly coloured South African birds. The day suddenly looked a lot brighter.

'Coffee?' her mother asked. 'You sit there and read them and I'll make some toast.'

Helen nodded absently and tore open the bright green envelope. A cartoon of a teacher in front of a blackboard adorned the bottom corner and she guessed it was from Anna-Marie.

Dear Helen, she read.
How are you? I'm fine. The teaching is going all right but the children keep asking when you're coming back!

How is your grandfather? I hope he is better.

My big news is that nice Mr Warren came back to do the trail again, and offered me a job in his clothing factory in Cape Town. He says he'll arrange for me to do a design course at the technical college there. Ma of course says no way but I'm working on her. Ouma is on my side, too. I wish you were here — you could talk some sense to her. Ma always listens to you!

And guess what, the TV people are coming to the farm next week to take pictures of Ouma's old bones down by the river. And that professor of hers says maybe I'll be in it! I'll be famous! Do you think you'll see the programme in England?

We all miss you. Do you ever think of us?

Love,
Anna-Marie.

Oh, if you only knew, Helen thought, smiling at Anna-Marie's enthusiastic exclamation marks as she opened the next letter, addressed to her in a big scrawling hand . . . Flippie.

Dearest Helen,

I hope your grandfather has recovered and that he was pleased to see you again.

I'm sorry you had to go away so quickly because I want to apologise for that night in the kitchen. I didn't mean to make you mad. My only excuse is one of too many beers, but Helen, you know I still love you, even though you don't love me right now. I'm certain that one day you will. We Smits never give up! Maybe I'll come over to see you and make you change your mind.

Love, Flippie.

Good News?

This letter exasperated Helen rather, but she couldn't help smiling.

She didn't recognise the handwriting

on the fourth envelope. Could this one be from Adam? She held her breath and quickly scanned down to the signature at the bottom of the page.

Much love,
Cora Smit.

Oh, well. She went back to the beginning of Cora's letter.

Dear Helen,

The house seems very empty without you, my dear, and I wish you hadn't had to leave us so quickly. I do hope your grandfather is getting better every day.

I know Flippie is writing to you; and we all want to catch the post before Adam goes into town this afternoon. Did he tell you how successful our little farm stall has become?

Anna-Marie has been enjoying the teaching, although the children don't listen to her as well as they did to you.

She's full of some crazy notion to

go and work for Richard Warren in Cape Town. But she is far too young for that. And I wish Ouma wouldn't encourage her. All this nonsense about living your dreams might be fine when you're eighty, but not eighteen, as I keep telling them both.

Things haven't been going very smoothly since you went, Helen. I think we all miss your calming presence! For some reason, maybe because we haven't seen a glimpse of Marita for ages, Adam growls at everyone like a bear with a sore head most days and Anna-Marie nags me to change my mind about Mr Warren's offer at every opportunity.

Flippie, I am sure, is missing you dreadfully as he has a very soft spot for you, but these days he is more in town than on the farm. He's talking of getting orders for the vegetables from restaurants in Cape Town and Port Elizabeth.

Do write and give us your news when you have a spare moment. I'm *sure you are very busy and enjoying being back with your family.*

There was another envelope full of coloured pictures, notes and photographs, from her pupils.

'Good news, dear?' Gwen poured the coffee and took up the morning paper. 'All from the Kasteelpoort family, are they?'

Helen nodded, recognising Amelia's upright handwriting on the next envelope.

My dear Helen,

Your sudden departure has cast quite a gloom on us all. Hardly a day goes by that someone doesn't wonder what you would think, or do, or say about whatever they are concerned with.

I've been thinking a lot about your grandfather and am hoping he has made a good recovery. I'm sure his positive attitude to life will help him in this regard. Of course, I have written to him under separate cover but I would like you to write back and tell me how he really is.

I expect he was delighted to see you again and your return must have given him a welcome boost. I wonder what your plans are now you are back with your family. Did your grandfather mention that some time ago he'd accepted my invitation to come out here for a visit? He hoped to stay three weeks and then return with you before Christmas.

You know what they say about the best-laid plans! But I'm hoping his visit will just be postponed until a later date, and not entirely cancelled.

If he is worried about travelling such a long distance, perhaps you could accompany him. Would another stay with us at Kasteelpoort be a possibility for you? It would make us all very happy to see you again, especially that handsome grandson of mine who hasn't been the same since you left . . .

Warm regards,
Amelia.

So her handsome grandson hasn't been the same since I left, Helen thought ruefully. Does *everyone* think Flippie and I were involved? Even Amelia? Then she read the letter again. Grandad had agreed to go out to the farm. And if I know my grandad, Helen thought, he's not going to let a little thing like a heart attack put him off!

★ ★ ★

Helen sat opposite her grandfather at his dining-table, surveying the neat piles of paper that separated them, and gave a small sigh of satisfaction.

'I really believe this is the whole lot done, Grandad,' she said.

'Angela did a really good job with everything.' Albert smiled. 'Needs to put her feet up now, I daresay.'

'She's so full of energy I doubt she's got her feet up at all.' Helen smiled. 'I know she wanted to stencil teddy bears on that old nursery chair she and Mark bought at the auction last weekend. The closer her due date becomes, the more she does.'

Then she remembered with a start that today was the date Angela's baby was due, although Gwen had warned her that most first babies arrived a bit late.

'You know what this means, don't you, Grandad?' Helen smiled as she pointed to the neat stacks of paper. 'No more excuses. The sorting stops and the writing begins!'

'Hmm, well, I'll take it slowly. I've got a few ideas worked out that I'd like to discuss with you some time . . . how about a cup of tea?'

'Good idea.'

Albert's Offer

Helen was on her way to the kitchen when the morning post plopped on to the mat. She spotted a colourful South African stamp immediately and recognised Amelia's distinctive handwriting.

Her heart leapt and she hurried back with it.

'Grandad, letter for you.'

'Ah . . . thank you. From Amelia, I think. Now, where are my glasses . . . ?'

Helen was in a fever of impatience to know what Amelia had written, but realised she couldn't hang over her grandfather's shoulder while he read it. She went to make the tea instead.

When she returned to the room, Albert was smiling at something he was reading.

'Sounds as though Amelia's been busy. She's an artist now and actually selling her work! Then she talks about the family. Anna-Marie's getting very involved with the farm stall, apparently, and Cora's thinking of breeding guinea fowl to sell to come fancy restaurants . . . '

'Does she say anything about the boys? Flippie? Or . . . Adam?'

Helen did her best to sound casual.

Albert grinned at her over his spectacles.

'Adam, eh?' Then he patted her arm. 'I'm sure he's still there, my dear.'

'Yes, but . . . ' Her voice caught. 'There's this girl, Grandad. She was his childhood sweetheart and she lives on the farm next door. Everyone expects Marita and Adam to get married because both parents have been planning it since they were children. Amelia doesn't mention anything about an engagement?'

He scanned the letter then shook his head.

'Ah, here we are . . .

'*I'm sure you want to celebrate Christmas with your family, but any time after the New Year would be lovely. I'm sure you would enjoy your visit. Please give it serious consideration, my dear Albert.*'

'Well, that's very nice,' he said, taking off his spectacles. 'How do you feel about that, Helen?'

'Me?'

'Going back to South Africa? To the Smits.'

'Amelia's invited me back?'

'She seems to assume you're coming back! She said so right at the beginning. Here, let me see . . . Oh, yes.

'*We all miss our dear Helen and can't wait for her return.*'

His eyes twinkled.

'Sounds like you don't need an invitation. Maybe we could go together, as soon as I'm strong enough?'

Helen swallowed, remembering her sadly depleted bank balance.

'Grandad, I'd love to go, but I really have to find a teaching post to start in the January term.'

'Well, how about if you carry on helping me here with a bit of secretarial work, then you and I could plan to go together once this conference is behind us? Say, the middle of January. And then you could start job-hunting after we come back.'

Seeing her discomfiture, Albert took her hand.

'I've got a bit put by, Helen,' he said gruffly. 'And it's not doing anyone any good just sitting in the bank. I'd just as soon spend it on two airfares to South Africa. So what do you say?'

Helen was silent, her mind in a whirl. Her first reaction had been to fling her arms around Albert's neck and say, 'Of course! I'd love to!'

But second thoughts told her she couldn't. Her grandfather wasn't a rich man.

'To tell the truth, I wouldn't want to travel such a long distance all on my own, so you'd be doing me a favour if you agreed,' he went on persuasively.

'Grandad, I couldn't let you do that. It's too much. You can go on your own. You'll have a lovely holiday. They'll look after you. Maybe I'll go back next Christmas.'

'But, sweetheart, wouldn't you rather go back sooner? Find out what's happening with this man of yours?'

'He's not my man, Grandad, and even if he were, I just couldn't accept.

But thank you anyway, you're a darling.'

Mother's Intuition . . .

Albert looked put out but let the subject drop for the time being.

'Well, can't sit around all day. I've got those two from the wildlife society coming this afternoon to discuss the paper they'll be reading at the conference.'

'I'll set the tea tray for you all before I leave,' she said, with a sudden longing to tell her mother about her grandfather's offer.

She was certain Gwen would applaud her restraint.

'But promise me you'll have a proper rest now. Doctor Helen's orders.'

'I promise,' Albert agreed. 'Can't seem to keep my eyes open anyway.'

When she arrived home, Helen heard her mother busy in the kitchen.

'Soup and sandwiches OK for

lunch?' Gwen asked, briskly ladling some lentil and carrot soup into big bowls.

Helen drew up a chair and sat down.

'Mum, Grandad's had a letter from Amelia inviting him out for a visit.'

'But that's such a long journey!' Gwen protested. 'Is he ready for that?'

'He's keen. And he's asked me to go with him.'

'But I thought you were hoping to get that teaching post over in Bramley? And it'd cost so much for the fare . . . ' Gwen finished uncomfortably.

'Grandad's offered to pay for my ticket but, of course, I had to say no.'

Helen's voice broke and Gwen looked at her keenly.

'You really miss the farm, don't you, darling?' She paused. 'Was the teaching so much more interesting or was it the whole different life you led?'

'Both, Mum.' Helen bit her lip. 'While teaching those farm children I just felt so — I don't know, fulfilled, I think. And the Smits were so good to

me and I loved life on the farm . . . '
Her voice trailed off sadly.

'And was there *someone* you loved, too?'

'How did you — ?'

'Mother's intuition.' Gwen smiled.

Helen grinned ruefully at her mother.

'Oh, Mum, it's no use. I know Adam feels something for me but he never actually said anything before I left. And he's probably going to marry Marita . . . '

'He's the one who runs the farm, isn't he? The older brother?'

Helen nodded.

'Cora depends on him so much. He's devoted to the farm and the land, and the animals. And he's such a kind man, all the farm workers love him . . . and . . . '

'And you do, too.' Gwen squeezed her hand. 'Well, it sounds to me as though you should do something about it. You should go back and see where things stand between the two of you. He hasn't announced anything formally with this Marita, has he?'

'No, but I'm sure he will.'

'If you don't go back, you'll always wonder if you should have. What might have been.'

'I know you're right, but how can I let Grandad pay? It's too much.'

'Darling, he's got savings and if he says he can afford it, then he can. And if he's determined to go anyway, then I think it's a very good idea that you go with him to keep an eye on him.'

'Do you really think so?'

'I do,' Gwen said firmly.

But before Helen could say anything the phone rang. Gwen answered, and it was Mark.

'I'm taking Angela to the hospital. The baby's on its way!'

Nine hours and three phone calls later, with the supper dishes washed and put away, there was still no news.

Gwen had stayed at home to be close to the phone but couldn't settle to anything and paced from room to room.

'I hope she isn't in labour for too

long. But first babies often take a long time. I remember with you, I was in labour for nearly a whole day. I was exhausted.

'But Mark will be with her, of course, he'll take care of her . . . '

'She'll be fine, Mum,' Helen pointed out. 'The doctor told her a fortnight ago that he didn't expect any problems.'

Helen felt a thrill of excitement to think of the baby coming but kept her voice calm to soothe her mother. Gwen watched for five minutes then jumped up.

'I can't wait! I'm going to phone the hospital again!'

'Mum, I'm sure Mark will phone us the minute the baby's born,' Helen said.

Gwen phoned anyway, but Helen was right. There was no news, and Mark was in the labour ward with Angela and couldn't be reached.

'I'll try his mobile!' she said. But Mark had very sensibly switched it off and Gwen was forced to sit on the sofa and watch a film without seeing any of it.

Just after midnight Helen yawned and stretched.

'Well, I'm going to bed, Mum. Are you coming?'

'How can you think of sleep when your sister's having a baby?'

'It could be tomorrow before anything happens, and if you stay up all night you'll be too tired to visit her.'

'I suppose you're right.'

Gwen got up unwillingly and started to lock up for the night.

Then the phone rang, sounding extra loud in the stillness, and they knew it had to be Mark. Gwen dashed to the hall.

'Yes?' she said. 'Yes? Oh, that's wonderful! And is everything all right? Oh, that's lovely! Aren't you a clever pair! Give Angela my love and tell her we'll be over to see them both in the morning.'

She put the phone down, her eyes shining.

'It's a boy! Seven pounds three ounces. And everything's fine! What a relief.'

'Fantastic! Just what Angela hoped

for. What are they going to call him? Have they decided?'

Helen found herself smiling like an idiot through tears which sprang from nowhere.

'Not the last time we talked. I know Angela liked Jessica for a girl. I forgot to ask!' Gwen blew her nose briskly. 'Isn't that marvellous news, though?'

'A nephew to spoil.' Helen giggled.

'A grandson!' Gwen smiled as they hugged again. 'I'll tell Albert first thing tomorrow.'

'Mum, I've decided to accept Grandad's offer,' Helen said through happy tears. 'It's what he wants — and what I want, too. What a kind old darling he is!'

Lights! Cameras! Action!

Anna-Marie went out on to the *stoep* where Amelia was seated in front of her easel, looking critically at her sketch of a leopard.

'Good morning, my child, you're

looking very fetching.'

'Thanks! I made a special effort today . . . D'you think they'll put me in the film, Ouma?'

Anna-Marie strained to see the cloud of dust that would herald the arrival of the camera crew from Cape Town. She was determined to be included in the shoot, somehow, even if it meant being extra nice to old Professor Philips who had arrived at Kasteelpoort the night before.

'Anna-Marie, stop day-dreaming and come and give me a hand.' Cora bustled out on to the *stoep*. 'I want a big jug of iced lemonade ready.'

'Did I hear the words iced lemonade?' Professor Philips came up the steps on to the *stoep*. 'That sounds like a good idea.'

'Let me get you some, Professor.' Amelia stood up. 'I know how hot it is down in that dry riverbed.'

But Anna-Marie beat her to it.

'Thank you, m'dear.' He folded himself slowly into the cane chair. 'Well,

Amelia, are you ready to face the cameras?'

Anna-Marie stood rooted to the spot on her way to the kitchen.

'Oh, go on with you, Professor. I have no intention of being part of this,' her grandmother bridled. 'You're the expert!'

'But *you* discovered these fossils,' he countered. 'If it hadn't been for you they would have lain here for another hundred years. No, the producer has already said he'd like a few words with you on camera.'

Protected Species

Anna-Marie cheered up enormously when the film crew arrived in a big van, disgorging an interesting array of young men and women loaded with strange equipment. Cameras, tripods, reels of electrical cord and folding white screens were all brought out and laid on the lawn in the front of the house.

One of them started talking to the

professor and giving directions to the rest of the team but broke off when he noticed Anna-Marie and smiled at her.

'Hi, there,' he said easily. 'Are you the daughter of the house? I'm Mike Andrews.'

'That's me, Anna-Marie,' she answered. 'Can I offer you all some coffee before you start? Or cold lemonade?'

'Thanks, cold lemonade would be great.'

Just then Flippie's pick-up turned into the garden and bumped to a halt. He jumped out and shook hands with the crew, and suddenly there was a crowd on the *stoep* and a babble of conversation as they helped themselves to the iced lemonade and home-made ginger cake.

Flippie, Anna-Marie noticed, was immediately deep in conversation with a petite blonde girl called Evelyn, and a few of them were admiring Amelia's sketch.

'Do you find leopards around here?' Mike was interested. 'I've heard they're under threat in these parts from farmers trapping and shooting them.'

'They're supposed to be a protected species and it's illegal to shoot them, but some of the locals just see them as a threat to their livestock,' Amelia explained. 'You should ask my grandson, Adam.'

Mike nodded.

'He's out on the lands somewhere,' Amelia explained, 'but I expect you'll see him at lunch. You could ask him then.'

Adam had been gloomy and silent for so long that privately Anna-Marie didn't think he'd agree to be on any programme, even to talk about his beloved leopards.

Mike stood up and turned to Anna-Marie.

'Would you like to come and show us the way?'

She glowed with pleasure, waiting while all the equipment was reloaded into the van. She climbed up into the seat next to Mike, directing him back down the rutted farm road and through the gate to the lands next to the riverbed.

At the last minute, Cora was persuaded to come, too, squashed on the front seat of the pick-up next to Evelyn, while Amelia and Professor Philips drove down in the professor's old black sedan.

A Star . . .

They took the vehicles as far as they could but the crew was forced to carry their gear the rest of the way to the riverbed, and seemed to take for ever fiddling about with it before they were ready. Reflective screens were set up, sound levels checked and Mike walked up and down with the professor.

'Prof, when we start recording, could you keep it simple?' Mike asked tactfully. 'No big scientific terms, please, or we'll lose the viewers' interest.'

'Oh, right. Well, over here, I'll just

indicate what I think might be the thighbone of an *Agriotherium Africanum*, shall I? That was an African bear that died out over two hundred million years ago. And I'm pretty sure we have the tusk of an extinct bush pig, *Nyanzachoerus*. It was three times the size of the bush pigs you'll find here today.'

'Monster bush pigs. That should do nicely.' Mike grinned.

But it was Amelia who stole the show. Wearing her big straw hat and with her grey hair blowing about in the breeze, she talked naturally and clearly and told Mike how she'd always enjoyed walking over the farm and had been fascinated by the odd shapes sticking out of the bank. She'd been convinced these were fossils and got down and slowly dug away the earth with her garden trowel.

'And I managed to dig out a small bone which I gave to my little granddaughter to play with, never dreaming it was a valuable find.' She gave him a dazzling smile.

'Your granddaughter? That would be Anna-Marie?'

Mike turned the microphone towards Anna-Marie, who was momentarily nonplussed. When had Ouma given her a bone to play with? Then she caught Amelia's wink and grinned.

'Oh, yes,' she agreed immediately, giving the cameraman her cutest grin and tossing her long red hair. 'I played with that old bone for ages when I was very small. It's my most precious possession.'

Mike nodded.

'Thanks, everyone. Now, maybe just a few long shots of the farmhouse and the mountains behind it and then that'll be a wrap.'

'You will stay for lunch, won't you?' Anna-Marie couldn't bear to think of them heading back to the city so soon.

'Of course they're staying,' Flippie said. 'I've promised to take Evelyn a little way up the adventure trail before she leaves.'

Evelyn smiled up at him.

Anna-Marie had hoped Flippie would see that Evelyn was just a pretty flirt, but he seemed completely entranced with her.

'I'd really like to meet your older brother,' Mike said. 'I want to discuss those leopard sightings with him.'

Shocked

He probably won't want to talk to you, Anna-Marie thought. Adam hadn't said more than three words for weeks now. Ever since he saw Marita flirting with Marcus the night before Helen had to leave, he'd been in a black mood.

Marita had continued to pop over for coffee most days but Adam seemed cold towards her, making a point of being absent during her visits and leaving her to chat to Cora and Anna-Marie.

'What's wrong with that man?' Marita asked crossly, when she saw his truck disappear towards the lands one morning. 'Have I done anything to upset him?'

'Of course not, dear,' Cora soothed. 'But he's got a lot on his mind. He had to fence off another camp for those angora goats of his and the pumps are always giving him trouble.'

'He's never here to talk to,' Marita complained. She turned to Anna-Marie.

'Oh — did I tell you Marcus is coming up next weekend? He's invited me to go up to the Pilanesberg Game Park with him. He's writing an article for some American wildlife magazine and we'll stay in the most luxurious thatched cottages in the *bushveld* and be given five-star treatment . . . I can't wait!'

'Surely you wouldn't go with him all alone, would you, Marita? Your father wouldn't like that, I'm sure.' Cora was shocked.

Marita just laughed and tossed her hair.

Neither Cora nor Anna-Marie had

mentioned this conversation to Adam and, strangely, he hadn't seemed to notice that Marita had been away for ten days.

But at lunch with the television crew, Anna-Marie was happily surprised to see Adam smiling and talking animatedly to Mike.

'How about next weekend?' Adam was saying. 'I'd really appreciate you taking the trouble.'

He sounded more cheerful than he had for a long time.

'No problem, and if we get any good shots, I'll use those in my programme,' Mike said. 'I'll do my best to make it for next Saturday.'

Flippie had been listening with half an ear.

'If you're coming to the farm again, Mike, maybe you could give Evelyn a lift, too?' he said hopefully.

Adam looked coolly at his younger brother.

'Now Helen's gone, it's Evelyn this, Evelyn that. Fast work, Flip.'

His brother flushed angrily.

'That's better than dangling Marita on a string like you do! How do you think she felt while you made sheep's eyes at Helen? You'll be lucky if she'll have you back.'

'Marita is absolutely none of your business.'

An icy shutter seemed to come down over Adam's face as he turned away from Flippie and strode down the steps to his truck.

Angela's Happiness . . .

At the hospital next morning, Helen waited patiently for Gwen to finish admiring her grandson before she reluctantly handed him over to her.

When she cuddled her nephew for the first time, she was entranced by his delicate perfection. She slipped her finger under five of his and he clutched it gently in his sleep.

'He's beautiful,' she breathed. 'Look

at his tiny fingernails! Oh, Angela, aren't you lucky?'

Angela flushed with pride.

'We are. Isn't he wonderful?'

Together they admired him, with Helen perched on the side of her sister's bed. Angela couldn't resist leaning over possessively and stroking his head.

'Have you decided on a name yet?'

'William. And second name Albert, for Grandad.'

'He'll be thrilled with that,' Gwen said. 'He's coming to see you this evening, and sends his love.'

'I can't wait to take William home tomorrow.' Angela said. 'And dress him up in all his lovely clothes!'

'And I can't wait to baby-sit for you! I claim Auntie's privileges!'

'That won't be for ages. He needs to bond with us first. The baby book says he should focus on his parents for the first few months so I don't suppose we'll go out much.'

'Well, Helen and I will pop in often

to help with the housework while you're focusing on him,' Gwen said comfortably. 'You'll be surprised how much time it takes just to feed and bathe him. I expect you'll be glad of a hand once you get home.'

'I'll be fine,' Angela said confidently, taking her baby back and gazing lovingly into his dark blue eyes. 'How much time can one small baby take?'

Two days later, the phone rang at four in the afternoon.

'Mum, he won't stop crying! I've fed him and changed him and he won't stop crying!'

'Have you burped him properly?' Gwen asked, amused.

'Well, I've held him up and patted him for ages but he won't burp!'

Gwen could hear Angela was near tears.

'Shall I come over?' she asked hesitantly.

'Could you? *Please*, Mum! I think Mark might be late this evening.'

Gwen looked at her watch. It was a thirty-minute drive over to Leighton in heavy traffic and the baby would probably have fallen asleep long before she got there. But it sounded as though her younger daughter needed moral support.

'I'll be there as soon as I can.'

She scribbled a note for Helen, then drove over to Angela's and knocked on the door.

Angela opened it, smiling sheepishly.

'Sorry, Mum. He's fast asleep. Just after I rang you he settled! I tried to call you but you'd already left.'

'Well, never mind, love. I'm here now. I'll just pop up and take a peek.'

Gwen was almost breathless from the surge of joy she felt as she gazed down at the sleeping baby. Who'd have thought a grandchild could be such a miracle?

Then she heard the sounds of Mark's arrival and he bounded up the stairs, followed by Angela.

'William's fan club!' Mark tucked his arm around Angela as they stood by the crib.

'So how did young Mr Milne behave today?'

'Just beautifully,' Angela said happily. Gwen smiled to herself.

'I'll just pop down and make some coffee,' she said, leaving them alone.

Mark hugged Angela and kissed her gently.

'Mum's come over for a visit,' Angela said. 'I was worried about William crying, but I was just being silly.'

'Nice for you to have company, anyway,' Mark said.

'Yes. Do you know, Maeve hasn't come across to see William? She knows I'm home but she hasn't even phoned.'

'She's probably arranging dinner parties and professional photographers!' Mark grinned. 'Her little girl must be three weeks old by now.'

'She has a nanny,' Angela said. 'I saw her going off with her gym bag this morning. Probably Maeve will be back in shape in a couple of weeks, like those celebs. And here's me looking like a sack of potatoes with sour milk on my shoulder.'

'And here's you looking as gorgeous

as ever, with the most beautiful baby in the world in your arms,' Mark corrected.

'Well, not really. But thanks for saying so.' Angela snuggled in his arms. 'I wouldn't swap places with Maeve for anything. Really, I feel quite sorry for her — I just can't imagine letting a nanny have all the fun of looking after our baby!'

They stayed gazing proudly at their offspring until the rich aroma of coffee took them downstairs again. They found Gwen, like good grandmothers all over the world, busying herself with the pile of ironing she'd spotted in the bedroom.

★　★　★

Cora and Anna-Marie were hard at work around the big kitchen table, sorting bunches of freshly picked carrots for the farm stall, when the phone rang and Anna-Marie went to answer it. Cora heard her voice rising and falling excitedly but when she returned, she said nothing.

'Who was that?' Cora queried.

'Margie Warren.'

'And what did she want? Trying to persuade you to go and work for her husband again in that clothing factory of his?'

'Leave it, Ma. Let's not discuss it right now.'

'She's a nice woman but she shouldn't interfere in our family plans. I'm your mother and . . . '

'Ma! Leave it, please. She just wanted to chat.'

'Hmm.' Cora wasn't convinced. 'So how's the teaching going?'

'I quite enjoy it, actually, although the children can be a bit of a handful.'

'It's good experience for you,' her mother said. 'Maybe you should think about training as a teacher?'

'Instead of being a typist, you mean?' She shook her head. 'I haven't got Helen's magic touch with children.'

'You could always learn,' Cora said

hopefully. 'If you went to training college . . . '

'I don't think so,' Anna-Marie interjected hotly. 'I'm not going to learn typing and I'm not going to be a teacher. I'm going to work in Cape Town as a designer, and if you won't let me go after Christmas, then I'll go when I'm twenty-one.'

'You're full of nonsense,' Cora said. 'And I partly blame your grandmother. She shouldn't encourage you.'

An Angry Visitor . . .

Anna-Marie rolled her eyes as Cora changed the subject.

'Now, how many bottles of gooseberry jam have we got left? Thombi said they sold ten yesterday. I'll have to make more. Could you go and pick some for me?'

Anna-Marie loved picking the golden Cape gooseberries in their little dry paper lanterns with the sweet round globes inside, and was glad of the excuse to stop talking about teaching.

'And don't eat more than you pick,' Cora called after her. 'There aren't that many left on the bushes.'

Cora was humming to herself as she put the carrots in a box for Flippie to take down to the farm stall and didn't hear a car arriving.

'Cora, my dear, it's Jacob de Wild.' Amelia put her head around the kitchen door. 'He wanted to see Adam but I told him he'd gone into town. So he says he'll see you, and he looks like a thundercloud. I've put him in the sitting-room. I thought you might need some privacy if he's come to talk business again.'

Oh, dear, I wish Adam were here, Cora thought, wiping her hands and taking off her apron before going through to greet Jacob. He was standing in the centre of the room, glowering like an angry old bull.

'Good morning, Jacob,' she said pleasantly.

'Morning, Cora,' he said abruptly, turning his battered old hat in his hands. 'We need to talk, you and me.'

'Jacob, if it's about selling my land, I'm not . . . '

'Not about selling, no.' He growled. 'It's about this baby Marita's having. Her and Adam.'

9

A Lot To Discuss . . .

'Adam's baby? Marita is having Adam's baby?' Cora sat down heavily. 'I don't believe it.'

'You'd better,' Jacob said grimly. 'It's due in seven months.'

He smiled thinly and shook his head.

'Can't believe they've been so stupid . . . '

'But Adam and Marita haven't been getting on very well lately.' Cora's mouth was suddenly dry and she could only speak in a whisper. 'In fact, he's hardly seen her. He seems to have been avoiding her . . . '

'Maybe he doesn't want to face up to his responsibilities,' Jacob said hotly. 'I'll have a word with that young man and make him see sense.'

'Adam would never shirk his duty,'

Cora said stiffly. 'Has she told him there's a baby on the way?'

She couldn't imagine her son knowing that he was to be a father and not discussing it with her.

'Apparently not. I don't think she'd have told me, either, but I asked her straight out. She didn't want to discuss it, just admitted she was expecting and took off in her car without another word.'

'And — and did she say it was definitely Adam's baby?' Cora asked hesitantly.

Jacob reddened angrily.

'Of course it's Adam's! Whose else would it be?'

'I'm sorry, Jacob. I didn't mean . . . I just thought Marita's been seeing that travel writer, Marcus. Didn't they go away together to a game park some time ago?'

'Not as far as I know. Marita went off to spend some time in Cape Town, shopping. And she went alone.'

So she didn't tell her father, Cora thought.

'She has her own flat there,' Jacob

continued. 'She begged me to buy it for her and it keeps her happy. I know, deep down, Marita's a farm girl at heart but she enjoys a bit of city life, and I can't deny her a little fun.' He pursed his lips.

'And if Adam has any sense, he won't keep her on a short lead once they're married. She likes to visit her friends and see the shops.'

Once they're married.

Cora had always assumed that this would happen, that when Adam and Marita felt ready to settle down they would marry. And when Marita inherited her father's farm one day, they'd consolidate the two properties and Adam would be running one of the biggest farms in the area.

The two sets of parents had laughingly predicted this while their children were still toddlers. It had all seemed so right, as if fate had given them a boy and a girl just meant for each other.

No matter that later on Jacob had been so devious about buying their land

. . . Their children had remained good friends, and she had always loved Marita.

But was Adam ready to commit to her? He certainly hadn't been acting that way! And neither had Marita. But surely they'd both see that a baby on the way changed things entirely.

Oh, what a mess, she thought wretchedly, but she couldn't help feeling a glow of happiness at the thought of a grandchild.

'The two of them must sit down and talk about this properly, Jacob,' Cora said firmly. 'It's quite wrong that you and I know about it but not Adam. When he comes back this afternoon I'll suggest he goes across to see Marita tonight. They'll have a lot to discuss.'

Jacob nodded.

'And tell him the first thing they're going to have to discuss is the date of the wedding.'

'I'll tell him no such thing. Marita should be the one to tell him he's going to be a father.' If that's true, Cora added silently. 'Now, can I offer you a cup of coffee?'

'All right,' he mumbled.

'Why don't you go through to the *stoep* and chat to Amelia? She's busy painting there. I'll bring the coffee.'

Jacob didn't mention Marita as they sipped their coffee with Amelia, preferring to chat easily about the drought and the price of wool.

'I like that picture of yours, Amelia,' he said as he got up to leave. 'A very good likeness of a leopard, if I may say so.'

'You may indeed, Jacob.' She smiled.

'Two of my men reported they'd seen one of those wretched animals up on the mountain and I'm going to have them set a trap. As far as I'm concerned, the only good leopard is a dead one.'

'If that's a joke, Jacob de Wild, it's in very poor taste,' Amelia said coldly. 'These are protected animals and any trap is illegal. If I were you I'd change my mind.'

'Or what?' he challenged.

'Or I'll report you to the conservation people.'

'You wouldn't! Anyway, I can claim my livestock is being threatened. They wouldn't have a case.'

'And exactly how many lambs have you lost?' she enquired coolly.

'None yet, although with this drought, it's only a matter of time. But I can see you've both turned into those — whatya call 'ems — Greenies. Tree huggers. So I'll say no more. Good day, Cora. Good day, Amelia.'

They watched as Jacob stomped off down the steps.

'Just make sure that when Adam comes over tonight, he's got a wedding date in mind,' he flung over his shoulder as he was getting into his pick-up.

In Love

'A wedding? What on earth is he talking about, Cora?'

351

Amelia looked at her sharply.

'Are Adam and Marita really thinking of getting married?'

'No. Yes . . . oh, Ouma, I don't know,' Cora muttered. 'You won't believe what he's just told me.'

Amelia didn't. She listened to Cora and then laughed uproariously.

'Don't be silly, Cora. If Marita is having a baby it's certainly not Adam's child! They've hardly said two words to each other for months, haven't you noticed? It's far more likely to be that good-looking writer man who comes up here so often — Marcus Retief. Anyone can see he and Marita are in love with each other.'

'Can they really?' Cora asked humbly. 'I must have been blind. I noticed her flirting a bit, of course, but that's just Marita.'

'And I'm quite sure Adam has his eye on Helen. Didn't you see the way those two looked at each other?'

'Helen? And Adam? My goodness.'

Cora was beginning to think she

didn't know much about anything. To think Amelia's sharp eyes had picked up signs that she, his own mother, had been oblivious to!

'But I've often spoken of Adam and Marita getting married one day and Adam's never said otherwise.'

'He didn't want to upset you, I suppose,' Amelia said.

'I expect Marita will clear the air tonight and tell her father it's Marcus' baby,' Cora said. 'Jacob will be disappointed. I know he's always expected to welcome Adam as a son-in-law. The trouble is, he's convinced it's Adam and wants them to be married as soon as possible.'

'Are Adam and Marita having a baby?' Neither of them had heard Anna-Marie join them. 'And they're getting married? Well, well, I'll be an aunt. And you'll be a granny, Ma. And Ouma — you'll be a great-granny!'

'Anna-Marie, calm down. Nothing has been decided yet. Please don't shout about it like that.'

Cora didn't want to suggest that the baby might not be Adam's. But if he denied it — well, Cora didn't want to think about the scene that would follow.

'So, when's the wedding?' Anna-Marie persisted. 'Why didn't Adam say anything? Do you think Marita will ask me to be her bridesmaid?' she bubbled on happily.

'That's enough, Anna-Marie,' Cora said sharply. 'We'll not discuss this again until Adam tells us. It's not our business. You're not even to mention it to Flippie.'

Anna-Marie looked at her in amazement.

'But he's got to know, surely? He'd be the best man, wouldn't he? What's the big secret?'

'Your mother's quite right,' Amelia put in. 'It's not our business so there's no point in speculating. It's best not to discuss it until we know more.'

Her grandmother sounded so uncharacteristically severe that Anna-Marie looked chastened. She helped herself to some coffee but didn't sit down.

'Ma, I'm just off to town to the post office. Do we need anything from the shops?'

'We need sugar.' Cora sighed. 'Get a twenty-five kilo sack, please. I'm going to need it for the jam. And you may as well buy some cake flour while you're there. Drive carefully, now. Just because you've got your licence doesn't mean you have to be a racing driver.'

Anna-Marie pulled up with a flourish outside the post office in Hartley's Drift, the car radio blaring forth with a throbbing rhythm. She was about to seal her letter to Helen and pop it in the box, but considered for a second and then scribbled one more line at the end.

She was sure Helen would want to know this latest exciting news from Kasteelspoort.

★ ★ ★

That evening Cora waited until after supper to speak to Adam.

As usual these days, he'd hardly said a word, but Flippie more than made up for his brother's silence, telling them enthusiastically about new outlets he'd found for their produce in Cape Town.

'There's a big craft market every month in one of the parks, Ma,' he told her. 'Everything has to be hand-made. They have pottery and woodcarvings and toys and so on but there's a big section for home-made food like cakes and jam. I reckon we could do pretty well there.'

'But that means someone would have to make a three-hour drive all the way down there to sell it all,' Cora pointed out. 'Who'd want to do that?'

'I would,' Anna-Marie said at once. 'I could drive down and sell it.'

'No, Anna-Marie, not on your own,' her mother said at once. 'It's much too far and you've only been driving a couple of months.'

Amelia cleared her throat.

'I wouldn't mind making the trip with her. Anna-Marie could do the selling, and I'm sure she'll be good at that. I might be able to interest people in my watercolours, too. I imagine they'd qualify as hand-made?'

'Oh, Ouma, would you? Thanks! You're a star!'

'We'll talk about it later,' Cora said hurriedly as she saw Adam rise to leave the table with a muttered, 'Excuse me.'

Scene

'I forgot to mention, Adam, that Jacob would like you to pay him a visit this evening,' she said. 'He wants to talk to you and Marita about something.'

'Why can't he just pick up the phone?'

'I really don't know,' Cora answered, shooting a threatening look at Anna-Marie who had a cheeky grin on her face and seemed about to say something.

'Well, if it can't wait . . . '

He shrugged and walked out. They

listened as his pick-up roared off into the night.

'Did you say Marita?' Flippie said casually. 'I don't think she's at home. I saw her this afternoon, tearing down the highway in the direction of Cape Town. She was heading for a speeding ticket, too, if a traffic cop spotted her.'

Cora bit her lip, imagining the scene that would shortly take place between Jacob and her son. She was confident that Adam would never shirk his duty towards Marita but she also knew he hated to be pushed into anything.

'Well, shall we have coffee on the *stoep?* I'll ask Tuleka to clear the table.'

The four of them played two games of Scrabble before Amelia left to go back to her flat in Hartley's Drift, unwillingly agreeing to leave her scooter at the farm and accept a lift with Flippie.

'Come on, Ouma, it's hardly any drive at all, fifteen minutes tops. I don't like to think of you riding that thing in the dark along the highway.'

'My headlight is perfectly good,' Amelia protested, but gave in quickly enough to make Cora realise her mother-in-law might be ready to agree to some other form of transport one day.

Cora was already in bed, staring into the darkness with her thoughts going round in circles, when she saw the lights of Adam's pick-up returning. The motor sounded as though it was going faster than usual and she was dismayed to hear the sudden squeal of brakes followed by a loud thump as something struck the edge of the *stoep*.

Vanished

A long silence followed and then the door was slammed. Cora heard a muffled groan as Adam's footsteps stumbled unevenly across the stoep and he fell into one of the old chairs.

Adam's been drinking, she thought in amazement.

She couldn't remember ever seeing her elder son the worse for wear and her first instinct was to go to him and get him to his own room. But then she realised he'd be unbearably embarrased for his mother to see him in this state.

The next morning Adam sought Cora out in the kitchen. He looked tired but remarkably cheerful.

'I gather you know about Marita's baby,' he began, helping himself to some gooseberries destined for Cora's jam pot. 'And that Jacob was convinced I'm the father.'

Cora let out a deep sigh.

'But you're not?'

'No, of course I'm not.' He looked at her in amazement. 'I don't know how you could ever have believed that I was.'

'I'm sorry, darling, but Jacob was so sure . . . But what did Marita have to say about it?'

'Marita's gone,' he said shortly. 'She vanished without a word yesterday afternoon, but while I was there she phoned Jacob and told him she'd gone to Cape Town for a few days and not to worry about her.'

'She's gone to see Marcus Retief . . . ?'

'I expect so.' Adam smiled ruefully. 'He's the one she's been seeing lately. But she refused to discuss the baby and Jacob lost his temper. He started shouting down the phone that she had to come straight back here and start making plans for our wedding.'

How can Adam be so casual, Cora thought in amazement.

'But that's ridiculous . . . '

'He should know by now that if you tell Marita to do something she'll do exactly the opposite.' Adam grinned. 'Jacob's got some notion that Marita and I have been promised to each other since we were kids. Just because we've always been good friends. OK, we did go to a couple of dances together in High School. But marry? He's crazy.'

'He's often said Marita needs a steadying influence and I know he's always liked the idea of you two marrying. Well, to be honest, we all did, but if she's not the girl for you then that's that.'

'Ma, I'm not the right man for her, either, and she'd be the first one to agree.'

'But it was so thoughtless of her just to drive away and not talk to her father properly. Look at all the trouble she's caused. Oh, it's too bad of her!'

'I don't suppose she thought that Jacob would react the way he did. I'm sorry you had to be put through all that. He told me he'd come over here looking for me.'

'That doesn't matter. What's important is clearing this whole thing up. Were you and Jacob on speaking terms when you left?'

'Not really. He started by apologising for assuming it was me, and then ranted on about Marcus not being the man he'd want as a son-in-law. As far as he's concerned, Marita should marry a farmer, never mind what she says about it.

'Before I left, we had a couple of

drinks to show no hard feelings, then he insisted we try his homemade peach brandy.'

'Dangerous stuff, that brandy.' She smiled.

'You're right.' He grinned ruefully. 'Anyway, then he made the most outrageous offer.'

Cora raised her eyebrows.

'He says Marita's too irresponsible to inherit the farm. And that no matter who the father of her child is, if I can accept the baby as mine and persuade Marita to marry me, he'll make over Blouberg in my name on our wedding day. As well as those three pieces of land of ours that he bought from the bank.'

'Oh, he's really gone over the score!' Cora exploded indignantly. 'Doesn't he know his own daughter well enough to realise how ridiculous that is? And how could he imagine that he could bribe you so shamefully?'

'Oh, I don't know,' Adam said casually. 'It could be one way of getting back what belongs to us. If you think about it from a practical point of view, it isn't such a bad idea.'

Then he caught Cora's horrified look and grinned.

'Don't worry, Ma, I'm joking! But when I told him he was crazy he flew into one of his rages and practically ordered me out of the house. So no, we didn't end things on a particularly friendly note.'

★   ★   ★

Helen and Angela were sitting in Angela's small sitting-room with William asleep in his carrycot between them.

'So you and Grandad are going out to South Africa after Christmas? Lucky thing. Mum told me you were.'

Angela's gaze slid over to her sleeping baby every few seconds.

'Yes. I was hoping to find a teaching post to start in January but Grandad made me an offer I couldn't refuse.'

'So Romantic . . . '

Helen still felt a bit guilty about accepting her grandfather's generous offer to pay for her trip.

'Oh, he really had to twist your arm, did he?' Angela grinned. 'This wouldn't have anything to do with a certain tall handsome farmer named Adam, would it?'

'No secrets in this family, I see,' Helen said wryly. 'Oh, Angie, it's pointless even talking about him. There's really nothing between us. It's all in my head.'

'Well, how do you know it's not in his head, too? He may be one of those strong, silent types that doesn't like to talk about his feelings.'

Helen pictured Adam driving up the mountain trail, stopping the pick-up to point out the unmistakeable signs that leopards had passed that way, remembering his infectious excitement.

'He's not the silent type when it comes to something he's interested in, but he doesn't just natter on, you know, like some men. He's just really . . . nice.'

'Oh, Helen, don't be so coy! Did he ever show you how he felt?'

'Well, he kissed me once,' Helen admitted. 'Just one kiss sounds a bit pathetic, I suppose. But we had long talks about absolutely everything and when we spoke I felt there was a connection, somehow. I think he feels something for me.'

'He's probably mad about you,' Angela said cheerfully. 'Maybe if you hadn't come back so suddenly he would have got around to declaring his undying love. Given you a cow or something to indicate his intentions. Don't they do that over there?'

Helen burst out laughing. It was such a relief to talk about Adam openly at last.

'I think this is just *so* romantic.' Angela wouldn't be stopped. 'You're flying back six thousand miles to claim the man you love!'

'You make it sound like one of those cheesy movies!'

Then Helen's smile faded. 'The thing is, any day now I expect to get a letter announcing the engagement of Adam and the girl next door.'

Angela dismissed this airily.

'Rubbish. It's you he loves, I know it. Now, if you were to get married, would his family all fly over here for the wedding, or would we all go over there? I fancy a trip to South Africa . . . '

'Angela, stop talking such nonsense!'

Helen threw a cushion at her sister. Luckily William stirred and snuffled in his carrycot and Angela turned her attention to him.

But I wonder what we would do, Helen mused, if it ever came to that . . . which it probably won't.

I'd love to get married on the farm, under the blue gum trees. Anna-Marie could make my wedding dress and all the children could sing at our wedding. Angela could be my Matron of Honour . . .

William's hungry yell brought her back to earth.

'I must be off,' she said. 'I promised to pick up Mum. We're having supper with Grandad tonight.'

'Give her my love,' Angela said, preparing to feed William. 'By the way, will you ask her what she'd like me to contribute to Christmas dinner? Mark says he'll buy the crackers and I thought I could make the pudding. I've got a great recipe and I've already bought those cute little silver charms to pop in.'

Helen bent and kissed her nephew's downy head.

'I'll tell her. 'Bye, William.'

* * *

At supper, Albert was full of plans for their trip.

'I've made enquiries about the flights to Cape Town. If we want to get seats we'd better look lively. There are seats available three days after the conference ends. It's a direct overnight flight, Heathrow to Cape Town. If that sounds all right with you, we'll book them tomorrow, shall we?'

'That will be perfect, Grandad.'

'It'll still be freezing cold, too, Albert, so it will do you the world of good to get some sun.'

Gwen's initial misgivings over the long flight had melted in the face of Albert's assurances. She looked at the pile of papers stacked neatly on a corner of the dining-room table.

'How's the book going?' she asked. 'Have you started actually writing anything yet?' She couldn't take the idea of Albert's memoirs seriously but was happy that it gave him such an interest.

'We're up to Chapter Three,' Helen said with satisfaction. 'I found loads of stuff at the library to add to Grandad's notes. A lot about *HMS Howe*, too, things Grandad had forgotten.'

'Really? That's wonderful.' Gwen was surprised. 'Have you got a title for it?'

'Tell her, Helen.' Albert smiled.

'You know that old poem, Mum, that goes 'I remember, I remember, the house where I was born . . . '? Well I can't think how it goes on but I thought 'I Remember, I Remember' would make a great title. What do you think?'

'Excellent,' Gwen said. 'And I can see half the village queuing up to buy it, hot off the press.'

'Yes, and checking that they're not mentioned in it!' Helen laughed.

'We'll do the washing-up quickly and then we'll be on our way,' Gwen said. 'It's nearly time for the nature programme you like, Albert.'

They had said their goodbyes and were just leaving when Albert thought of something.

'Tell you what, Helen, when you come over tomorrow I'd like to get a letter off to Amelia, giving her our dates,' he said. 'I wonder if you could pick up an aerogramme at the post office on your way?'

'Of course, Grandad,' she said. 'And

I'll phone that travel agent first thing, too. We don't want to lose those seats.'

The Happy Couple . . .

'That girl has no business disappearing like this,' Cora fumed. 'Jacob's health isn't so good at the best of times and the worry of it all has aged him ten years this week. Why doesn't she phone him?'

Marita had stayed away for five days without contacting anyone, and her father visited Cora almost every day on some pretext or other, when all he was hoping for was news of his errant daughter.

'I don't see why he's worrying,' Flippie argued. 'She's obviously gone to find Marcus and tell him the good news.'

'I hope *he* thinks it is,' Cora said darkly. In her opinion Marcus was too slick, too handsome, and too much the polished man of the world for Marita.

'How's he going to be a proper father if he's always halfway round the world taking those photos of his?'

'Relax, Ma. By the way, Adam, I had a call from Mike Andrews, the TV man. He says he's got enough footage from that camera of his on the mountain to make an entire programme on the leopards. He wants to come up this weekend and give us a preview.'

'Great,' Adam said. 'He told me he's actually got pictures of three cubs. All shot at night but you can see them quite clearly. So they're settled in and breeding well.'

'And what about the film he did of me? I mean, of Ouma and her old bones? He said he'd show us and he never did.' Anna-Marie asked crossly.

'Oh, that? Apparently some awful face on the film cracked the camera and the whole thing's a dud,' Flippie joked.

'Don't be so horrible.'

'I'm sure he'll bring that video, too,' Adam comforted.

'Ma, what about that market in Cape

Town? I want to book a stall for us, so let's settle on a date.'

Flippie pulled out his notebook expectantly.

'I think we should wait until after Christmas,' Cora said. 'That would give me and Anna-Marie time to build up stock. It's difficult when the jam gets sold almost as fast as I make it.'

She looked at her daughter.

'If you could give me a hand, we could make sure we had enough to make that trip worth it.'

'OK, if that's what it takes!'

Anna-Marie was prepared to go to any lengths to have a day in Cape Town, even if it meant hours of stirring jam over a hot stove.

'And I'll make a lot of those buttermilk rusks, they keep well. And those sesame seed crunchies are very popular . . . and the shortbread. We can make all those in advance and then the evening before we can make a lot of milk tarts and lemon tarts and so on. They really need to be freshly made.'

'I'll phone to remind Ouma,' Anna-Marie said. 'She should do as many paintings as she can. People love her animal pictures. And I'll make sure I have loads of funky labels ready for the jam.'

'Right. I'm off to check the windmill.' Adam rose from the lunch table. 'Oh — who's this?'

A four by four drew up in a cloud of dust and Marcus climbed out, then went round to the passenger door to help Marita down. She linked her arm in his and they both grinned up at the Smit family on the *stoep*.

'Ta-da!!' Marita sang. 'Say hello to Mr and Mrs Retief!'

She waggled her hand proudly, a big diamond sparkling in the sunlight.

'You're married? Sweetheart, how wonderful!' Cora ran down the steps and hugged Marita, then turned to Marcus.

'Congratulations, young man. I hope you know what a treasure you have here.'

'Oh, I do.' Marcus grinned. He turned to Marita and kissed her. 'I had the devil of a time persuading her to marry me, but she agreed in the end.'

They crowded round the couple, laughing and congratulating them both. Adam shook Marcus's hand and kissed Marita lightly with no sign of anything but genuine pleasure for them both. Cora was pleased to note that he really didn't seem the least jealous or upset.

'Does Jacob know?' she asked suddenly. 'You have told him, haven't you, Marita? He's been beside himself with worry, with you just dashing off to Cape Town like that. He didn't know what to think.'

'I told him I was in my flat. But the next day his line was down and I couldn't get through for ages. I spoke to him briefly this morning, Auntie Cora. The line was still bad but I think he got the general idea of a new son-in-law!'

'His line was down all that time? Oh, dear. I wish you'd phoned us. We could have driven over and told him.'

'No, I wanted to tell him myself. He's going to think it's bad enough that we just got married in a magistrate's court without consulting him.'

So Blind

'I think that's so romantic!' Anna-Marie said dreamily. 'Didn't you tell your father why you were coming down to Cape Town?' Marcus turned to her in surprise. 'Oh, boy, we're going to have some explaining to do!'

'And there was such a funny mix-up!' Anna-Marie continued happily. 'When you told your dad you were going to have a baby, he thought Adam was the father.'

'What?' Marita blushed scarlet. 'How could he possibly have thought that? Oh, my heavens. Did he come over here and make trouble for you? Knowing him, that's just what we would do. Oh, Adam, I'm so sorry!'

'You told your dad you were

pregnant and you didn't tell him it was mine? And that I'd been begging you to marry me long before we knew about the baby?' Marcus looked indignant.

Marita pulled a face.

'I'm sorry, I just didn't handle things very well. I just assumed Pa would know that Marcus and I — well, I can't imagine why he thought Adam . . . '

'Neither can I,' Cora said a bit guiltily. Looking at Marita's face glowing with love for Marcus, she wondered again how she could have been so blind.

'And I always intended to marry Marcus. When I told Pa about the baby I just thought, well, I'll come back as a married woman so he can't be cross with us!'

'I'm sure he'll be delighted with your news, dear,' Cora said doubtfully. 'He'll just need to get used to the idea of Marcus as a son-in-law.'

'Oh, I know he's going to absolutely love him,' she said happily.

'Come on, darling, let's go and show

you off to my pa!'

Marcus grimaced.

'Somehow I don't think I've started out on the right foot,' he said. 'Love might be too strong a word.'

'See you all tomorrow!' Marita shouted as they left. 'We need to plan a party!'

The Smits watched them drive away.

'I wouldn't like to be in Marcus's shoes,' Flippie said. 'Marita's right about Jacob. I'm sure he was expecting to be asked permission to marry her, then have a big church wedding. The whole traditional bit.'

'Well, things don't always work out as planned.' Cora sighed.

'Big News'

'I wonder if we're going to have a white Christmas?' Helen mused, looking at the leaden grey skies. 'Or if it's just going to keep on raining?'

'The forecast was for a bit of snow

this week,' Gwen replied. 'It's certainly cold enough.'

'Not in here!' Helen had turned on all the heaters and the fire crackled cheerfully in the sitting-room, which was strewn with wrapping paper and ribbons. She found that after her months in South Africa she still felt the English cold a lot more than her mother.

'What time are we expecting Angela and Mark tomorrow?'

'They'll be over just before lunch and they're going to give Grandad a lift.'

'And she's bringing the pudding and the brandy sauce. I hope that milk tart I made tastes all right. It doesn't look quite like Cora's although I followed her recipe exactly.'

'I'm sure it will be delicious.' Gwen smiled. 'I wonder if we should have crackers this year? Maybe not, the noise might upset William.'

They settled down to the pleasant task of wrapping gifts and writing notes to go with them. Helen had bought her grandfather a soft white cricketer's hat with the brim lined in dark green to shield him from the sun, the kind that both Adam and Flippie wore on the farm.

Albert would find that wide brim very useful on holiday.

'What are you giving William?' she asked.

'That baby has more than enough clothes and he's too small for toys, so I'm starting his library.' Gwen smiled. 'I've bought him an illustrated copy of 'The Just So' stories. You two used to love them.'

'And I remember how you loved reading them to us! All about how the elephant got his trunk . . . and the grey, green slimy Limpopo River . . . that was my favourite. Oh, there's the post.'

Helen rose and went through to collect a pile of mail that had clattered on to the hall carpet.

'Mostly Christmas cards,' she called, then spotted an envelope with Anna-Marie's handwriting and ripped it open eagerly. She probably doesn't know Grandad and I are coming out, she thought. His letter to Amelia wouldn't have reached there yet.

She stood in the hall, reading the news of the schoolroom and the farm stall with pleasure.

Then she froze as she read the casually scrawled last sentence.

Big news! Adam and Marita are having a baby so they'll be getting married soon.

Helen felt as if her heart would burst from her chest. She dropped the cards and ran upstairs, slammed her door and threw herself on to her bed, letting the hot tears spill unchecked.

'Helen? Is anything wrong?' Gwen called up the stairs.

'No!' Helen's voice was muffled by the pillow. 'Just leave me alone.'

Her mother picked up the dropped envelopes and the open sheet of paper Helen had been reading. Something in the post had definitely upset Helen and she couldn't help herself as she glanced at the contents of the letter. The last sentence was written in bright blue ink and hit Gwen between the eyes. Adam was marrying Marita.

My poor girl, she thought. My poor baby. How could this happen to such a lovely girl twice? But there was nothing she could say to Helen to comfort her until she decided to tell her mother about it.

Guiltily she went back and slowly started to pack away the wrapping paper, knowing that Christmas wasn't going to be the joyful family occasion she'd expected . . .

10

Christmas Day

'It's snowing. So we're having a white Christmas after all.'

Helen's voice was flat and disinterested as she gazed out of the dining-room window. Her mother's garden was already lightly dusted with white and the snow looked set to continue.

'Lovely,' Gwen said positively. 'A white Christmas seems just right, doesn't it? I can't remember when we last had snow on Christmas Day, though. I hope Mark drives carefully in this weather.'

'I'm sure he will.'

Helen hadn't mentioned the letter she'd received the day before, but Gwen felt she had to say something to encourage her to discuss it. The day would be ruined for everyone if her daughter remained sunk in this misery.

'What's wrong, love?' Gwen put her arm around Helen and they both looked out at the garden. 'I can see there's something the matter.'

She felt Helen's shoulders tremble beneath her sweater.

'Adam's going to marry Marita. They're having a baby.'

She turned blindly towards her mother and buried her head on her shoulder, sobbing. Gwen hugged her until the storm had passed. There was nothing she could say that would comfort her, but at least now it was out in the open.

'I'm so, so sorry, my darling.' She hesitated for a while. 'But you did say everyone had expected them to marry all along.'

'I know.' Helen sniffed and blew her nose. 'Marita warned me ages ago that Adam belonged to her. I was just being stupid. I'll get over it.'

She sighed tremulously and continued to speak more resolutely.

'We'd better start the turkey if we're

to have it in the oven before church. Sorry I haven't been much use, Mum.'

Gwen had mixed the stuffing the night before, with Helen silent in her room behind a closed door. She'd also decorated the small tree and finished wrapping the gifts, which were piled at the foot of the little fir.

'That doesn't matter, darling, I understand.' Gwen hugged her again. 'We'd better get started, then.'

Harmony

So together they prepared the turkey, put it in the oven, chopped the vegetables ready for lunch, then set off for the early service. As they walked to church, the icy wind whipped some colour into Helen's cheeks, and Gwen was pleased to see she cheerfully greeted old friends as they took their place in the pew. The small church was packed.

'I always love the carol service, don't

you? The choir master's really good this year.'

Helen smiled. She wished her mother could hear the children from Kasteelpoort singing in such perfect harmony without any training at all. She suddenly remembered how she'd dreamed of entering them in the Eisteddfod in Cape Town. She doubted Anna-Marie would think of it.

The organ notes swelled and she sat back, allowing the familiar words of the Christmas service to flow over her, and gradually felt herself relaxing. By the time the vicar pronounced the final blessing and wished the congregation a happy and joyful Christmas, she felt ready to face lunch.

Soon after their return, the rest of the family exploded noisily into the sitting-room. Angela was carrying William, who was letting everyone know he was hungry. Albert was carrying the Christmas pudding and Mark brought up the rear, laden with baby gear and gifts.

'Who would have thought one small

boy needed so much stuff,' Mark said, gasping. 'Right, who else is ready for a glass of wine?' He proceeded to open the bottle and pour some for everyone.

'Cheers! Happy Christmas.'

'I hope this pud's going to be all right, Mum. The recipe sounded wonderful. Anyway, I've made loads of brandy butter and an egg custard to go with it, so if it doesn't taste right we can just drown it!'

'I'm sure it will be excellent.' Gwen beamed. 'I really love having my daughters doing most of the work this year!'

'We just did the puddings, Mum,' Helen protested, laughing. 'Come and look at the dinner table, everyone. Mum's outdone herself.'

Gwen had laid the table with a dark green cloth and decorated it with fat red candles and red serviettes, with little plastic robins holding the place names.

'Mum found these specially for you, Grandad,' Helen said. 'Aren't they sweet?'

'I've put Mark's beautiful crackers on the tree for now.' Gwen smiled. 'I didn't want to waken the Sleeping Prince!'

'So no silly paper hats, then?' Albert said. 'Good thing, too!'

But once fed, baby William obligingly slept through the meal and didn't even wake up to the applause when Angela doused the lights and brought in the flaming pudding.

'Careful, everyone, don't swallow the silver charms,' she said.

'Grandad, I hope you'll get the plane. Or Helen. That means travel.'

A Phone Call

But just then Helen bit into something hard, and inspected it. A small silver bell. She tried to conceal it but Angela was too quick.

'The wedding bell! Just right for you!' she teased, but Helen just smiled briefly and looked at her plate.

Angela looked enquiringly at her

mother but Gwen just shrugged and shook her head. There hadn't been the time or place for Helen to confide in her sister since receiving Anna-Marie's letter the day before.

Later, the dishes washed and the leftovers put into the fridge, everyone settled in the sitting-room around the tree, pleasantly relaxed. Presents had been exchanged and Albert had just poured everyone a small glass of sherry to toast the Queen at the end of her speech when the phone rang.

'Who can that be?' Gwen asked, from the depths of her armchair. 'Be a dear, Helen, and get it?'

Helen went through to the hall and picked up the phone.

'Hello?'

There was an electronic humming on the line and a voice which sounded as though it was coming from the moon.

'Helen? Is that you?'

It was Adam. Helen's legs buckled and she sat down on the lowest step, struck dumb.

'Hello?' he said again. 'May I speak to Helen McLeod, please?'

'Speaking,' Helen answered, clearing her throat. 'Hello, Adam. Happy Christmas.'

'Helen . . . oh, happy Christmas to you, too. I just wanted to tell you something. I don't know if you think it's at all important but I wanted to let you know that Marita and I . . . '

'I know,' Helen said calmly. 'Anna-Marie told me. You're getting married. I hope you'll be very happy.'

'No! That's the point! We're not. We . . . ' The electronic humming took over again, louder this time. Then Adam's voice faded in briefly ' . . . to Marcus. She got it all wrong . . . we were never . . . '

Helen strained her ears.

'Adam? Are you saying you and Marita aren't going to get married?'

A series of crackles, then Adam's voice came over clearly.

' . . . written to you. You should get my letter before you leave in January.'

Then there was a long, final hum

before Helen found herself staring in disbelief at the silent receiver. Anna-Marie had got it wrong! Adam and Marita weren't going to marry. As if in a dream, she walked to the window and looked out at the snow-covered garden for a long time. He wondered if I thought it was important . . .

If only she'd been able to hear Adam properly. But he'd written to her. They were leaving in just over three weeks; she should get his letter well before they caught the plane.

She walked back into the room, unable to stop smiling from ear to ear, and wanting to scream with happiness.

'My goodness,' Gwen said. 'Who on earth was that, Helen? You look all lit up!'

'I am,' Helen said simply. 'That was Adam, phoning from South Africa.'

She still couldn't believe what she'd heard. Just the sound of Adam's voice had set butterflies doing somersaults inside her.

'And . . . ?' Angela squealed in

delight. 'Was this a long-distance proposal?'

'Don't be silly, Angie, love,' Gwen reproved, looking anxiously at Helen.

'No . . . ' Helen grinned hugely. 'He just said happy Christmas. And he says he's written me a letter.' She looked across at Gwen. 'Everything's all right, Mum. Anna-Marie got it wrong.'

'I told you the wedding bell was perfect for you,' Angie said smugly.

'Shush,' Albert said. 'You girls can gossip later. It's time for the Queen's speech.'

Helen was in such a happy daze she didn't hear a single word.

Exotic

'Now that Christmas is over, Mike Andrews is finally coming up to show us his films!' Anna-Marie carolled, replacing the telephone receiver. 'He's cancelled so often I'd given up on him. But he promises he'll be here the day after tomorrow and he says he's got something very interesting to show us. Flip, is the video machine working?'

'Sure, last time I looked.' Flippie shrugged. 'We just have to hope the generator doesn't pack up again. Ma, we're really going to have to think about getting a new one. That one's almost past the point of no return.'

'It is pretty old,' Cora agreed. 'Well, you'd better see about it, then.'

'I'll ask Adam to do it,' Flippie said. 'I'm driving down to Cape Town tomorrow, to see the fruit and vegetable buyer from the big supermarket chain there. He's interested in buying our entire gooseberry crop next year. He wants to know how many we can supply.'

'Our gooseberries?' Cora asked in disbelief. 'But they're just good for jam making!'

'Apparently they're considered exotic by people in the city and they'll pay a fortune for them. I was thinking we could plough up that field behind the barn that we've always used for the lambs and plant the whole thing with gooseberries. Maybe send some up to Jo'burg, too. I must work out how many kilos we could reasonably expect next year.'

Silence

Cora shook her head, smiling. Flippie's ideas had leapt so far ahead of her own she could only wonder.

'If Mike's coming up, we'd better make sure Ouma is here, too,' she said. 'I wouldn't want her to miss the preview of that fossil film.'

'Ouma's screen debut!' Anna-Marie laughed. 'Mine, too. I wonder what I'll look like? They say being on film adds at least ten kilos.'

'I shouldn't worry, Mike told me he'd cut the bit with you in it,' Flippie joked, making for the door. 'You had a huge spot on your chin and it just ruined the whole thing.'

'Just go away and play with your vegetables,' Anna-Marie said lightly. 'Shall we put Mike in the outside flat, Ma? I'll go and make up the bed there.'

'Good idea. When Helen and her grandfather arrive I thought we'd put Mr McLeod in the flat, too. He might want to sleep late and it's quieter out there. And Helen can have her old room, of course.'

'Ma, he'd have to be awfully deaf to sleep through that wake-up call for the men!' Anna-Marie pointed out. 'Nobody sleeps late here, or haven't you noticed?'

'No-one's ever complained,' Cora replied comfortably. 'Early morning's the best time of day, anyway.'

Cora liked nothing better than walking through her enormous vegetable garden just as the sun was rising over the mountains, breathing in the crisp morning air and pulling the odd weed.

She loved the great silence of the farmlands around her, and the feeling of peace before the start of her busy day. Cora couldn't understand how anyone could possibly want to lie in bed a minute longer than necessary.

Caught On Camera . . .

Two nights later, the Smit family and Tuleka were ranged expectantly in front of the video machine with Mike.

'I'll run the footage of the fossils first,' Mike said. 'It's been edited and it's ready for the programme. I'm really pleased with it and I hope you are, too. Ready?'

First there was a shot of a windmill turning slowly and the chunk-chunk of the water being pumped up into the cement dam next to it. Then the camera panned down to the stony riverbed.

'Water,' a man's deep, cultured voice said. Anna-Marie recognised it as belonging to one of the television news readers. 'A few million years ago, the Karoo was covered in it. These days, farmers in this vast dry area have to rely on boreholes for their lifeline. This river on the farm Kasteelpoort, belonging to the Smit family, has been dry for nearly fifty years, but thanks to the sharp-eyed Amelia Smit, the riverbed has recently yielded up a treasure chest for paleontologists all over the world.'

And there was Amelia, smiling and talking to the camera. She gave a little gasp of surprise.

'Ouma, you look lovely!' Anna-Marie was thrilled, listening to Amelia's crisp voice explaining how she'd found the fossils. 'And I gave it to my little granddaughter to play with,' she ended, 'never dreaming it was a valuable find.'

The camera moved to Anna-Marie and she watched, transfixed. Was this really her? Not bad at all! Then she heard herself speaking and was horrified.

'Oh, I sound dreadful!' she wailed, covering her face in dismay.

'So squeaky! Like a chicken squawking!'

'No, you don't,' Cora said stoutly.

'You sounded very good. Didn't she, Flip? Adam?'

'You come across very nicely actually, Anna-Marie,' Mike said.

Her brothers nodded in agreement.

'Very natural,' Adam said.

The programme continued with shots of the half exposed fossil bones and the professor talking about them in a rather dull voice, then ended with a long shot of the farmhouse shimmering in the heat with the blue mountains rising up behind.

'That's it, folks.' Mike went over to the machine. 'Five minutes. We're going to use it on a magazine programme in four weeks' time.'

'Only five minutes?' Anna-Marie complained. 'But you were here for about three hours!'

'I had to edit it down to fit the slot. But I've got something else here I'd like you to see — especially you, Adam. Your leopards. I've got a lot of good stuff from those cameras I left on the mountain, as well as some lucky footage

I got on my own.'

They watched with interest as two leopards walked across the track and proceeded to play, cuffing each other and standing on their hind legs. Although it was shot at night, they could be seen as clearly as though there were a full moon shining. Mike had used special film for it.

'Just as if they knew the camera was on them,' Mike said happily. 'Born stars, these two are. Wait till you see the cubs.'

He had some wonderful shots of the parents and the cubs playing and eating.

'Feeding their cubs,' Mike said. 'At that point they were still hidden in their den. Now you'll see some shots of them when they're older . . . '

The film continued to delight with the antics of the leopard family. Then suddenly there was a daytime shot of two male figures carrying something, oblivious to the camera fixed in the tree, set to record whenever movement occurred in front of the lens.

'See that?' Mike said. 'Those fellows are setting a gin trap. A big one, by the look of it.'

'Those guys are trespassing on our land!' Adam said, stunned. 'Who are they?'

'They're Jacob's men,' Amelia said. 'He said he was going to set a trap but I didn't really think he would.'

'When was this taken, Mike?' Adam was furious. 'How long has that trap been there?'

'About a week. I only saw it when I was editing the film a couple of days ago. Unfortunately the camera didn't show where they placed it. It could be anywhere above the road. You can see they're walking up the hill.'

'We'll go up first thing tomorrow and find it,' Adam said. 'I just hope they haven't caught anything.'

'What if one of the cubs is caught?' Anna-Marie cried. 'How can Jacob be so cruel?'

'Once we've found the trap, we'll pay

him a visit, too,' Adam said grimly. 'This time he's gone too far. What he's done is totally illegal.'

Furious

The following afternoon Mike, Adam and Flippie drove across to the farmhouse at Blouberg, with the rusty gin trap in the back of the pick-up. Fortunately it had been empty when they found it.

'The drought's affecting Jacob,' Flippie said, looking at the dry brown fields almost with satisfaction. 'I heard his last borehole is starting to dry up. No wonder he's got his eye on our bottom lands. We've got the best water in the district and he knows it.'

Jacob was on the *stoep* and rose to greet them, smiling.

'If you've come to see Marita and Marcus, they've gone into town,' he called genially. 'But there's hot coffee in the pot. Like some?'

'No, thank you, Jacob,' Adam said shortly. 'I've brought you this.'

He pulled the trap out of the back and flung it at Jacob's feet.

'Your men set this trap on our land.'

Jacob started to bluster.

'My men? Who says so? I know nothing about it.'

'Jacob, we have them on film. Piet and Longman — they're clearly recognisable. Mike here has been photographing the leopards for a couple of months now.'

'So I told them to set a trap. So what? Leopards are vermin,' Jacob muttered. 'Any farmer has the right to look after his own livestock. They destroy sheep — yours as well as mine.'

'Exactly how many sheep of yours have these leopards eaten?' Adam asked coldly.

'None so far. But once they've killed off all the small game up on the mountains they'll come down and start on my sheep, you can be sure.'

'Sir, I think you're aware you've broken the law,' Mike put in. 'The ruling is that if you have suffered repeated loss of your stock, you call the Nature Conservation people and they set a cage trap. Perfectly harmless to the animal. Then they relocate the leopard somewhere in a wilderness area, away from stock farms.'

Jacob snorted.

'Why should I wait until I've lost a few valuable merinos? It's all very well for you city busy bodies to come here and . . . '

'These traps are illegal and your men were trespassing on our land,' Adam said hotly. 'I'm going to Hartley's Drift tomorrow, to lay a charge against you. I'm taking this trap as evidence and we have the video footage as well.'

'Now, now, Adam, my boy . . . ' Jacob looked as though he couldn't believe his ears. 'We've been neighbours — friends — for a very long time. Calling in the police? What are you thinking of?'

Just then a big four by four drove up and Marcus and Marita jumped out, laughing.

'Hi, guys.' Marita greeted them. 'Coming in for coffee? Sorry we were out. We've been shopping.'

'They've come to tell me they're going to the police,' Jacob blurted out, his face red. 'Some nonsense about this little trap I put out to scare the leopards away.'

'Pa!' Marita was horrified. 'That awful trap? You set it? How could you?'

Marcus gave a startled grunt and looked up at Jacob, shocked.

'I didn't believe these things still existed. Weren't they outlawed years ago?'

'Marita, you know how bad leopards can be.' Jacob was almost pleading with his daughter. 'Maybe you don't remember, but when you were a baby we lost so many — '

'That was more than twenty years ago! No-one uses these awful traps any more. How could you even have it on the farm? It makes me feel ill just to look at it! I'm ashamed of you!'

Marita swept inside the farmhouse,

leaving Jacob shamefaced and uncertain. Clearly Marita's furious disapproval meant more to him than anyone else's.

'Well, Adam,' he muttered. 'You must do as you see fit. I can't stop you. But if those leopards are so important to you all, then I suppose I won't . . . '

'Too right you won't,' Adam snapped, picking up the trap. 'Good day, Jacob.'

'That shook him.' Flippie smirked as they drove away, leaving the older man staring after him. 'Jacob can't bear to think of being involved with the police. He's always thought of himself as such an upright citizen, a pillar of the community.'

'Marita will make his life hell!' Adam agreed. 'But what's the bet we get a phone call tonight?'

A Guarantee

He was right.

It was just after supper when Marita called.

'Adam, my sweetie,' she said. 'Are you serious about reporting my pa to the cops?'

'If it's the only way to get his attention about trapping leopards.'

'What if I told you he'd smashed his traps? And he absolutely promises not even to think of using them ever again?'

'*Traps*? He has more than one?'

'Well, you know my pa. Listen, Adam.' Marita was serious. 'I know my father's been terrible about the leopards. Marcus also says he can't believe what he did. But Pa's just very old fashioned. He's so upset about you going to the police. I've never seen him like this. I'm certain he'll never do it again.'

'So, are you asking me not to lay a charge?'

'Yes, I am,' Marita said in a small voice. 'Adam, he's my pa, after all. And if you lay a charge, everyone will know, all his friends. His name will be ruined around here.'

'Are you imagining that your father

will be carted off to jail in handcuffs? I don't think that's going to happen. There'll be a court case and he'd probably get a big fine, that's all.'

'I know, and he deserves it, I told him so. But we're trying to plan a party, Adam, and if you lay a charge against him, everything will be spoiled.'

Respect

Adam was silent. As far as he was concerned, the more people who knew what Jacob had done, the better. But he couldn't deny the pleading in Marita's voice and he certainly didn't want to cast a pall over her celebrations.

'OK, Marita,' he said heavily. 'If you can guarantee he's destroyed all his traps — and that his men will stay off our land.'

'I can guarantee that, Adam! Thank you!' She was about to ring off when she spoke again. 'Oh, by the way, Marcus and I are having a small party next Saturday. You're all invited! Will Helen and her grandpa be here by then?'

'No, they're only getting here on the eighteenth. Are you sure it would be such a good idea if we came? After today, I can't see your dad welcoming the Smits on to his farm for quite a while!'

'Oh, he'll be fine with it,' Marita said airily. 'Anyway, I wouldn't have the party without all of you. You're practically family.'

'Well, if you're sure,' Adam replied.

'He's not used to anyone standing up to him, and I think this afternoon made him realise you're not the little boy who lives next door any more. He's always liked you but it's as though he's got a new respect for you.'

'Pity it took a leopard trap to make him see it,' Adam said briefly.

'You know, we had a long talk after you left this afternoon, and for the first time he actually spoke of leaving the farm. He says he's been lonely since my ma died and said he might move to Cape Town — to be near Marcus and me, I suppose.'

'I'll believe that when it happens!' Adam said. 'What on earth would your father do in a city?'

'I don't know, but he'd have to do something more than sit on his *stoep* and drink coffee, which is what he's been doing lately. Maybe new surroundings would do him good. He seems to have lost interest in the farm.'

'Can't say I've noticed that,' Adam mused. 'Anyway, see you on Saturday night. And you can tell the old reprobate he's got one last chance, but only because his daughter is so charming.'

★ ★ ★

Cora looked about her at the crowds of people milling around the craft market in the park and wondered how much longer they'd have to stay at their stall. Luckily their table was under a shady tree, but she was tired of standing and wished they'd remembered to bring a couple of folding chairs. Next time . . .

There would definitely be a next time, she was sure. They'd almost sold out of everything they'd brought and Flippie had already taken orders for the following month.

But so many people and so much noise! I really couldn't stand to live in a city, she thought, wishing they hadn't agreed to stay the night. She'd far rather have driven home, even if they got there at midnight . . .

But the others had been so thrilled with Marita's offer to stay in her flat that Cora had gone along with the idea.

'It's yours for as long as you want to stay in Cape Town!' Marita had said on the night of her party. 'You'll want to do some shopping after the market, so why don't you go and see a movie in the evening? Or have dinner out somewhere at the waterfront? There are some lovely restaurants on the harbour front.'

'Oh, yes!' Anna-Marie had been thrilled. 'Ma, you have to come, too. Please! We'll have a great time, all of us.'

Really, Anna-Marie's a strange mixture, Cora thought fondly. I imagined she'd be only too keen to explore Cape Town without me, but she insisted I come. You'd never say she'd been brought up on the farm; she's enjoying the crowds and she chats so easily to total strangers.

Besides heaps of red-leafed lettuce, freshly-picked carrots, crisp green peas and baby courgettes on the laden trestle table, there were loaves of home-baked bread, bottles of jam, packets of rusks and biscuits, fruit cakes, milk tarts, and a big cooler box filled with cream and packets of yellow farm butter.

On one end of the table, Amelia had laid out her framed watercolours of the farm and wild animal sketches.

Cora had been amazed at the response. Even before Flippie had finished unpacking, people were crowding round to buy their goods.

'Real farm butter, I can't believe it!' one grey-haired lady said as she scooped up four packets. 'I haven't seen this since I was a child! I'd better have two of those huge loaves to go with it. Oh, and is this a ginger loaf? You made it yourself? How wonderful!'

Poor things, it's as if they've never seen fresh food before, Cora thought. The vegetables were gone within twenty minutes and the baked goods and bottles of preserves were all bought by ten o'clock. Amelia had also done brisk business with her paintings.

'People told me I priced them very low,' she said. 'But I'd rather have sold them than take them home again.'

'That's the first principle of marketing, Ouma.' Flippie nodded. 'Next month, if we bring a truck, I reckon we could sell twice as much.'

'So can we pack up now and wander around the rest of the market?' Cora pleaded. 'I'd like to take a look at that pottery over there.'

What's Going On?

Anna-Marie seemed strangely unwilling to leave the table, which was practically empty.

'Let's stay until we sell these last three bottles of jam,' she protested. 'Oh! look who's here!'

'Hello!' Margie Warren, carrying a big empty basket, beamed at them. 'What! Almost everything gone already? Even your lovely bread, Cora?'

'What a coincidence, Margie!' Cora smiled. 'Imagine seeing you here. Yes, we've done pretty well and I'm afraid they're all sold.'

'No, actually, Mrs Warren, I saved you a loaf.'

Anna-Marie dived back into the truck and produced one.

'Whole wheat, the kind you like.'

'You knew we'd be here?' Cora was mystified.

'Oh, yes, Cora. And your daughter and I have a little surprise planned for you, haven't we, Anna-Marie?'

Anna-Marie grinned a bit guiltily.

'Yes, Ma. Mrs Warren's offered to take us around Cape Town a bit. You and me.'

'We'll see you back at the flat this afternoon then, shall we? Ouma and I thought we might take a trip up the cableway to the top of Table Mountain.'

So Flippie and Ouma knew about this surprise, too! What was going on?

Margie Warren nosed her big sedan out into the Saturday morning traffic, made for the freeway along the side of Table Mountain and pointed out the sights as they passed.

'That's the Baxter Theatre on our left, and the university up there on the other side of the bridge. And this big building on our right, that's Groote Schuur Hospital where Chris Barnard did the first heart transplant. Now, look at this gorgeous view of the city!'

'I'm Not Promising'

Cora gasped.

The whole of Cape Town was laid

out before them, stretching as far as she could see, round the harbour and along the huge bay to the opposite horizon. A stiff breeze was blowing and little yachts scudded about the bay.

'They're racing this afternoon,' Margie told them. 'I'm afraid that's where Richard is, on his beloved boat! So it'll be just me showing you around.'

'It's very kind of you, Margie,' Cora murmured, still puzzled. She was even more so when Margie turned down off the freeway, past a crowded area of small, run-down shops, wove her way through a crowd of hooting taxis and buses and took them to a big industrial building down a side street.

'Here we are.' She smiled. 'Gladrags. Our clothing factory, Cora. I wanted you to see it before you made up your mind about Anna-Marie's future.'

Cora stiffened, but Anna-Marie took her arm.

'Ma, just take a look, please,' she begged. 'First see the factory and then have a look at the college where I could study.'

'And the hostel where she could stay,' Margie added. 'I've got all the details, Cora. The design course runs for one term, and then the students have to do three months of practical work. She could work here, with me. I'm the head of the design room so I'd keep an eye on her, and make sure she works hard!

'Then the following term it's back to full-time study and then another session of practical work, and so on, for two years.'

Cora looked at the appeal in her daughter's face and sighed.

'All right. I'll have a look. But I'm not promising.'

Entranced

The factory was enormous, with long rows of sewing machines and big cutting tables at one end. Huge rolls of fabric were stacked along the side.

'No-one's working today, it's Saturday,' Margie pointed out. 'Usually the radio's playing full blast, and with the machines going you can't hear yourself speak.'

Cora shuddered but Anna-Marie was entranced.

'Is this an embroidery machine? I've heard about these.'

'Yes, we use it for the children's designs. It's all computerised. Come and see our design room. You'll love it.'

This was a big, airy room with windows letting in plenty of natural light. Paper patterns, drawings and swatches of fabric lay everywhere in what looked like total confusion, and pages torn from fashion magazines were pinned to the walls. Anna-Marie fingered the fabric of a dress that was fitted to a mannequin in the corner.

'Meet Miss X!' Margie laughed. 'Our model. She's a perfect size thirty-four. Everything we dream up has to fit her, then the pattern-makers in the room next door enlarge our designs to fit the different sizes.'

'It's wonderful,' Anna-Marie said

wistfully. 'Imagine spending your days in here, just drawing clothes!'

'Well, there's a lot more to it than that,' Margie said briskly. 'That's why you go to college, to study the different fabrics and the history of fashion and the economics of clothing and so on.'

The Right Decision

Cora looked out of the window, straight up to the mountain rearing proudly above the dreary industrial building around her. She could make out some small figures walking slowly along a path and watched as a thick waterfall of white cloud spilled over against the skyline.

'A lovely view,' she commented. Really, what else could she find to say? The whole place depressed her, but Anna-Marie seemed to be in her element, discussing fabrics with Margie and examining the sketches.

'This is the table you'd be working

at.' Margie pointed. 'Right next to mine. If you decided to come, that is.'

Anna-Marie looked at her mother, imploring her.

'Let's take a look at the college, then,' Cora said in resignation. 'And you mentioned a hostel? So Anna-Marie wouldn't have to stay all by herself in a flat?'

'Goodness me, no,' Margie said. 'She'd have her own room in the college hostel, of course, but they have strict rules for first-year students. They're expected to be in by midnight over weekends and ten o'clock on weekdays.'

'That's sensible.' Cora nodded, comforted. 'And is there someone responsible in charge of all these students?'

'Yes, the supervisor, Miss Harrison. I've heard she's quite a dragon. You'll meet her this morning.'

'I bet you'll love her, Ma,' Anna-Marie added. 'She sounds your kind of dragon!'

'And of course, until she made new friends, we'd love to have Anna-Marie visit us over the weekends,' Margie continued. 'Richard could take her sailing. He's always looking for hard-working crew.'

'So, Ma?' Anna-Marie held her breath, searching her mother's face for signs of agreement. 'What do you think?'

'I think I'd better say yes,' Cora said slowly. 'I can't fight the two of you. And if Margie says she'll keep an eye on you, then — '

Anna-Marie squealed and threw her arms around her mother.

'But we'll just try it for a term or two,' Cora added quickly. 'If I hear that you're lying around on the beach instead of attending classes, or Margie says you're not pulling your weight, then you'll come home and do that secretarial course.'

'I'll work hard!' Anna-Marie promised joyfully. 'I'm not interested in going to the beach, Ma, I just want to be a designer.'

'And you're to phone home every

week and tell me how you're getting on.'

'Of course I will!'

'And I'll be down here to the market on the first Saturday of every month, so I'll see you then.'

'Now, Ma, don't be — no, you're right. It will be lovely to see you,' Anna-Marie said hastily. 'Oh, thank you, Ma! Thanks, Mrs Warren!'

Looking at her daughter's radiant face, Cora knew she'd made the right decision. And later, driving past the modern college and then meeting Miss Harrison, the hostel supervisor, and seeing the students' rooms, laid the last of her doubts at rest. Miss Harrison had a no-nonsense look about her that Cora approved of.

Anna-Marie would probably be in her element and she'd been silly to worry about it all this time.

When Margie Warren dropped them off at Marita's flat later, Anna-Marie was bubbling over with the news that she'd be returning to Cape Town in three weeks' time, as a student of clothing design. Amelia hugged her and winked at Cora.

'I knew you'd see a bit of sense,' she said cheerfully. 'This granddaughter of mine is going to be a big success!'

'That's great, sis,' Flippie said. Then he faced Cora awkwardly and bit his lip.

'I've also got an announcement, Ma. But I don't think you're going to like it very much. I've accepted a job here in Cape Town. I'm leaving the farm.'

Cora looked shocked.

Flippie's life seemed to be going in a different direction from Adam's. But then he'd shown real flair for spotting business opportunities, so she shouldn't have been surprised. Everything was changing at Kasteelpoort . . .

11

'Lovely To See You'

'Someone's sure to be here to meet us, Grandad. You gave Amelia all the flight details, didn't you?'

Helen and Albert were standing next to the carousel in the airport, waiting for one last bag to appear.

'Of course, dear. I told her we were arriving at eight this morning. And we're right on time. Ah, there's my other bag.'

She scooped it up for him and they pushed their laden trolley out into the concourse, which was thronged with smiling, expectant families meeting travellers from Britain.

Helen craned her neck but couldn't recognise anyone in the crowd.

'I don't know who'll be here,

Grandpa, but it'll probably be Adam.'

Helen had no idea how she'd act when she saw him again. Although she'd rushed to collect the post every day, the letter he said he'd written still hadn't arrived by the time they'd left England.

'Helen! Over here!'

Flippie's deep voice boomed out across the crowd.

'Sorry I'm a bit late . . . '

Flippie? Helen felt a small stab of disappointment, which was swept away in delight as he lifted her off her feet with a great bear hug. She'd forgotten how tall and tanned he was, and hardly recognised him in a smart grey suit and tie.

'Oh, Flip, it's lovely to see you again!'

He shook hands with Albert.

'You must be Mr McLeod, Helen's *oupa*? Good day, sir, I'm Flippie Smit. Welcome to South Africa.'

'Thank you, young man. I see you've arranged some real sun for us!'

A New Job

The heat hit them as they stepped out of the air-conditioned building and made their way to the carpark, but Helen couldn't help smiling. She was back!

'Oh, a new car? What happened to the pick-up?'

Flippie was loading their luggage into the boot of a sleek sedan.

'I'll tell you all about it in a minute.' He grinned. 'Let's just get out of here.'

The outline of Table Mountain beckoned majestically on the skyline, but Flippie headed towards the national road which led out of the city.

'I hope you don't mind if we just head for the farm,' he said. 'You'll probably come back for some proper sightseeing, but everyone's dying to see you, Helen, and I promised to get you there in time for lunch.'

'Fine with me,' Helen said. 'So, Flippie, tell me the latest news. For starters, what's the suit for?'

'Ah . . . ' He grinned. 'I have to dress up for this new job of mine.'

'Job?'

'Started last week. Helen, you're looking at the national buyer for exotic fruits and vegetables for Pick 'n' Purchase. The head office is here in Cape Town, but I get to go all over the country finding fancy food for the customers.'

'So you're not on the farm any more?' She couldn't believe her ears.

Catching Up . . .

'A lot's happened since you went back, Helen,' Flippie said. 'For starters, Ma fell in the dairy this morning. Adam thought she'd broken her wrist, so he had to take her to the clinic at Hartley's Drift. Otherwise he'd have been here to meet you.'

'Oh, Flippie, that's awful. Poor Cora!'

'Well, you know Ma,' Flippie went

on. 'She won't make any kind of fuss. She'll be there when we get to the farm. Luckily, I'm based in Cape Town so I've taken the day off. Got to get back tonight, though. I'm due to fly to Durban tomorrow.'

'Durban's a nice town,' Albert remarked. 'I remember shore leave there during the war when I was on *HMS Howe*. Got to watch out for the sharks in the sea around there, though.'

'I doubt I'll have time for a swim, sir!' Flippie grinned. 'I'm visiting lychee farms near there to sign contracts to buy their crop.'

'I'm impressed,' Helen said, and she was. Flippie sounded so different from the farm boy he'd been when she first met him. 'So what else has been happening?'

'Anna-Marie's finally got her way. She's at college here, doing fashion design, but she'll be coming up next weekend.

'And you know about Marita and Marcus, don't you?' he continued.

'They're going to live in Cape Town, too.'

'I did hear something about it,' she murmured. 'I wasn't sure . . . '

'Old Jacob was cross as a snake,' he said cheerfully. 'He always wanted Marita to marry a farmer — preferably Adam! But I'm afraid my brother had other ideas.' He grinned sideways at her.

'Anyway, Jacob's come round now and thoroughly approves of Marcus. And, of course, he's thrilled he's going to be a grandfather. I bet he'll be camping on their doorstep once the baby's arrived.'

'And how's Amelia?' Albert asked.

'Ouma? Flourishing! She's selling her paintings almost every weekend to the visitors. And she's moved back to the farm for a while, to help Ma with the farm stall during the summer. Actually, I think coming over from town on her scooter every day was getting a bit too much for her.'

As the car ate up the miles, Helen

watched the countryside turn from lush mountains and neat green vineyards to flat dry land stretching away endlessly into the heat haze on the horizon.

Sheep dotted the lands on either side, nibbling at a grey-leafed bush.

'Dry countryside, isn't it?' Albert remarked. 'It's incredible that those animals find anything to live on.'

'Best lamb in the country,' Flippie stated. 'It's the herbs they eat — gives the meat a good flavour.'

Flippie's comfortable car was a far cry from the Mawasa bus Helen had travelled in the first time, and the journey to Kasteelpoort seemed much shorter than she remembered. They passed the little farm stall at the turn-off to the farm and Flippie waved to the women behind the counter but didn't stop.

She saw enormous yellow pumpkins arranged in a pyramid on the counter.

'Remember Tandiswa? She and Thombi are running the stall now and doing really well. They write down everything that gets sold and Ma's paying them a percentage of the profits.'

'Everyone's a businessman!' Helen laughed. 'I'm glad the farm stall took off, Flip.'

'It was your idea, and the best thing we ever did. That and the adventure trail.'

They turned a corner of the farm track and the house came into view.

'Great Scott!' Albert exclaimed with pleasure 'Nothing's changed in fifty-five years! It's exactly as I remember it.'

Helen felt a thrill of excitement as she opened the door and stood looking at the cascade of bright pink bougainvillea tumbling across the wide verandah. It was as comforting as if she were coming home, but at the same time exciting enough to cause butterflies.

'Helen! And Albert, my dear!'

Amelia came out of the house in a great rush and opened her arms for a hug as Helen ran up the steps.

'How very nice to see you back. And Albert — well, my goodness!'

'My goodness!' Albert was smiling from ear to ear.

He looked as though he might shake hands with her, but Amelia gave him a resounding kiss on the cheek.

'After all these years! And don't you look well!'

'You're not looking too bad yourself.' Albert laughed.

Amelia looked striking in a gold turban from which her grey hair escaped in curly wisps, and a loose black and brown leopard-print top. Helen thought she recognised Anna-Marie's hand in the design.

Then Cora came out, her arm heavily bandaged but beaming a welcome.

Overwhelmed

'Helen! I'm so glad you're back! And Mr McLeod, how nice to meet you. Sorry I can't shake hands right now . . . a bad sprain. Come and sit down. Hello, Flippie. My, I still can't get over the sight of you in a smart suit! Quite the city gent. I'll just ask Tuleka to bring some nice, cold lemonade.'

In all the bustle Helen looked for the person she most wanted to see, but there was no sign of Adam.

Tuleka came out bearing a big tray of iced lemonade, her face split in a wide grin. There were more kisses and greetings, then Helen sank gratefully back on to the bamboo chair and sipped her drink.

'Miss Helen, the children so glad you come back!' Tuleka said. 'Miss Anna-Marie, she gone now. Children go to proper school in town. But they be so happy to see you!'

'I'll be happy to see them.' Helen smiled.

'Meanwhile, Marita is coming over for lunch, with Marcus,' Cora said. 'We couldn't keep them away! They're dying to see you, Helen, and meet your grandpa.'

Helen felt quite overwhelmed. She'd have preferred just to sit on the verandah absorbing the atmosphere of the farm for a while.

She realised how much she'd missed the peace of the wide-open space, with only the distant sound of a tractor or sheep to break the silence.

The conversation bounced back and forth and Helen felt as though she'd never left Kasteelpoort, except that instead of faulty pumps and sheep dip, the talk between Flippie and his mother was all about buying chives and cherries and the best way to package Cape gooseberries for the supermarkets.

When Marita and Marcus arrived in their big four by four there was another round of greetings and laughter. Marita was quite noticeably expecting and glowing with happiness. She sat down next to Helen.

'Congratulations,' Helen said hesitantly. 'On your marriage. And your baby. And everything.'

'Thanks,' Marita said. 'Aren't I the lucky one? Marcus is a lovely man. I'm so sorry you missed our party. But there'll be plenty of time . . . you are staying a while?'

'Only three weeks,' Helen said.

'Nonsense!' Marita cried. 'The Smits won't let you go this time!'

Then she took Helen's hand impulsively.

'Helen, I owe you an apology. I must have been crazy that day, telling you that Adam belonged to me. He never did, really, and I knew it. I was just jealous.'

'Of me?'

Helen couldn't believe her ears.

'Of course. I saw Adam couldn't take his eyes off you. But anyway, I knew we weren't meant for each other, no matter what my pa said, and Cora. He's like my older brother, and ever since I was fifteen I just practised my flirting on him! He knew that, too. He was never serious about me. Not like he is now.'

'Hello, Helen'

Everyone seems to know more about Adam's feelings than I do, Helen thought ruefully. I wonder where he is?

As if in answer to her thoughts, Cora spoke.

'Adam had to see to his goats as soon as he dropped me back here, but he'll be here as soon as he can. In the meantime, I'm sure you're all starving. Shall we have lunch?'

Albert broke off his conversation with Amelia in the corner.

'I remember these farm lunches! Lead the way.'

'Tuleka's done something extra special for you, Albert,' Amelia said, taking his arm as they went into the dining-room. 'I remember how you used to love my mother's mutton pie. She does one almost as well.'

Besides the delicious pie topped with a feather-light crust of puff pastry, Tuleka had also grilled some home-made spicy sausage and served it with golden baked sweet potatoes, yellow rice studded with raisins and a bowl of tiny green beans and baby carrots, still crisp and tossed in olive oil.

There was an appreciative sigh as Cora started to cut the crust and ladle the pie on to their plates.

'We won't wait for Adam,' she said. 'I don't know how long he'll be.'

'Here I am,' a deep voice said. 'Sorry I'm late, folks. Hello, Mr McLeod.'

He shook Albert's hand and slid into the empty seat beside Helen.

'Hello, Helen.'

He took her hand and held it firmly, his skin warm against hers. And the look in his eyes told her that everything was going to be all right.

'So, Helen, did you get my letter?' Adam's voice was low against the buzz of conversation around the table.

'No. It was held up with the Christmas mail, I suppose.'

Helen found it difficult to keep her voice from trembling. The warmth of Adam sitting next to her sent a tremor through her and she wished they could be alone to talk openly.

'After lunch, let's take a drive up the mountain, just the two of us,' he said quietly, obviously feeling the same.

Then he turned to Albert, asking him about his war experiences and his memories of Amelia and the farm.

Helen couldn't concentrate on what the others were saying, but she could see Albert was in his element, teasing Amelia and telling Adam and Flippie stories about their grandmother as a young girl.

'And do you remember that time, Amelia, when you tried to get me to believe in the *tokolosh*? And you put that piglet under my bed and I was convinced I was being haunted?'

'Go on, Ouma, you didn't believe in that *tokolosh* yourself!' Cora chided. 'That's just a story the workers tell their children to make them behave!'

'Of course I didn't, but I knew that one of the men had told Bertie that the *tokolosh* was an evil little man who lived under the bed and punished naughty children. I don't think he was too sure what to believe, were you, Bertie?'

'Well, he was pretty convincing and I was pretty green.' Albert laughed. 'After all, I reckoned anything could happen in Africa! So Amelia put this piglet under my bed just before I turned in and it was grunting and thumping about all night long. I was too scared to look under the bed and I didn't sleep a wink.'

'Ouma, you were a terror,' Flippie said fondly.

Tuleka cleared the plates and brought in the dessert of plump stewed guavas.

'Lovely, but I don't think I have room for another mouthful.' Albert eyed the big bowl of whipped cream regretfully.

'Is very nice pudding,' Tuleka said firmly.

'Oh, well, just a small helping, then.'

'Grandad, I can see you're going to fill out a bit while you're here!' Helen grinned.

After lunch, they finished their coffee on the verandah. Adam had just stood up and turned to Helen when a cloud of dust and a squeal of brakes informed them of Jacob's arrival. He got out of his truck and walked stiffly to the steps but didn't come any further.

'Afternoon, everyone,' he said peremptorily. 'Adam, I'd like a word with you if I may?'

Adam muttered under his breath, clearly put out.

'I'll be back as soon as I can, Helen.' Aloud he said, 'Certainly, Jacob. What can I do for you?'

'You can come with me,' Jacob said. 'I want to talk in private.' They got into his truck and drove off down the farm road.

'Goodness me.' Amelia sighed. 'What's that all about?'

'A Young Man's Game'

Jacob drove until he found some shade under a pepper tree, then stopped the truck and turned to Adam.

'Adam, I've got a proposal for you. How would you like to take over Blouberg?'

'You mean — manage your farm?' Adam was stunned.

'I've decided I'm going to live in Cape Town to be near Marita and her family. I've realised one thing, my boy, and that is a man's family is the most important thing. And since my Aletta passed away, Marita is all the family I've got. Her and her baby. And Marcus,' he added, rather unwillingly.

'I'd have to think about it,' Adam said, his mind racing. 'Did you have in mind a monthly salary? Would you still make all the decisions? Oversee everything?'

If that was Jacob's idea, then he'd refuse.

Jacob shook his head.

'Once I'm in Cape Town, that's where I'll stay. Farming's a young man's game and I've made my decision. I'm sure it's no secret that we could do with more water at Blouberg. You've got more than enough under those bottom lands of yours. What I had in mind was that you amalgamate the two farms and farm them as one concern.'

'And your labourers?'

'You're responsible for them, too. Run the place as if it's your own. Make any changes you want to.'

'But it would still be your farm?'

'Well, I suppose I'll have to sell it one of these days. Marita certainly isn't interested in running it, not with that city boy she's married. You're the best man for the job.'

Adam was silent for a minute.

'I'm not interested in working for you as a manager. But I'll take over the farm on one condition — that while I'm running it I can buy it from you on terms. Say, over twenty-five years. Your lawyer could draw up a mortgage agreement between us.'

'You're a couple of jumps ahead of me there, Adam.' Jacob smiled wryly. 'I hadn't thought that far down the line. But I suppose that would make sense.'

'And we get Blouberg valued by an independent agent,' Adam continued firmly. 'The whole property is badly rundown. Your fences need replacing, and you haven't fertilised the lands for the last couple of years. And I know you're pretty short of water, with your three boreholes dried up.'

'No secrets around here, are there?' the older man grumbled. 'All right, I'll speak to my lawyer in the morning about arranging a mortgage. You know, I always imagined it would be you running my place anyway, but married to Marita and giving me grandsons to carry on the farm.'

He gave Adam a sly look.

'But I suppose that lass from overseas will make you a good enough wife, if she'll have you. Asked her yet?'

'Not yet,' Adam said.

His mind was racing ahead. Running both farms, especially now Flippie was no longer working alongside him, would be a big undertaking. On the other hand, it was a huge opportunity, and the answer to a problem that had been worrying him for some time.

'Right,' Adam said at last. 'It's a deal,

Jacob. We'll talk some more tomorrow. But can you take me back to the house now? I have something I must do and it won't wait.'

When Jacob dropped Adam back at the farmhouse, the verandah was deserted. He could hear his mother in the kitchen talking to Tuleka, and from inside the house came Flippie's raised voice, discussing delivery dates on the phone with someone. The curtains of Helen's room were drawn, and he assumed she was probably resting after her long flight.

He wandered disconsolately towards the barn, thinking that he might as well check on the men who were replacing parts on the old tractor, when he caught sight of a blonde head hurrying towards the schoolroom and grinned with relief.

Helen pushed open the door and looked around, with a lump in her throat. The walls were bright with pictures and hand-written stories and she walked around slowly, admiring their work. It looked as though Anna-Marie had been teaching them some geography, and there was a big map of the world on one wall.

Closer study revealed a big red sticker over England with *Miss Helen lives here* written on it. There were pictures of the Queen and Buckingham Palace and a Beefeater in full dress regalia. Helen wondered what on earth the children made of these. Perhaps they thought she lived in the palace!

The workbooks were piled neatly on the desk in front and she started paging through them nostalgically.

'Helen?'

She jumped. Adam stood silhouetted in the doorway against the sun.

'Sorry about that. Jacob had something he wanted to discuss with me and it took rather longer than I expected. Still feel like a drive up the mountain?'

'Yes, of course.'

She climbed into his old pick-up, pushing aside some leather harness, and revelled in the familiar smell of animal feeds and hay. They bumped their way up the mountain trail, with Helen holding on to the dashboard for support. She'd forgotten just how exhilarating the road could be and she couldn't stop herself from laughing out loud as they hit the bumps and potholes.

Well before they reached the summit, Adam braked to a halt under a thorn tree.

'No need to suffer any more than this.' He grinned. 'There's a great view from here.'

'I remember,' she said softly. 'This is where we saw the baby zebras the first time you brought me up here.'

'That's right. They're doing well. We had seven zebra at the last count. And the leopard family was filmed here, too, at night.'

'Leopard family?'

'I forgot. You weren't here when we

discovered them.'

They left the pick-up and he brought her up to date with the news of the television cameras and how they'd used infra-red film to record Jacob's men laying the trap.

Majestic

So much had happened since she left . . . The success of the farm stall, Flippie's job, Anna-Marie leaving for college, Marita and Marcus . . . Helen was silent, looking out over the distant plains that seemed to ripple in the heat of the setting sun.

The big canvas of the farm never changes, she reflected. We're just a few small figures that move about it. The bleating of the angora goats wafted faintly up from the lands, and from the scrub nearby an unseen bird called harshly.

'What's that bird — ?'

She turned to Adam questioningly,

but he took her in his arms without a word and kissed her, at first gently, then more fiercely. He pressed her to him so closely she could feel the beating of his heart through his shirt, and she returned his kisses eagerly, giving herself up to the pleasure of being held at last by the man she loved.

Breathless, he drew back a little and gazed into her eyes.

'Do you think you could marry me, Helen?' His voice was husky.

'Yes, Adam, I could. I think I'd die if I didn't!'

She embraced him closer again, rubbing her face against his chest and breathing in the strong male smell of his sun-warmed skin.

'But I was so worried you'd think that Flippie and I . . . when you saw him kissing me in the kitchen the night before I left. I didn't know what you'd think . . . ' She felt foolish, but it had to be said.

'I wasn't too worried.' Adam smiled. 'I knew he had a crush on you. But when you left there was Evelyn for a while, then lots of girls in Hartley's Drift who were glad to help him forget.'

'But you didn't?'

'How could I? I thought of you every single day. Ever since you left I've been miserable. There was no-one I could talk to, because I wasn't sure if you felt the same way. And I wasn't sure if you'd want to stay on the farm for ever, with me.'

'How could you not be sure? And why didn't you write to me?'

'I'm not much good at writing small talk,' he muttered. 'But when I heard that Anna-Marie had told you that Marita and I — well, I tried to phone you but that was a disaster. So I wrote to make sure you knew the truth. I couldn't bear you to think that I might marry Marita, then you'd never have come back!'

'Never mind, I'm here now. No need to write letters.' She cuddled against him, her whole body alive with happiness. 'Look, the sun's just about to set. Isn't this beautiful?'

They held each other close together while they watched the sun dip behind the far blue mountains and the sky changing from pink to dark blue and shades of lavender.

'The sunsets here are wonderful,' she breathed. 'But this is the best I've ever seen.'

'Ordered it specially for you,' he murmured. Then he went very still.

'Don't move. But look next to you,' he whispered. 'On the rock.'

A big leopard had leapt on to a boulder near the pick-up and was surveying the sunset, his great golden eyes unblinking as he majestically raised his head, sniffing the breeze. Then he seemed to look right at them for a long time, before lightly jumping down and disappearing into the gathering darkness. It was a magic end to a perfect day.

'He was giving us his blessing,' Helen murmured.

'I think you're right.' Adam kissed

her tenderly once more before they headed back to the pick-up. 'Let's go back and tell everyone our news — if they haven't already guessed.'

He drove all the way down the mountain, not letting go of her hand even to change gear.

So Happy . . .

It was almost midnight before they all went to bed. Adam and Helen's announcement was greeted with kisses and hugs and handshakes, with Albert and Flippie both proposing a toast, and Cora shedding a few tears.

'I'm so glad, my dear,' she whispered, hugging Helen tightly. 'From the first day I always felt you were like another daughter to me. I know you're going to make my boy very happy.'

'I told you Adam was going around with a face like a boot, didn't I?' Amelia said triumphantly. 'I could tell he was missing you, but of course he never said a word. But you can't fool your ouma, can you, Adam?'

Adam hugged her.

'Never could, Ouma!'

'Oh, your 'handsome grandson'!' Helen exclaimed. 'And here I was thinking that you meant Flippie!'

'I heard that!' Adam said in mock annoyance.

'It's only eight o'clock,' Cora said suddenly. 'Wouldn't you like to phone your mother and tell her, Helen?'

'She'll be just back from work,' Albert said. 'It's teatime over there.'

'I'd love to.' Helen smiled. 'Come on, Adam, you'd better introduce yourself to your future mother-in-law!'

When she heard Helen's news, Gwen was so choked with emotion she could hardly speak. It was a bad connection and over the static crackles Helen heard the tears in her mother's voice.

'Mum, Adam is dying to talk to you but it's a bad line so we'll phone again tomorrow, all right?'

'Please do that. I'm so happy for you,

darling. So happy.'

'That's my mum.' Helen laughed as she replaced the receiver. 'So happy she's going off to have a good cry!'

'And then she'll phone Angela,' Albert prophesied, 'and they'll have a good cry together.'

'So when do you two plan to be married?' Cora asked, when they were sitting together over the remains of the champagne.

'We haven't thought that far ahead,' Helen remarked.

'Why not as soon as we can?' Adam asked. 'While your oupa is here? We don't need to plan things for months ahead, do we?'

'Good idea!' Albert said cheerfully. 'I'm sure your mother would get on the first plane available.'

'But what about Angela and Mark?' Helen worried. 'I couldn't get married without my sister here, too . . . But you're going back in three weeks' time, Grandad. What if Mark can't get leave? Oh, dear, there'd be so much to try and arrange . . . and only three weeks!'

'Things have a way of working out,' Amelia said comfortably. 'Wait until tomorrow and you'll see, everything will just fall into place. Don't worry.'

Amelia was right, of course. In the morning Gwen phoned, excited and happy and all emotional waterworks well under control. She heartily approved of their plan to marry while Albert was still there.

'Angela said that's just what you'd do!' she exclaimed. 'She said there was no way at all the Smit family could just drop everything and fly over here for the wedding; they've got a farm to run. It makes far better sense for you to be married there.'

'Oh, Mum, I'm glad you see it that way.' Helen was relieved that her practical mother understood. 'Will you be able to come over here within, say, a fortnight?'

'Wild horses wouldn't keep us away!' Gwen laughed. 'Mark's already said that he could apply for leave if you decided this. And a bit of that sun will do us all good. It hasn't stopped raining since you and Albert left.'

'Mum, tell Angela I want her to be my bridesmaid — no, I mean, matron of honour,' Helen said, remembering. 'And I'll ask Anna-Marie, too.'

'What are you going to do about a dress?' her mother asked, typically thinking ahead. 'Should I buy you one and bring it out with me? I know your size; just tell me what style you fancy. Something sleek and plain? No lacy frills?'

'Heavens, Mum,' Helen protested. 'We have a designer right here in the family! Anna-Marie would be terribly hurt if I didn't ask her to make my dress. I'm sure she'll come up with something special.'

Precious Moments . . .

Anna-Marie was thrilled with the news and the invitation to be bridesmaid.

'What's your colour scheme?' she asked immediately.

'Colour scheme? I'm leaving that all up to you, the expert.' Helen laughed. 'And if you could find time to make my dress . . . '

'Oh, Helen, I was dying to ask you but I thought maybe you'd want something fancy from overseas!' Anna-Marie laughed. 'Of course I'll make your dress. It will be the most fantastic, wonderful dress, you'll see!'

'Nothing too overboard, now,' Helen warned. 'Just something pretty. Like that dress you made me for the dance in Hartley's Drift, remember, but full length.'

'Just you wait.' Anna-Marie smiled. 'I've already got an idea. Leave it to me.'

For Helen the days before the wedding seemed bathed in a golden light, each one happier than the last. She and Adam stole precious moments together whenever they could, but during the day he was busy on the farm and they only saw each other at mealtimes, or at night when the rest of the family was sitting around playing Scrabble or just talking.

There was no teaching to do, so instead she helped Cora in the garden with the vegetables and asked Tuleka to show her a few favourite recipes, writing them down in a notebook she bought specially.

'You really don't have to worry with that, my dear. Tuleka's still going to do all the cooking for us,' Cora remarked one day, smiling complacently at Helen, who was intently watching the cook kneading the dough for the wholewheat loaves.

Helen suddenly understood that Cora expected them to carry on living with her once they were married. And why shouldn't she expect this? They'd never discussed where they'd live, although she supposed it would be in the outside flat Adam had made from the old storeroom.

But she certainly intended to do her own cooking there, although there was only a tiny sink and a two-plate gas stove.

Helen decided to speak to Adam about it at the first opportunity, but Amelia was ahead of her and brought up the subject that afternoon around the tea table while they were discussing wedding preparations.

'So where are you and Adam going to live, my dear?' she asked. 'Is Adam planning to build a little house for the two of you somewhere on the farm?'

Helen looked enquiringly at Adam, who had just come from town and was still dressed, uncharacteristically, in a pair of grey trousers with a tie.

'We haven't thought about that yet, Amelia,' she said softly.

'Well, yes, actually, I have.' Adam looked mischievously at Helen and took her hand. 'Thought about it, I mean. How does the farmhouse at Blouberg appeal to you, my darling?'

'Jacob's house?' She gasped. 'That gorgeous place?'

'*Our* house,' he said firmly. 'Or it will be when we're practically grandparents ourselves . . . I signed the papers this morning.'

Above the excited babble of questions and exclamations, he explained Jacob's offer and the terms of agreement.

'I'll run the two farms as one,' he said. 'I've got it mostly worked out. Jacob's got two fairly new tractors and all his equipment is a lot better than ours. His men have been working for him for years and know their jobs. We've got the water and the ideas. A perfect combination!'

'What a change in Jacob,' Cora marvelled. 'First he cheats us out of our land and then practically gives it back.'

'Not gives, Ma,' Adam corrected. 'I have to make regular payments to him or the whole agreement falls away. He's still as sharp as a flint, is old Jacob.'

'Wonderful News'

'More than double the land, eh,' Flippie said excitedly. 'You can do a lot with that. Maybe you could try putting down a few of those plastic tunnels for growing out-of-season stuff like celery and cherry tomatoes. They'd fetch top prices.'

'We can talk about that.' Adam nodded. 'It's double the land but double the work as well. It'll take some managing.'

'Well, I can start a vegetable garden, too,' Helen said. 'If you'll give me some advice about planting, Cora?' She turned to the older woman. 'Isn't this wonderful news?'

'Yes, indeed. I was so worried you'd be staying on with me! Not that I wouldn't have loved having you both,' she added quickly. 'But I feel that once she's married, every woman needs her own kitchen.'

And you had to wait more than twenty years for Amelia to move out so you could call your kitchen your own, Helen thought. She impulsively leaned across and kissed Cora.

'I couldn't have a better mother-in-law!'

she exclaimed. 'Aren't I lucky?'

'I'm the lucky one.' Cora smiled.

'Can this mutual admiration society please come to order so we can discuss important items like food for the reception?' Amelia queried. 'So far, all we have as a definite is the wedding cake.'

'How many guests are we thinking of inviting?' Helen asked tentatively. 'On my side there's my mum, Angela and Mark, and Grandad . . . '

'Goodness, you haven't met all the Smit family yet!' Cora laughed. 'We have aunties and uncles and cousins all over the place — Durban, Pretoria, Windhoek in Namibia . . . they wouldn't want to miss the wedding. And of course all the neighbours must be invited. Probably about a hundred people altogether, I should think.'

'How about we just elope, darling?' Adam said, only half in jest.

'Less fuss all round.'

'Don't even think of it,' Cora said. 'Helen wants a proper wedding, don't you, dear?'

'I wouldn't mind eloping, but Anna-Marie would never forgive me,' Helen said faintly.

Surely it wasn't possible to arrange a wedding in three weeks and invite a hundred people?

'And Adam, before you get married you need a haircut,' his mother said firmly.

Details

'Helen, you haven't got anything blue!' Gwen was unwinding Helen's hair from rollers and doing some last minute fussing around as she stood in front of the big mirror in Cora's room. Cora and Amelia sat on the bed watching, with Anna-Marie and Angela unwilling to sit down as they were already in their bridesmaids' dresses.

Tuleka kept popping her head around the door to admire them.

'Something old . . . that's Granny's gold cross and chain. Something new

. . . that's your dress. Isn't it lovely?'

Gwen put her hands on Helen's shoulders and smiled at their reflection in the mirror.

'It's exactly right for you. And so personal. Anna-Marie, you're really clever.'

Mum's right, Helen thought. My dress is perfect. The thick cream satin fitted her to perfection and swept gracefully to the ground with a small train, short sleeves and a low neckline which showed off her grandmother's heavy gold cross beautifully.

Around the hem of the dress Anna-Marie had hand-painted a border in subtle shades of darker cream and coffee, so delicate and feathery that the subjects only became obvious after a while.

She'd taken something from every part of Helen and Adam's life — leopards, sheep, goats, books, flowers and vegetables, heads of maize, an aeroplane, posies of herbs and even Albert's old battleship, *HMS Howe*.

'After all, if it wasn't for that ship, your *oupa* would never have visited the farm during the war and you'd never have come here, either!' Anna-Marie said as she explained the pictures. 'And you can cut it short later for dances, and use the bottom part and the train as an evening wrap.'

'Something borrowed — well, that's my gold bracelet,' Angela added. 'But blue . . . haven't you got a blue garter?'

'I forgot to buy one,' Helen admitted. 'But it doesn't matter.'

'Of course it does,' Angela insisted. 'You should have everything right, or it's bad luck. Although I know you don't believe that.'

At first, Angela had been dismayed at the speed and casualness of her sister's wedding arrangements, compared with her own. The preparations for the wedding were simply included in the daily running of the farm and Tuleka and Cora had put the finishing touches to the wedding cake only the night before.

'If you two would only wait another year or so, then William could toddle down the aisle as a page boy.'

It was the night before the wedding and she was only teasing. Once Angela had met Adam and the rest of the Smits, she admitted she'd have done the same.

'He's exactly right for you, sis,' she said. 'Completely different from Mark but perfect. So's Flippie. All the Smits are great and just think, we can have holidays in Africa from now on!'

'Working holidays,' Helen corrected. 'I don't think any of this family has ever taken a holiday.'

'But you're at least having a honeymoon, aren't you?'

'Only three days. And no, I don't know where. Adam says it's a surprise.'

'Something blue? Wait!'

Cora left the room and returned with a small blue enamelled hairclip in the shape of a bird.

'I've just remembered this. I wore it on my wedding day and was keeping it for Anna-Marie. A blue bird for happiness!'

'Just right.'

Helen waited while Cora pinned it carefully into her curls and both mothers exchanged a smile of satisfaction.

Helen was delighted that Gwen and Cora had got on so well from the minute they met. Somehow, between them, they'd taken over all the details of the wedding leaving almost nothing for her to do except answer the telephone and speak to her future relatives who would soon be converging on Kasteelpoort for the wedding.

'The food? Don't worry, all the neighbours are lending a hand,' Cora smiled. 'The music? Flippie will arrange that. And the invitations? Amelia's phoning everyone; it's too late to post formal invitations. We'll hire chairs and crockery. Stop worrying, everything's going to be fine!'

From the garden, the deep tone of an ancient bell suddenly rang out.

'What's that?' Helen asked puzzled.

'Our old farm bell.' Cora laughed. 'The closest we could get to a church carillon, I'm afraid.'

'It sounds wonderful,' Gwen enthused. 'This is going to be a most untraditional wedding.'

Amelia grinned at her.

'Not your average English festivities, I agree. Did you know the farmhands have slaughtered a cow for the wedding feast tonight? Provided by Adam, of course.'

'Oh, my heavens,' Gwen said in alarm. 'I thought those huge pots of beer Tuleka showed me were quite enough!'

'*Umqombothi*? That African beer is an acquired taste and they brew it for every celebration. But the cow is to honour Adam and Helen's marriage,' Amelia said. 'It's goats for a funeral, but a cow for a wedding. There'll be a huge party down at the huts after the reception, long after we've gone to bed.

'But I think it's time to leave,' she

added. 'No point in being late for your wedding when you're just walking down the steps!'

Amelia adjusted her purple-feathered hat and handed Helen the dainty arrangement of miniature yellow and orange marigolds, brilliant against her dress.

'Don't forget your bouquet!'

She swept out past Albert, who was pacing around in the corridor.

'My, sailor, you look handsome,' she teased. 'Almost as good as in your uniform!'

'Flattery will get you the first dance,' Albert said. 'And the one after. So save them for me.'

Then he turned to his granddaughter and crooked his arm gallantly.

'Helen, my girl. Don't you make a beautiful bride? In fact, all you ladies look a picture.'

'So do you, Grandad,' Helen said, kissing him. 'But you've forgotten your buttonhole!' She pinned a huge golden marigold to his lapel. 'Now we're a matching pair,' she said approvingly.

Thanks

Gwen hugged Helen hard, a suspicion of a tear in her eye, before she and Cora went ahead to take their seats. Summoned by the bell, the guests were already seated in rows, with an excited buzz of conversation coming from far-flung family members who only met at weddings and funerals.

But as the two mothers sat down in the front row, an expectant silence settled over the crowd.

Adam and Flippie had erected a big wooden arch under the pepper trees and all the farm workers had decorated it with long tendrils of green ivy and pieces of fern. At the last minute Anna-Marie had studded it with bunches of scarlet bell-peppers and the total effect was charming.

The minister from the church at Hartley's Drift waited beneath it.

Helen took a deep, tremulous breath and looked out over the sea of guests, across the lands to the blue mountains behind — the land she would now call home for ever.

'Thanks for everything, Grandad,' she whispered, squeezing his arm. 'Anna-Marie was right. If it wasn't for you, I wouldn't be here and I wouldn't be marrying Adam.'

Look Of Love . . .

As the small procession stepped out of the dark coolness of the house on to the verandah, a choir of African voices rose in soft, glorious harmony from behind the arch. All the labourers and their wives were singing, swaying from side to side with the women clad in traditional long dresses and faces decorated with whirls of white paint.

The children were in front, dressed in their new school uniforms, waving at her and grinning broadly as they sang and clapped. Helen smiled back, a lump in her throat from the beauty of the melody.

The guests rose to their feet and every head turned to watch as Helen and Albert walked slowly down the steps on to the lawn, with Angela and Anna-Marie two steps behind, resplendent in gold silk with smaller posies of marigolds and scarlet zinnias.

Helen was dimly aware of the admiring smiles and muted exclamations as she passed. But she had eyes only for one man, standing rather awkwardly in an unaccustomed suit, with his recent haircut leaving a pale line on his tanned farmer's neck.

Adam turned and their eyes met as she walked towards him, his look of love surging through her and warming her more than the hot African sun that shone on them all.

Albert gently disengaged his arm and gave her hand to Adam.

'Now you look after her well, my lad,' he whispered as he pecked Helen's cheek and stepped back.

'I will,' Adam murmured. He gripped her hand tightly, and with their palms touching they turned to face the minister as he opened his book of prayer and recited the time-hallowed words.

'Dearly beloved, we are gathered here today in the sight of God . . . '

THE END

We do hope that you have enjoyed reading this large print book.

Did you know that all of our titles are available for purchase?

We publish a wide range of high quality large print books including:
Romances, Mysteries, Classics
General Fiction
Non Fiction and Westerns

Special interest titles available in large print are:
The Little Oxford Dictionary
Music Book, Song Book
Hymn Book, Service Book

Also available from us courtesy of Oxford University Press:
Young Readers' Dictionary
(large print edition)
Young Readers' Thesaurus
(large print edition)

For further information or a free brochure, please contact us at:
Ulverscroft Large Print Books Ltd.,
The Green, Bradgate Road, Anstey,
Leicester, LE7 7FU, England.
Tel: (00 44) **0116 236 4325**
Fax: (00 44) **0116 234 0205**

Other titles in the
Linford Romance Library:

HER HEART'S DESIRE

Dorothy Taylor

When Beth Garland's great aunt Emily dies, she leaves Greg, her boyfriend, in Manchester — along with her successful advertising job — to return to live in Emily's cottage. Feeling disillusioned with Greg and his high-handed attitude, she finds herself more and more attracted to her aunt's gardener, Noah. But Noah seems to be hiding from the past, whilst Greg has his own ideas about the direction of their relationship. Surrounded by secrecy and deceit, how will Beth ever find true love?

PRECIOUS MOMENTS

June Gadsby

The heartbreak was all behind her, but hearing her name mentioned on the radio, and that song — their special song — brought bittersweet memories rushing back through the years. It had to be a coincidence, and was best forgotten — but then Lara opened the door to find her past standing there. The moment of truth she had dreaded for years had finally arrived, and she wasn't sure how to handle it . . .